TEATIME
WITH
MONSTERS

—·—

SHAYNA GRISSOM

CONTENTS

1

—·—

The unemployment office was hopping on that Tuesday morning. The blue plastic chairs were all but full in the lobby. The air conditioner was grinding through the Georgia heat that stifled my labored breath. I checked my phone. Fifteen minutes past my appointment time. Ten minutes was the latest you could be to one of these, but Renee would do me a solid. She had to. I didn't have anyone else to turn to.

Please, Renee, please help me one last time.

I sat by a dust-coated plastic plant and scratched the dirt clump off the back of my heel. Someone's perfume filled the waiting room and stung my sinuses, prompting a headache within moments. One match and the room could go up in a blaze. I suspected the old lady with bright orange lipstick and plastic dangly earrings, though the other twelve individuals were just as likely. Then again, no one occupied the seats on either side of her and opted to stand.

"Jayme Coleman," a familiar voice boomed.

Renee was a short, stout black woman who owned nothing but maxi skirts and cardigans. This would be our third appointment in four months. She must have been sick of seeing my face, and I didn't blame her.

Inside her office, the sting of the perfume dissipated, and I was able to breathe my first real breath of the day. "Renee, thank you."

She shook her head and slid the reading glasses chained around her neck onto her face. "You're just lucky I got to you before my manager did. She's a stickler about no-shows and late appointments."

"I'm sorry."

Excuses would dry my good fortunes faster than any bank account I ever had, so I kept them to myself. Renee observed me from over her readers. "You still with that man?"

I didn't respond, and she made a tsk noise before sitting in her chair. She knew he was the reason I was late. He was always the reason. Greg was just going through something, and he needed time to heal. Everyone goes through a rough patch. I had faith that he would turn things around. If I just loved him back from the brink, we could do anything. I had always believed that love could conquer all, and I was going to prove it with Greg.

"Did he take your car again? Tell me it was because he got a job."

"He's in the middle of a divorce," I explained.

The caseworker raised a brow and shook her head. "And what does that have to do with being out of a job for nearly a year?"

She had a point. Everyone else could work through a divorce–why not Greg? Claire was why. "His ex is a piece of work. She's rich but is doing everything she can to take every cent from him."

Her lips were pressed together so tightly, I feared she would burst with a differing opinion on the matter. Instead, Renee pulled a manilla folder out of a bin and dropped it on the desk before me. "I'm a case worker, not a therapist," she said, more to herself than to me. "I plucked this one out of the bin just for you. It's a real opportunity if you stick to it."

"I will," I promised.

"You had better," she warned. "I can't keep sticking my neck out for you."

I didn't deserve to be angry at that, but I was. I didn't ask her to risk her job for me. My words sputtered out before I could reel them back. "Then why help me?"

Renee paused as if she needed to contemplate the reasoning. "I had a dream about you last night. I'm probably spending too much time at work, but my grandma always said to listen to the angels if they come to you in dreams."

The caseworker didn't strike me as a woman who put much thought into dreams or premonitions, but this was the South. We put a lot of faith in God. Christianity was the beating heart that kept many folks going when there was nothing left. Faith left me the day I ran from the altar.

There was a knock on the door behind me. Renee's face was impassive, but it was a mask. The manager had it out for me. I didn't even know her, but the last time I came, there was a similar knock. The caseworker stood by me for a moment as if she were preparing for a battle. "Excuse me, I'm going to need to take this. You should take that."

Renee opened the door. "Can I speak to you in private?" a woman said.

That was my cue to leave. Inside the manilla folder was a single sheet of paper waiting expectantly. I thought about leaving it. Maybe I could find something else, something that wouldn't get Renee in trouble. Then again, to assume the case worker was stupid enough to get caught was outright insulting.

Renee was giving me a chance. To leave it was wrong.

I slid the paper across the desk. The sheet was so crisp and rigid, the scent of ink still lingered on the page. Few hands had touched this. She must have snatched it up just for me before anyone with a better work history could take it. "Renee, you're a freaking lifesaver," I muttered as I folded the paper in half and put it in my purse.

Renee was still talking with what was probably her manager as I bolted. I gave an audible whimper and exaggerated a sniffle—just loud enough for the manager. The hushed berating had ceased, and I made like I was wiping my eyes and sniffed loudly. Hopefully, my performance was enough to get Renee off the hook.

This was my last chance before having to change employment agencies again. The next agency was in Alabama, and I didn't want to have to drive an hour each way if I could help it. The Kia did all right on gas mileage when I had it, but I couldn't afford gas. I couldn't afford life at this rate.

On the bus ride home, I unfolded the job letter. Tears welled in my eyes when I saw that it was a salary position, not hourly. Using my calculator on my phone, I choked back a sob when I realized it was more than I had ever been paid. There were benefits. It was a job assisting a woman less than thirty minutes from my apartment.

An assistant position that listed cleaning as the primary job. No experience required. No diploma required. Yet it paid more than a teacher's salary. I only knew that because Greg used to be one. I was a high school dropout. When I couldn't find work, I went up to the college and took GED classes. Thought that maybe I could further my education. That didn't work out, but I did manage to get the Good Enough Degree.

Why did this assistant job pay so much? I read the single sheet of paper so many times I almost missed my stop. Getting off the bus was a blur, but there I was, standing on the lawn before my apartment with its paint-chipped siding and cracked parking lot. The echo of the bus's breaks in the distance should have jarred me from this dream, but I was floating in possibilities. With this kind of money, Greg and I would stand a chance against Claire. Our fights over money and cars would be over. Love could win if I did this right.

This job was too good for the likes of me. Perfect, even. There must have been a catch. If thirty-three years of life taught me anything, it was that there was always a pitfall. Offers too good to be true were like good guys. I didn't deserve them, and it was only a matter of time before they were gone.

2

— · —

It took me forty-five minutes to find the place. The driveway was unmarked and overgrown with Clematis vines strangling the heavy trunks of the trees that marked the dirt road. The Kia tossed me around in the driver's seat as I barreled down the driveway. The shocks were shot to shit, but they would have to do.

I was late—again. This time, it was my fault. I should have looked up the directions before I went driving through the sticks. When would I not be late? I couldn't afford to lose this opportunity. It doubled the wage of my last job, and it had dental! Imagine just calling up a dentist and getting an appointment. No barriers, no extra hoops, just a golden ticket to reputable service. I hadn't had that since I was a teenager under my parent's insurance.

My stomach churned as my phone attempted to reconnect to the GPS for the third time. At least I had the car. I could drive up and down these old roads for miles with nothing but the cows and horses to observe me. I'd like to think I wasn't the first lost driver they had seen. There were no buses out this way for several miles. Though Greg was not liable to take the car again, I kept the keys hidden the night before, just in case.

He knew he was in trouble as he walked in the door. His hands were up in surrender. "I know," he said. Greg's face was clean-shaven, and he was wearing slacks and a blue button-up shirt. It was hard to be mad when he looked that good. "I took the car, and it was wrong, but Claire texted me. She wanted to talk."

"Your ex-wife?" That was unexpected. The only conversations she had with Greg were in the form of served notices delivered by the sheriff. I set aside my anger momentarily for him to explain. If he told me something dumb, like he was going back to her, I'd drop-kick his ass on the concrete steps in the stairwell. No, he'd never go back to her, not after everything she put him through.

His eyes went wide. "Crazy, right? She wanted to meet clear in Atlanta. I had to get up at four in the morning just to get there in time. I tried to get her to change the time or location, something, but you know how she is."

I plopped on our third-hand beige loveseat, anger evaporating like the morning due on the lawn. Claire was not one to meet anyone halfway. When she initially hinted that they *needed to talk*, he asked if it could wait until after work—lunch break even—instead, she served him divorce papers in the middle of a lecture.

"So, what did she have to say?" I asked, shifting my body opposite of his.

Greg shook his head and closed the front door. Casually tossing the keys on the kitchen counter before striding toward me. "I had hoped we were going to talk about the alimony payments."

The alimony payments. Greg had refused to pay them by quitting his job for the past three months. It was a nasty, bitter divorce. The kind you read about in the magazines. They were going on two years, and there was still no end in sight. "Did she agree to rescind them?"

"In a way," he said, joining me on the sofa, resting a gentle hand on my knee. I wanted to slap him, but I also wanted his hand to move just a little bit higher. It was awful how good-looking he was. He could get away with murder, and I'd still be waiting on him.

"She proposed a lump sum. I don't know what else she thinks she can get out of me. She got the house, the cars, and half my retirement."

That heinous bitch. She left him but had to suck him dry in the process. Not everyone's wealthy daddy could pay for a whole army of attorneys. When they met in college, Claire had thought she hit the jackpot. It was only after they got engaged that she learned he got there on scholarships and a heap of student loans. No well-to-do parents, just a single mother, and a part-time job. When he decided to be a biology professor, that didn't sit right with her either.

"Well, she got all your retirement; you used the rest on a legal defense."

Greg's face was sullen with guilt, a common bond we shared. Did Claire feel guilt for putting him in such a sordid position? I doubted it. Rich folks didn't feel remorseful when they trampled over the poor like us. In their minds, it was a privilege just to consort with them.

In Claire's mind, he could just get a job, even two and all their problems would be solved. When the bills piled up anyway, she blamed him for being extravagant while ignoring her own luxury car payments.

"I'm so sorry you had to meet me at my worst," he said. "I'm going to make this up to you one day, I swear it."

My anger over the car fell away. I couldn't stay mad at him. He was trying to defend himself, and that was more than I ever did. I always relied on my brothers to take up for me, but they hadn't talked to me in months. They must have given up on me just like our parents did.

I could forgive just about anything, but Greg couldn't keep doing things like this, not if I was going to get a solid job that could keep us both afloat. I understood not wanting to pay Claire alimony when she already had money, but she would suffocate the both of us. I couldn't make it on my own, and at the rate we were going, we'd be evicted in a few months.

"How much does she want?" I asked.

Divorce was an ugly thing. It tore his entire life asunder. I watched as he divvied up friends with his ex-wife like they were allocations and prized possessions. Ten years of marriage was being snipped away day by day. Had I gone through with my own marriage, would it have ended the same way? I couldn't afford to think about that. Lars moved on, and I was happy for him. He deserved a good woman. Not like me.

Greg shook his head and refused to look at me. More than he could afford and more than any loan he could take out. I pressed the question, but he refused. "Any job I get, she will have my wages garnished. At least while unemployed, I can postpone my student loans and her cut."

Claire may be spiteful, but he was too. He'd rather remain penniless than give her anything, but what good would that do? It would only delay the inevitable and cause more strain on our relationship. He said he was holding out just until she gave up on the alimony. That he'd work on his thesis in the meantime. He'd get a PhD and get a raise. That was the plan anyway. While I was out working minimum wage jobs, maxing out my credit cards, and catching up on late fees, his laptop held only blank pages.

"Well, I have a job interview," I said.

I called the woman the moment I got off the bus. The phone rang four times while I paced the concrete. A raspy voice answered, "Swollas residence."

My throat tightened with anticipation. I needed this so bad, but I couldn't sound desperate. "Hi, I'm Jayme Coleman. I'm from the employment agency."

The woman on the other end huffed. "About time. I was starting to wonder if no one was going to respond."

I checked the paper. The job was posted yesterday. "I'm sorry about that, Ma'am. I'm more than happy to assist you in any way I can."

"Are you now?" she said in a way that made me regret saying it. "Come to the house at nine AM. That's not too early. I know how you young ones do not like to get up early."

"Nine AM will be fine, ma'am."

Okay, so not a perfect start, but I had an interview. I probably wouldn't be working with that old sourpuss anyway. Despite the rocky morning, I looked forward to telling Greg, and he did not disappoint when it came to celebrating good news.

Despite his dismay, my partner did his best to smile. "That's wonderful!"

My grin wouldn't cease, and he mirrored it before saying, "Okay, what's with that face?"

I showed him the paper. His eyes lit up when he saw the salary. Half laughing, half yelling, Greg embraced me. "How did you get this?"

"Renee did me a solid, that's for sure."

Greg was on his feet and breaking out the IPAs I had been saving for a really hot day. "This calls for a celebration! I can't believe you got an interview for that kind of money."

I couldn't believe it either, but the way he said it was unsettling. Renee had a dream and said it was an angel who told her to give me the job. So, what if I didn't have a fancy degree, but maybe I had something better. "I got an angel on my side."

If Greg had heard me, he wasn't at all phased by what I had said. His mind was still whirling in the dollar signs. "I don't want to get our hopes up too much," he said with a gentle frown. "There's a chance you're not what they're looking for."

I wasn't good enough—that was what he meant. He was right. I was a Podunk girl with no real credentials and a spotty work history. There was a good chance this woman would take one look at me and slam the door in my face. Anxiety was beginning to set in. If I didn't get this, we might be living out of the Kia at the end of the month.

"I really need you to be on board with this," I said.

"I know."

"I need the car, and I need the smartphone."

"I won't screw this up for you," Greg promised.

He kept that promise. That morning, he made the coffee and was tidying up our studio apartment. He even packed me lunch—an apple with a ham sandwich with my mustard, not that runny yellow shit he slathered on all his sandwiches. Greg kissed my forehead with a longing that made me want to go back to bed. "You're going to be great."

If only I didn't lose service on the road. I had to pull over several times, searching for cell service, to memorize the directions. By the time I blazed through the driveway, I was late. Still, it was better than never.

When the trees gave way, I pulled up to one of the strangest houses I had ever seen. It was a dry, grey-shingled thing nearly devoured by the greenery. Rooms jutted out in corners and edges, and turrets faced the morning sun. It rested on what initially appeared to be stilts, but as I got closer, they were more like archways that led to yet another story of the house.

I had seen a lot of different types of homes in my time. Colonials, Georgians, trailers, but never anything like this. It was like an attempt at a modern house with scraps. The closer I got, the more expansive it became. The overgrown foliage hid much of it, but walking under the archways, the home stretched onward. It was bigger than my whole apartment complex.

Where was the front door? I emerged from the arched corridors to a set of stairs. The warmth of day hit my back, reminding me of just how chilly it was in the shadows of the home. Behind the stairway, the house carried onward.

I made my way up the steep steps and knocked on a solid wooden door. There was no answer, so I knocked again. There was no doorbell that I could find. Nervousness has me sweating in my skirt suit. The tag stated "Dry Clean Only" in bold lettering. I couldn't afford that, so I'd have to stop sweating. Poverty is absurd like that.

I hesitated to knock again. What if I got the wrong house and unwittingly stumbled on an abandoned home? What if there was a serial killer waiting inside? Or worse, methheads.

The door swung open wide, and I stepped back. A short, ancient woman with a big hairdo stared up at me with green, watery eyes. "You must be the woman from the agency," she said with all the briskness of a woman who didn't have time for Southern hospitality. Her foreign accent strained my mind as I tried to establish where she was from. I was pretty sure it was the same woman who answered the phone. I hoped she was just interviewing me.

"Hi, I'm Jayme," I said with a weak smile.

"You're late."

I cringed. "I got lost, and there's no service out here."

"Waste no more of my time, then. Come in."

Scratching at my dry arms underneath the jacket, I followed the woman through the darkness. She was too small to hurt me, but the tightness in my chest suggested otherwise. I rounded the corner and was greeted by daylight once more. I must have found the back door because this was a kitchen. It had a stale, unused smell to it, as if the kitchen hadn't been in service for a decade. My eyes were vulnerable with all the dust and threatened to water.

It was a nice kitchen too, well, it was at one point. A double baby blue enamel oven matched the small fridge dotted with rust and tarnished silver lettering across one side. Lights dangled from ropes of painted-white chains. Huge, blocky beams lined the walls. The windows were cloudy but spanned from the floor to the high ceiling. There was a kitchen island with a wooden counter. Everything was painted white but stained by dust and time.

"This is quite the house," I said. "I've never seen anything like it."

"I gathered when I heard knocking at the back door," the woman said dryly. "Come along."

The woman's demeanor left no room for idle conversation, so I followed her silently through a wainscoted hallway, but what I saw next took my breath away. She led me into another expansive room with a high, curved ceiling and bay windows with ornate stained glass. The room was the size of my apartment, but only a few worn floral couches and a coffee table adorned the room.

With the shiplap ceilings and floral stained glass, I wouldn't want to heavily decorate either, but it was all so forlorn. Much like the woman, who was no doubt a beauty in her prime, the house was lost in some other time. "Sit," she commanded as she seated, stiff-backed and scowling.

"Are you Mrs. Swollas?" I asked, sitting on the soft canvas sofa. It was an expensive couch once. Unlike the kitchen, this room carried residual scents of lavender and roses. There was no sign of a vase. Perhaps she moved it recently.

"Who else would I be?" There it was again, that accent. I couldn't quite place it. It was far removed from the southern drawl I knew and loved, but it was so subtle I thought her a Northern transplant.

"I thought you might be an assistant," I said.

"That's what you're here for." Crisp and proper, but there was an underlining of something else, something wilder and more feral. The brightness of her eyes and the sharpness of her teeth... It was strange. She had a fierceness to her that made me envious.

"Have you ever been an assistant before?"

"In an office setting," I said. It was my daddy's office I worked for, but I wasn't about to tell her that.

She nodded in approval. Her faded black gown covered her from neck to shoe. A large red gem on her neck was the only adornment. Judging by the narrowness of her belted waist, I suspected a corset or a girdle. Not uncommon for older women in the South—they wore Lycra until the day they died—but the formality was jarring. I glanced at my own apparel, and the inadequacy was apparent.

"What about housekeeping?" she asked, folding her thin, bony fingers in her lap. "I need someone to keep up with all the housework. I recently acquired this home, and I was not prepared for the state of it."

That explained a lot. The home was likely abandoned until this woman bought it for its uniqueness. An investment property that needed renovations before she could resell it, though I wasn't certain that backwoods Alabama was a great location for high-end properties.

I nodded with a hard swallow. "I worked in housekeeping for a hotel."

"Goodness, you've worked a little bit everywhere, haven't you?"

I didn't have a response for that, though I suspected she didn't expect one.

"How old are you?" Mrs. Swollas asked.

It was a fair enough question, I guess. "I'll be thirty-three in July."

Her scrutinizing glare told me what she thought of that. A thirty-three-year-old woman with no college education, a blotchy work history, and not a lot to show for herself. Mrs. Swollas glanced at my unadorned hand and gleaned another fact. That's right, you old hag. I'm not married, and I have no kids. Make what you will of that.

"Unmarried, I presume."

In the South, a childless, unmarried woman was about as useful as a pickle jar without vinegar. I had my shield up and was ready for the onslaught, but to my surprise, Mrs. Swollas gave a nod of approval. "Good," she said. "No attachments."

I relaxed at that. This wasn't a Southern Belle; this was a woman of the old world who held a different set of ideals, whatever those were. Did she have children? Perhaps not anymore; otherwise, why wouldn't they have been here to help her? I wouldn't have left my mother out in the boonies like this. Then again, this was not my mother. My mother baked cookies and volunteered for the PTA when I was in school. This woman wouldn't be caught dead in a school gym with a Tupperware full of brownies. This was not the Avon-selling housewife who went to First Methodist.

"You'll be expected to arrive *promptly* at nine, and you must leave before evening," Mrs. Swollas explained. "I am old and need my rest. I won't be bothered past sundown for any reason."

I nodded eagerly, and my heart rose with the prospects. This could happen. It would change my life. I wouldn't need to worry about rent or utilities with the salary she offered. I could move into a better apartment. If things worked out, I might move closer. Rent was cheaper out here, and it wasn't like Greg had any prospects in town anyhow.

"I have other rules, but we'll get to those later," Mrs. Swollas said. "I need a great deal of housecleaning. I expect you to dress informally—a step down from what you're wearing now, perhaps. Trousers, I should think."

"Yes, ma'am." I pressed my hands into my lap to keep from shaking. I didn't register the backhanded insult until after the meeting.

She smiled at that. "I do love that southern politeness. These days, manners are lacking in most of the world. Not unless they're paid to be courteous, of course."

It struck me that Mrs. Swollas was embittered by isolation and loneliness, but she was too strong and proud to admit it. She was stiff and uncomfortable to be around, but I suspected that underneath that brittle exterior was a kind woman with a tragic past.

"One more inquiry..."

"Ma'am?"

"Do you believe humanity worth the trouble?"

I straightened at the philosophical question. I was accustomed to all sorts of questions at interviews. I had learned to answer the "weaknesses" question in a way that also seemed like strengths. I was asked my opinion on whether pineapple belonged on pizza or how I would deal with a zombie apocalypse. Mostly out of humor and a tension breaker at interviews, but never something so bleak.

"Worth it?"

"Are you a parrot, girl?" Mrs. Swollas cracked a slight smile. "That is what I asked. Do you think people are worth all the trouble they make? Are they beyond redemption?"

It was a strange question, but at the heart of it, she wanted to know whether I was an optimist or not. Either that or she wanted to know if I was a fool. She no doubt already had her mind made up about the latter. Still, Greg came to mind.

We met in college when I was flunking out of classes. He was teaching at the time. I didn't take biology, but we often found ourselves talking in the cafeteria. It was a slow, gradual friendship that started with holding the door open, chit chats in line, and one day, we sat together.

Greg and his wife had been legally separated for almost a year, and there was no reconciliation in sight. Still, when I asked him out for more than lunch, he declined. "I know things between me and Claire are over, but I'm still married, even if she doesn't agree."

"Say what you want, but it sounds like you're not ready to move on," I told him over our deli sandwiches. "And that's okay. I think it's romantic, to be honest."

"At least someone does." He shrugged and dropped his roast beef. "Her version of romance is making me sleep in my car while it's being repossessed."

That was when I first learned he was homeless. It wasn't long after he took residence on my couch that we discovered she had also gained access to his bank accounts and credit cards. His reputation was in shreds after she served at work multiple times. She cornered him into what he was now.

Greg had his faults, but in his heart, he was a good man. He just needed the support and love that his wife never provided. Was he worth it? I'd like to think so. Despite leaving a good man at the altar years ago, I could be redeemed, right? If my father was still alive, would he still be angry with me for the cost of the failed wedding? I'd like to think one mistake—no matter how big—did not make me unworthy of love and forgiveness.

"Yes," I said at last. "Everyone makes mistakes. It's what we do about them that defines who we are."

The ancient woman's eyes glimmered with approval. I passed whatever test she had set before me. Whether kinship in belief or a deep understanding of human nature. It wasn't what I wore or my experience that the lady approved of. It was what I thought and believed that mattered. Something about that sprouted hope where it hadn't been for a long time. This was not another dead-end job. It was the start of something life-changing for both of us.

"Well spoken, Ms. Coleman. When can you start?"

I withheld my joy as far as the end of the driveway before tearing onto the road. Punching my foot on the gas, I screamed as I drove down the road. The cows watched vacantly as they chewed. This wasn't the first time they had seen a crazed woman shrieking as she barreled down the road. There were some tears as I went down the interstate and a small anxiety attack pulling into my parking spot. It was too good to be true, and I couldn't wait to tell my boyfriend.

Greg stood as I walked in the door. "Well?"

I was about to tell him the good news, but when I opened my mouth, I burst into sobs instead. Greg's face fell, and he rushed to take me in his arms. "Oh, honey, I'm so sorry."

"No," I managed. I couldn't say anything else, so I began nodding profusely.

He braced my shoulders and stared into my eyes. "You got it?"

"Yeah."

"Yeah?"

"Yeah," I wailed. We hugged with the front door still wide open, letting all the air out. This was the Greg I could make it work with. Someone who shared in my ups as well as my downs. We could overcome anything just so long as we stuck together.

3

— · —

Mrs. Swollas was waiting outside the home when I pulled up. She pointed to an archway indicating where the car was to be parked. It wasn't like any covered parking I had ever seen, but when I rolled in, the smoothed concreate was the size of a two-car garage and there was a shelf full of old car soaps, rags, buckets, and unused lawn equipment.

I stepped out and followed the old lady up the steps and through the garage door. "I understand your confusion regarding the entrance," Mrs. Swollas said. "The front entrance is on the other side of the house that faces a private road."

So, we were on the backside of the home. "It's such a beautiful home, I've never seen anything like it," I said.

"It's a Shingle-style home," Mrs. Swollas explained. "Made in the sixties. Back then, they assumed the private road would become the busier main road and built the home in that direction. The previous owner was old money with a most eclectic flavor."

She practically purred those last words. I got the sense that business and pleasure mingled for her. "Did you know the previous owner well?"

"You know how intimate a purchase this large can be," she said. "By the time we were done, I knew more about Montgomery than his doctor did."

I didn't know whether to laugh or not. I had heard buying a house requires a lot of evaluation. It was just the way she spoke; it was so unsettling, like everything was a private joke. She must have been by herself for a long time.

We passed through a small mud room where I took off my shoes and hung my sports jacket. Mrs. Swollas looked me up and down and said, "Good, you're dressed for cleaning."

I was wearing my best pair of leggings and button-up flannel that I had found at the thrift store last week. "Yep."

"The house is rather expansive, so I will give you a tour. You're familiar with this wing of the house; the kitchen and living room are just over there. Downstairs consists of two bedrooms and what I think is a playroom. Upstairs is a master and a loft. All three stories have bathrooms, of course."

Apart from the sheer space of the rooms, the woodwork was the most striking detail. Doorways arched in half circles overhead and railings curved with an asymmetry I wasn't accustomed to. Some rooms had curved ceilings, and others were long and narrow with built-in shelving and seats with rounded arm rests. It was like the builder had a split personality or something. It was fragmented, yet beautiful. Rounding stair railings gave way to acutely angled spaces. The classic mixed with the contemporary.

Mrs. Swollas showed as much interest in the home as she did anything else. A woman who had seen so much in her lifetime that nothing surprised her anymore. The world had lost all its wonder for her. Whatever pain she endured in her life left her empty and withered.

I didn't want to go like that. I was meant for something special, even if I didn't know what it was.

"I have rules," she reminded me as we went up the square-posted stairs.

"Yes," I said. "I'll be gone before nightfall."

The entryway jutted to the left of the stairway and opened to an observation deck that bridged the two sections of the house. I paused to take in the view of the woods and the swamplands in the distance. Mrs. Swollas waited until my eyes had their fill before resuming her tour. Her hands remained clasped in front of her as if she wanted to hold something. With her long dress and coal-colored hair swept into a perfect bun, I imagined she needed a candelabra to carry, but this was the South and not a crumbling castle like in novels.

"The second rule is that if you happen to injure yourself, a cut perhaps, you must leave immediately. No need to alert me or explain. Just leave for a few hours until the bleeding has fully stopped and the wound is properly bandaged."

Mrs. Swollas did not go on to explain this rule, but I suspected I already knew the reason. I had an aunt who would faint at the sight of blood. I'll never forget the time my cousin fell off her bike and scraped her knee. My aunt collapsed on sight. Mrs. Swollas was proud and not one who would allow the help to see her in such a state. "I understand," I said as we moved into what was intended to be the front of the house.

"No one is allowed to accompany you," Mrs. Swollas went on. "You are the only visitor I want on this property."

Again, a perfectly valid rule. She was alone here, and I couldn't blame her for relishing the safety in obscurity. We had toured half the home, and not one sign of wealth adorned its halls. If someone were to break in, they would be in for a disappointment. A disgruntled thief expecting a treasure trove would likely threaten the elderly woman.

"Is there something wrong, Ms. Coleman?" Mrs. Swollas asked, her back still turned to me.

Jolted by the sudden self-awareness, I frowned, but not before releasing my fists from their balled position. "You're alone here all the time?"

Mrs. Swollas peered at me from over her shoulder. "There are many strengths of old age—not all of them are easily understood by the young."

I wanted to argue, but this was not the woman to argue with. What if someone broke in, threatened her at gunpoint? We were in backwoods Alabama, and there wasn't a phone to be found. She must have had one, but where? Not that calling anyone would do a lick of good, the only ones close enough to rescue the old lady were the cows.

"I can assure you," Mrs. Swollas said. "I am quite capable of caring for myself. I have thus far, and I'm still here despite the odds. Besides, I don't plan on remaining for much longer."

I sighed. She had a point. I was blending my personal experience with this woman. This was not my mother, and to treat her like some feeble, confused woman was doing her a disservice. I wasn't about to trouble her with my own situation. She didn't hire me to tell her about myself. Still, the way she said she wouldn't be remaining for long...it was like she was waiting to pass away. A terminal illness, maybe? That was why she wanted someone to help her with the house. There was a profound sadness in those green eyes. A despair I only saw in the homeless veterans on the side of the road.

I wanted to ask more, but I swallowed my questions for her sake. "Yes, Ma'am."

The disjointed house maintained its unique style in the front wing, but it did not have the covered porch with the archways. It, too, was three stories. The third story held two spacious master bedrooms with their own bathrooms; Mrs. Swollas inhabited one of them. Her bed was a great heavy thing with a solid wood headboard depicting a fox on a hillside being chased by hunters. Draped across the end of her bed was a massive wolf pelt with the head still attached. Enormous, yellowed teeth as long as my fingers barred at the door as if warning intruders. Its glass bead eyes stared into me. A chill ran my blood cold, numbing in my veins.

"You're afraid of my pet?" Mrs. Swollas asked with a dry smile.

"It's huge," I said, trying to admire the thing. The matted tangle of black hair still had some luster despite its age, just like Mrs. Swollas.

"That beast murdered several of my family," she explained. "In a different land, long ago, it was kill or be killed."

"I understand." I didn't understand. Not really. Just where had this woman come from that would make life so dangerous? I scratched at my arms again, setting my pity aside.

"What do you do in your spare time, Miss Coleman?"

I couldn't afford to do much of anything, but she was attempting to strike up polite conversation, and I had to come up with something. "Well, my boyfriend and I watch TV. Sometimes we go for a drive."

"Tell me about this boyfriend of yours."

"His name is Greg. He's real smart and handsome."

"Hm."

We descended the square staircase with the same peculiar rosettes with iron balusters that bowed outward beyond any promise of sta-bility. The second story was void of a kitchen but otherwise mirrored the second story in the other wing of the house. "For guests and entertaining, though impractical since the kitchen is on the other side of the house," Mrs. Swollas mused.

Why live in a home she deemed so impractical? She wasn't wrong; I didn't know any party that didn't congregate around the kitchen. I supposed Mrs. Swollas didn't have a choice on where she lived any more than I did. With this salary, I'd have more of a say on the matter, and I couldn't help but smile at the thought.

The ground floor held four rooms and a bathroom. Two of the doors were locked. "The next rule," Mrs. Sallow continued. "Is to stay out of the locked rooms."

"I can respect that," I said. All women were entitled to their privacy, and it made for less work. Judging by the state of things, I had it cut out for me.

"What does your boyfriend do?" she asked.

"He's a biology teacher," I said.

"Teachers do not get paid well in this country," she said. "I imagine he wasn't thrilled when he learned of your salary."

"He was very happy," I said. "I know some men don't like the idea of their woman getting paid more, but he isn't like that."

She took me out of the home through stained glass double doors that did not dome at the top like the interior. Still, it suited the curved ceiling in the rectangle room. I was beginning to understand the intent behind the unusual design.

"That's good. Tell me, do you like to read?"

"No," I confessed. "I never really got into it."

"That's a shame. My daughter loved reading."

So, there was a daughter. With each curve, there was a sharp edge, much like its owner in a way. With each long, rectangular room, a rounded high ceiling. It was the classical mixed with the modern, the new world melding with the old. Instead of forcing the two worlds to change into a single cohesive style, they remained unique but together.

"The curb appeal is lacking," Mrs. Swollas said. "I'll be sending you into town for some plants as well."

Another chill took hold of me. The AC was running hard in this house. Suddenly wishing I had my jacket. I wrapped my arms around my chest. I gazed up at the trees that surrounded us, they might have been the culprit of the chill, but they did not account for the eerie sensation of being watched.

I turned to regard the house. Two stone eyes smiled at me. I gasped and backpaddled away from the creature.

"Oh," Mrs. Swollas chuckled. "I see you've met my companion."

It was a gargoyle and the nastiest one I had ever seen. Its long tongue flopped out of a jaw full of protruding, broken teeth. Wings fully spanned, it was perched like a dog with talons bracing the balcony railing. Though it was old, I could see details of scales and feather texture under its scant moss loincloth.

I was at a loss for words. It wore a mocking smile as if it enjoyed how horrifying it appeared. "It's...so," I was taught to say something nice or not at all, but the words failed me.

"Disgusting?" Mrs. Swollas finished for me, her accent particularly choppy with the word.

"Maybe put that thing away when it comes time to sell the home."

"Have no fear in that regard," she said. "He will follow me to the grave."

I fought the shutter that racked my body. There it was again. The hint of death. She was dying. It was rude to pry. I supposed she would tell me in her own time, but how the hell did she plan on buying the gargoyle with her? Maybe he was to be her tombstone. Another joke she kept private from the world she no longer knew.

"Come," Mrs. Swollas said. "Let's have tea."

I suspected she didn't mean the sweet kind in the pitcher, but maybe I could turn her on to it. My mamma's sweet tea was the best on the block. Her mind went before she could give me the recipe. I never did get it quite right.

"Yes, Ma'am."

As I followed the woman toward the stairs, the little hairs on my arms raised as the air in the hallway went dead. Faint whispers echoed in my mind. What were they saying? I shook my head as if it could free my mind from the intrusion, but the voices faded away before I could think to panic. It was an old house with a strong AC; it probably made all kinds of noises.

"Ms. Coleman?" Mrs. Swollas called from the steps.

"Coming!"

It must have been my imagination brought on by stress. Last night I woke up gasping from a dream, but I couldn't remember a thing about it. Greg rubbed my back until I fell back asleep. I wanted to say it also involved tea, but why would that be so scary? I always got a little edgy around the beginning of the month—that was when rent was due. It would be late again, but when I got paid, it wouldn't be late again if I could help it.

In the kitchen, Mrs. Swollas seated herself at the dinette. "I assume you know how to make tea."

"Yes, ma'am," I said, putting the kettle on the burner. "We drink tea a little differently around these parts, but the first part is the same."

"Montgomery didn't drink tea. He only had coffee with enough flavored cream to bury the flavor. You don't use milk, do you? I know most Americans don't."

The water boiled as I got myself acquainted with the kitchen. The mugs were in the cabinet closest to the sink where my mamma would have put them. I grinned at the prospect of horrifying Mrs. Swollas with sweet tea. This was not America; this was the South. We were our own breed down here. "Well, we boil a bunch of teabags in a glass pitcher before dumping a whole lot of sugar in the hot tea..."

I glanced over at Mrs. Sallow as she gritted her teeth. "How much sugar?" she asked.

"Well, I think my mamma used about three cups, but everyone has their own preferences. She also put lemon and orange slices in hers."

Mrs. Swollas blanched and did her best to restrain her upper lip from curling in disgust. "I take mine plain, thank you."

"You have to understand," I said. "It gets so hot and humid here, the only thing that keeps us cool is iced tea or coke."

I joined her at the dinette and sipped on the bitter tea. The steam that rose from my cup was an earthy with a hint of sweetness. It wasn't my mamma's sweet tea, but it was nice. I felt sophisticated with the cup between my hands.

"That would make sense, but must the amount of sugar be so wasteful?"

"It's not wasted if we drink it," I teased.

Mrs. Swollas cringed. "No wonder the people here are so heavy."

Based on her slim frame, I could only guess she came from a place where sugar was a luxury that could not simply be picked up for a few dollars at the store. I couldn't begin to imagine what she thought of me. I was always a sturdily built girl. I wasn't fat, but I was never slim either. When the other girls in school ran track or played tennis, I lifted weights.

"I'm sorry," I said. "Do you want me to fix you something to eat?"

Mrs. Swollas grinned. "Your accent is simply delightful."

The heat rose to my cheeks at her praise. What was it about this woman that I wanted to please so badly? It was probably the desire to please my own parents. That was probably why I said yes to Lars all those years ago, but I'd never gain my parents' approval again.

"Your accent is even better," I said. "If you don't mind my asking, where are you from?"

Mrs. Swollas looked to the ceiling as she pondered the question. Was it so hard to remember?

"Europe has undergone many changes in my lifetime. The name has changed many times. I'm not even certain it is a place anymore."

Suddenly, the gargoyle made more sense. It must have been a keepsake from her old life. I didn't know spit about Europe apart from what I learned in high school, and history was never a good subject for me. I was familiar with parts of it being renamed. Lands being redistributed and whatnot. Poor thing probably didn't even know herself. Not wanting to push the topic further, I changed my line of questioning. "How long have you lived here?"

"Oh, not long. A few months, perhaps. Had I known this home would be such an undertaking, I would have reconsidered the purchase."

"You mean you bought it sight unseen?"

Mrs. Swollas shrugged. "The offer was too scrumptious to refuse."

Now that was something I knew all about. Greg used to kid that if there was a deal to be found, I could sniff it out from the bargain bin. I found him some real good clothes that way. "You've got to take every opportunity thrown your way," I agreed.

The woman's green eyes glowed for a moment as she leaned toward me. "That is precisely the way of things."

Something in her excitement made me nervous. We weren't talking about Nike's in the bottom of a thrift store bin anymore. She straightened as if she had forgotten herself and said, "Today, I'm going to have you dust the house, but tomorrow, I'm going to have you go to town to pick up some cleaning products."

Dusting proved to be more difficult than I expected. I had to bring a ladder in from the covered parking, and even then, I struggled to reach the heights where cobwebs mocked me in the corners of the rooms. Mrs. Swollas would appear out of nowhere to inform me that I had missed a spot before vanishing once again.

The silence made me nervous. If only I had a radio or something, it wouldn't have been so bad. I thought I saw one outside, but I wasn't about to climb down the ladder and walk halfway through the house for a radio. The thing probably needed batteries.

Standing on the kitchen counters, I wiped an inch of dust and dirt off the top of the cabinet when a gust of unexpected wind pelted my face with debris. My face scrunched as I hacked and wheezed. My eyes snapped shut in defense. My damn allergies were going to make this even harder than it already was. A wave of vertigo came over me, and I grappled at the cabinet in a state of panic.

Steadying myself, I stood frozen on the countertop for several minutes before I opened my stinging eyes.

"What are you doing?"

I looked over my shoulder to find Mrs. Swollas standing below me. Her head was tilted like she was observing an idiot in her natural habitat. "Some dust flew into my eyes," I said. "I got a little dizzy."

"Come down from there before you hurt yourself," she demanded.

Prying my hands away from the cabinet, I did as I was told. One shaky leg at a time. It was an awkward descent, but once my feet were on solid ground, I finally took a solid breath. "The wind," I said, searching for the source of it. "It came out of nowhere."

Mrs. Swollas frowned. "I've not opened any windows."

Neither had I.

"Try not to injure yourself if you don't mind."

"I'll try—"

And just like that, she was gone again. She only seemed to show up when I did something wrong or stupid. I had been dusting for hours, and there were no signs of cameras anywhere. Maybe she just had a nose for trouble. Then again, if she had some kind of radar for disasters, she would have stayed clear from me.

On the drive home, I turned up the classic country station and sang all the way home. Rent would be partially covered by my last unemployment check, but the rest of the bills could wait until my first paycheck in a week. Even a week's worth of pay would cover them. I was eager to be home. I wanted to tell Greg every detail and revel in our success.

Smells of garlic and oregano hit me when I opened the apartment door. Well ahead of me with celebrations, Greg was in the kitchen making spaghetti. My eyes lingered on his pants. He filled out those jeans in all the right places. It wasn't all bad having a man at home all day. The apartment was spotless, and the washer was empty.

"Hey, good looking," I said.

"How was your first day?" he asked as he poked at the red sauce with a wooden spoon.

I wasn't quite sure how it went. On one hand, I learned a little bit about my strange employer, but I almost fell off the counter. I supposed she thought me a bit clumsy and dumb, but I hoped I could grow into the position over time. "Well enough, I suppose."

He glanced up at me to assess my face. "She wasn't mean, was she?"

"No," I said. "She's not hateful. A little strange, I guess."

"You said she's not from around here."

I poured a bit of the red wine into a cup and sat down at the dinner table. "Yeah, she's from Europe, though she doesn't know where anymore, bless her heart."

Greg frowned. "Like she can't remember?"

"No," I said, sipping the merlot. "She remembers but I think it was like a war situation. She said the name has changed so many times that even she doesn't know anymore."

"Damn," he said, plating up the noodles. "She must have been around post World War Two. A lot of things changed and collapsed after that mess."

"She's all alone up there," I said, staring into my glass.

If the clink of the plate on the table didn't get my attention, the smell of the sauce did. I scarfed it down while Greg seated himself. "She's not alone; she's got you to look after her now."

"She's a proud old bird," I said, slurping up a noodle. "You should have saw her face when I explained how we make sweet tea."

Greg laughed and dug into his dinner. Afterward, we sat together on the couch, watched old sitcom reruns, and held hands. Occasionally, he'd sweep my hair off my shoulder and kiss it. He was always the affectionate type. Sometimes, I'd find him staring at me for no reason at all, and it made me giggle. I was never the prettiest girl in the group. I never entered the pageants, and I didn't make the cheer squad in the four years I tried out. Greg always treated me like I was the most beautiful woman in the room.

That night, after a little celebratory sex, I was lulled into an easy sleep while the air conditioner hummed in the window. I dreamt that I was on a grassy hill, only I was a little kid. I was wearing a white woolen dress despite the sun bearing down on me. It was long-sleeved with lacy bits, and the bonnet was making my head itch.

On the grass before me, there was a little tea set. It was hand-painted with little blue flowers on the smoothed wooden cups and saucers. A heavy, silver teapot sat in the middle.

"Would you like some tea?" a child's voice asked. It must have been my own because I picked up the pot and offered to pour. It was like living in someone else's head. I was a silent observer with only one perspective in a story that wasn't my own.

A teacup was held out, but my bonnet obscured whoever I was serving tea to. I poured what looked like water into the cup. A broken, impossibly crooked finger weaved around the cup's handle. I wanted to scream, but the little girl did not.

"Eat your cookies, Auntie," my voice rang.

On one of the wooden plates there were indeed cookies. Little plain shortbreads like from the Danish tins you bought at the supermarket, only these were fresh, and I could smell the butter. A hand from a different direction took the cookie. It was a normal enough hand, but the fingernails were caked with dirt and bloodied.

I desperately wanted to lift my head to see past the bonnet, but I had no control over this body. It was like I was weighted in place. Something about all this wasn't right, and I couldn't do a thing about it. Where was I, and who were these people?

The little girl sang a sweet song in a foreign tongue while topping off her own cup of tea. Only this time it wasn't water. Dark, thick blood poured from the pot. Cups were now being eagerly shoved in my direction. "Now, now," the little girl said. "There's enough to go around."

Blood poured into the cups and overflowed onto the saucers. It clashed against grass so green it must have rained daily for years. The little girl lifted her head. Out from underneath the bonnet, I saw them. One was a body broken so many times, it was hard to make out head or tail. The nose was smashed to one side against the face. The brow bones were broken so badly, the eyeballs were missing. A sizable dent of the temple crushed inward, and the neck was swollen and contorted with sharp, jutting pieces in every direction.

The one the kid called Auntie was just monstrous. Her body wasn't broken and healed back up countless times, but her long, stringy brown hair laid flat across her head and all the way down the body. The bottom half of her jaw was at the bottom of her neck and her tongue was big and flat, the tip of it lapped up the blood in the teacup.

Powerless to do anything else, I screamed. I shrieked as loud and as hard as I could inside the girl, but she didn't seem to hear it. Next thing I knew, my body was being shaken by the shoulders. I had my body back! I swung my arms out in front of me and began slapping anything I could, but it was dark now, and the humming of the AC was back.

"Jayme," Greg said. "Jayme, are you alright? You were having a night terror."

I stopped smacking poor Greg and felt my face. I was covered in sweat. The cold air from the AC soothed my heated body, and after several breaths, I finally had enough air to cry.

"Baby, what happened?" Greg's voice was raspy and strained. "Sweetie..."

"It was awful," I cried. "I was a little girl, or I was in a little girl's body, I don't know, but she was feeding monsters tea!"

It sounded so stupid out loud, but it was so scary. How could I explain it? Those creatures... the blood in the teacups.

"It was just a dream," Greg said.

"I know it was a dream!" I spit at him. I wanted to hit him, but he was just trying to make me feel better. "I used to have night terrors all the time as a little girl. I thought I grew out of them."

"I used to wet the bed," Greg told me. "Be thankful I haven't relapsed."

That made me giggle. He nuzzled my neck and stayed up with me for hours as I told him about the nightmare. He held me close and stroked my back until I relaxed in his arms. "I think it's probably your mind trying to process your new job. You mentioned that gargoyle the lady has, and you had tea."

The rationalization made sense. "She has these rules. One of them is that if I cut myself, I need to leave immediately until it stops bleeding. Greg, I think she just hates the sight of blood but doesn't want to look weak."

"Probably for insurance reasons, too, I bet," he added.

He was probably right. I was mashing together all the things from work and turned it into a freaky ass dream. "I think I just got a little worked up over this job. It's just so much money; I don't want to screw it up for us."

Greg took my head into his hands. "Hey, don't talk like that. You are not the screw-up here. If anything, it's me. I can't keep holding out just to get back at my ex."

What was he saying? That he was finally going back to work? "You mean you're going to go back?"

"I am," he said. "My wages will be lower than ever, but at least then you won't need to put so much pressure on yourself. I'm not going to let Claire win anymore."

I fell asleep in his arms that night with the assurance that things would turn out no matter what. They had to. That was how life worked. Things could go from bad to worse, but that didn't mean you stopped moving. We would get through the debt and the divorce together. I just hoped those monsters wouldn't be waiting for me when I went back to sleep.

4

— • —

It had been a week since the dream, and nothing like it had happened again. Chalking it up to a weird stress reaction, I laid in bed and basked in the glory that was sleep after all the bills were paid. For the first time in years, there was a positive remainder in my bank account. I could get used to this. As I stretched across the bed, there was a disturbing amount of space. I turned to find Greg's side of the bed empty. Panic seized my brain as I clambered out of bed.

Not again. He wouldn't. He didn't fucking dare. If he took that car again, so help me...

Shoving the blinds to one side, parking spot number fifty-seven was vacant. "Son of a bitch!"

Inside, I discovered that not only did he take the car, but he took the smartphone too, leaving me with an old pre-paid cellphone we got when we couldn't pay the phone bill and it got disconnected. I paid the late fees and the service charge, so it was agreed that it was my phone. I yanked the old phone off the charger, and the cord came with it as I punched at the push buttons of the cell phone.

"Hello?" he answered. He had big brass balls to answer as though he weren't expecting my call.

"What the fuck?" I screamed.

"I needed to attend this seminar. I think this could be bigger than any professor job."

Oh, not again. How the hell did he keep finding these things? This was not the first time he'd been whisked into a scam. For women, it was cosmetics or diet pills, but Greg always managed to find the kind that promised millions by recruiting others to sell junk.

"You couldn't have asked? How am I supposed to get to work?"

"I was told to dress nice and not be late. There are some millionaires in this group. They have this great opportunity—I can possibly earn money without Claire even knowing about it."

"Oh, Greg, not another pyramid scheme!"

I attended the last meeting with him. It resulted in a fight where I slept on the couch for a week before he finally agreed it wouldn't work. How could he jeopardize a good paying job I had only worked for two weeks? One paycheck was all it took to make him forget about everything we went through while unemployed. How could he do this to us again?

"This one is different," he started.

That was what he said last time, too. I knew better than to fall for his promise that he'd go back to the college. I was so stupid sometimes. Sure, he was the college graduate who fell for the pyramid schemes, but I was the one who kept forgiving him.

"Greg, listen to me. If you don't turn that car around and get your ass back home right now, I'm going to pack your bags and change the locks."

There was no answer. I held my phone in front of my face and pulled it to a distance until the screen came into focus. The call ended. He hung up on me. The bastard hung up on me.

I let out a scream in frustration. No doubt the neighbors had heard it before.

Without a phone with internet, I was forced to use his laptop to schedule a driving service. While I was at it, I changed his background image to the most disgusting thing I could find on the internet—the image of a severely infected vagina—before snapping the lid shut. Let his students see that when he plugs his computer into the projector screen...if he ever goes back to teaching.

I arrived at work only a few minutes late, thanks to the driver. No thanks to my boyfriend. Still fuming and stressed from the awful morning, I marched down the driveway, muttering under my breath. This was the last time. I was going to sleep with the keys taped to my wrist.

All was peaceful outside the house, despite the spring warming the nearby swamps. In the place of the chirping of birds, the clicking of crickets, and the low burps of frogs, there was nothing. Only the occasional rustle when the breeze caught the leaves.

I was greeted by the mocking smile of the Gargoyle. It was like he was laughing at my morning. The thing gave me the willies. There were all sorts of statues at plant nurseries, and I never got the urge to talk to them. Their eyes didn't follow me as I walked. They were nowhere near as hideous.

Refusing to give breath to my suspicions, I shook off the stiff hairs along the nape of my neck and pushed one of the front doors open. For all her precautions, Mrs. Swollas did not lock her doors, but the silence did not fool me. I had worked here for two weeks and had never caught the woman asleep. She was likely in one of the locked rooms and would make herself known soon enough. I was late, and she'd be certain to point that out.

I draped my jacket over the back of a dinette chair in the kitchen before putting the kettle on. Time to summon the beast.

Steam was billowing out of the spout but not quite ready when a sudden chill filled the room. An irrational urge to run took hold, and my heart thumped in my chest. This wasn't all that unfamiliar, though it usually didn't happen unless bill collectors were calling. Bracing the counter, I took deep, intentional breaths.

It's okay. Bills are paid. Money is in the bank. Job is steady.

But Greg had still taken the car. Stupid asshole. He was bent on these get rich quick schemes instead of a real job. What was he thinking? The driving service was more reliable than my boyfriend—what did that say about our relationship? I was willing to drag him into a better life if that's what it took, but maybe he didn't want that. Maybe my love could only do so much.

I braced the counter and trembled. I hated these. Usually, I could talk myself out of a panic attack, but this one came on so quickly. My breaths were visible in the air, and the hair on my arms shot straight up. I tried rubbing the goosebumps down, but it hurt when the palm of my hand raked over them.

There were whispers then. Faint and melodic. My eyes sought the source, but the singer was out of my peripheral vision. A window rattled as something smacked against it, and I let out a little gasp. Jarred from my anxiety attack, I went to the window to investigate. A scarlet, oozing smear slid down the window. It must have been a bird, bless its heart.

The kettle screeched. I whirled around and came face to face with a withered old scowl. "If you're quite finished," Mrs. Swollas said.

Clutching my chest, I stifled my cry.

Mrs. Swollas frowned at my reaction. "Are you all right?"

"A bird hit the window."

The kettle raged on, insolent from neglect. I took it off the burner and reached for the cups with shaky hands. Mrs. Swollas tilted her head as she regarded the window. "Yes, that happens frequently here. You'd think the birds would have something better to do in spring."

"I think it's because the windows are so large."

"Perhaps."

She seated herself in the chair opposite mine, and I set the tea before her before joining.

"Are you having car troubles?" she asked.

I didn't think she had seen me come in. The only thing outside to greet me was that nasty gargoyle.

"My boyfriend..." I didn't want to finish the sentence. Greg took the car after promising he wouldn't to go to a pyramid scheme event he promised not to. Broken promises were a norm with Greg, but it was my fault for putting up with it.

Mrs. Swollas eyed me. "Men are a troublesome sort."

"He's had a rough few years," I said. Telling her about my issues wasn't something I prided myself on, but I had no one else to talk to about it. "His divorce changed him."

The old lady sipped her tea. I moved to do the same but when I did, the hot water scalded my tongue so badly, I had to spit it back into the cup. If Mrs. Swollas saw, she said nothing. I was embarrassed, but I couldn't swallow that; it would have burned the shit out of my throat.

"I once had a daughter," Mrs. Swollas said. "I urged her to marry. A mistake if there ever was one."

"Was he a dud?"

Mrs. Swollas's lips puckered into a smile. "A dud?"

"Like, he was a bad guy."

The lady giggled. "Oh, he was the worst sort. He loved her too much. It proved to be their demise."

Oh. I forgot my blistered taste buds for a moment. "What happened?"

"A story for another day, I think," Mrs. Swollas said. "Today, we must wash the linens. It's a good day for it."

Poor Mrs. Swollas. I knew her past was tragic, but to lose her only child must have been unbearable.

I followed the lady out of the kitchen as she said, "We will need to wash that window as well."

"Yes, ma'am."

I stripped the beds that had been made and balled the sheets and comforters at the top of the steps before kicking the mountain down the stairs. I imagined it was Greg instead of a heap of laundry. Booting his ass would be more satisfying, but that would have to wait until I got home. Mrs. Swollas was right. Men were more hassle than they were worth. He could move in with his mom and drive her crazy with his bullshit.

The lump of laundry flopped onto the middle landing. I followed and kicked it again, sending the pile to the ground.

"What are you doing?" Mrs. Swollas materialized beside the linens.

I froze in place, not sure what she was referring to. I was doing what she asked. "Bringing down the laundry."

Hands on her waspish waist, the lady was unimpressed. "Is that how you treat your own bedding?"

It was a bunch of sheets. What was I supposed to do? "I didn't mean any harm."

"Well, I'd appreciate it if you didn't kick my belongings around the house."

They were just going to be washed anyway. My cheeks flamed, and I swallowed the angry lump in my throat. "Yes, ma'am. Where should I take them?"

"Outside, of course."

She'd given me a tour of the home, and over the last two weeks, I had the run of the place. I was sure there was no washer outside. What were we going to do? Wash the linens in the swamp?

I gathered the mass of beddings and followed Mrs. Swollas to the carport. Outside, there were two halves of a barrel, separated and each filled with water. She had a shelf clear and motioned for me to put the laundry there. Oh, no. She meant to wash this all by hand. I know my grandparents did this back in the day, but once washing machines became affordable, no one turned back.

There was no dishwasher either, but with one woman living on her own, it made sense she didn't need one. The sink was always empty; Mrs. Swollas was already in the habit of washing her dishes and putting them away. But no washing machine?

One of the barrels had a hand crank and the other a washboard. I had seen those used for making music but never for laundry. The image of shoeless men in overalls with banjos and guitars came to mind. Straw hats and summer heat. Fireflies flittering among the trees. It was a cartoony stereotype for the most part, but not the worst one.

I had been to many reunions where folks would pick up guitars and collaborate. Banjos were much harder to play than people realized. The only person I knew who could play one was my great uncle, and even then, he could only do a few licks.

Mrs. Swollas knew nothing of this. I wished I could share it with her, but she was in a foul mood, and nothing amused her in this state. It was a good thing I was wearing a t-shirt today.

I grabbed a few sheets off the top only to be corrected. She snatched the sheet from my hands and replaced it with a heavy woolen blanket.

"Blankets first," Mrs. Swollas said. "They need to dry the longest."

Still stinging from the last lecture, I ignored the irritation around my eyes and did as I was told. I didn't mean to be so sensitive, but I couldn't help it sometimes. Between the bad morning and the anxiety attack, I was raw and ready to cry at any moment.

"You do know how to wash, correct?"

"Well, I've never washed anything by hand before."

The old woman's cheeks puffed. "Goodness, what use are you?"

I was beginning to wonder that myself.

Mrs. Swollas ripped the blanket from my hands and shoved it into the water. "Plunge, scrub, plunge, scrub."

Blinking back hot, angry tears, I observed as Mrs. Swollas washed the blanket. It wasn't necessary to be so gruff about it. Why was she so angry with me? I was barely late and hadn't done anything to deserve this. Not everyone was born centuries ago.

In her wrinkled, pruned hands, Mrs. Swollas held up a white bar of soap and said, "Soap. Any dullard can manage."

She rubbed the bar over the edge of the blanket not submerged in the water and repeated the process before resuming her patronizing "plunge and scrub" lecture. She wrung the blanket as much as she could before transferring the wet mass to the other barrel where she plunged the blanket into the clean water and said in a softer tone, "You can leave a blanket in this while starting on another."

Was it guilt the old lady was feeling? After patronizing me for the past ten minutes, it was too little too late. I needed the money, but did I need it this bad? I had been on the receiving end of many angry bosses, but none of them had ever left me so shelled.

The bags under her eyes drooped more than usual, and she was panting. She was too old to do this work. Her shoulders slumped with a heavy weight, too. I couldn't help but link this outburst to her daughter.

"If you want, I can find a washing machine for you," I said quietly, tugging at the edge of my shirt. "That way, it won't be so exhausting.

And winters here can get rough. It'll be too cold to go outside and get all wet."

Mrs. Swollas straightened. "I wouldn't have the slightest idea what to do with it."

"I can show you," I offered, pulling a blanket from the pile before taking it to the wash barrel. "I'd just hate to have you out here washing in a foot of snow come winter."

"That's why I have you," she replied glibly.

She was just teasing, I knew that, but after being berated over the wash it still hurt my feelings. "What if I'm not here come winter?" I asked.

The suggestion put the old woman on her heels. It was as if the fact that I could just drive off and not come back was something she hadn't considered. Mrs. Swollas's chin jutted out as if she were chewing on an unsavory morsel. How about them sour apples?

"I won't have any delivery boys here," she said at last. "You can buy this thing with my money, but you'll need to find a way to put it in yourself."

One of her rules in action. Fine. "I can have them delivered to the front door and—"

"No one else must know I'm here but you," she insisted.

"I'd need to rent a truck."

"So be it." The old woman waved me away with one hand and massaged her brow with the other. "I trust you have this in hand. I need to rest."

So, it does sleep after all. "I'll be fine."

The laundry took up several hours of the day. I hung everything on the lines she had strung up along the side of the house while listening to the country station on the radio I found on one of the shelves, singing along to the songs I knew even if I didn't like them.

Maybe I'd get her one of those clothes umbrellas while I was at it. While a dryer would be useful, it couldn't beat the scent of air-dried clothes. It would be more compact than this elaborate system she had strung around the edge of the hill, too.

Cell service was nonexistent out here, and Mrs. Swollas didn't have internet. I would need to drive into town and buy the washer and dryer from a local store. There was a hardware store about an hour's drive from here, but I didn't have the damn car.

I took out my frustration on the sheet, wringing the life out of it until my knuckles went white. I couldn't decide if it was Greg's neck or Mrs. Swollas's neck I was wringing, but it felt good. I was so tired of being the pushover, but I didn't know how to not be. I needed to buck up. It was for Greg's best interests that I did. As for Mrs. Swollas, who knew what she would do if I put my foot down? She frightened me the way I imagined she frightened everyone else.

Whatever soap she used left my skin feeling tacky and coated my hands. It resisted the scrubbing in the clean water and caked every pore and crack in my skin. What was this stuff? I rubbed my thumb and index fingers together. It was almost glue-like.

Bringing my fingers close to my nose, I sniffed at it. It was that fresh, clean scent most cleaning products had, but there was a hint of lavender and something else, something sickly sweet. I would have to introduce Mrs. Swollas to laundry detergent. This soap would gunk up the pipes faster than cheese fondue.

Instead of cutting through the house to get to the bloodied window, I walked around. The dead leaves and twigs from the neglected property crunched underfoot. They were herded and piled high in corners by the wind, and the occasional breeze wafted from the swamps from down the hill. Stagnant water-filled air billowed against the hanging linens, making large wavy shadows against the house.

It might have been the shadows playing tricks on my eyes, but I could have sworn the gargoyle had shifted slightly. Closer now than I had ever dared to go, I could still feel its eyes on me, but that couldn't be right. Its head was facing the driveway. Still, from this angle, his wings appeared lower than before, and its head was tilted slightly in my direction.

Racked with a shiver, I shook my hands as I ran under the balcony and to the other side of the house. "Eck, that thing gives me the heebie jeebies," I said, hoping it could hear.

There was a water spigot, but no hose. I found a tin bucket half rusted over, filled that, and sort of flung it at the window. It wasn't the most efficient job, but it was cleaner than before. I never found the poor bird. It must have been a big blue jay or a small hawk, judging by the size of the blood splatter and the way the window rattled when it hit, but there was no evidence in the gravel. Maybe it had survived somehow and flew away.

My stomach twisted and rumbled. It occurred to me that I didn't bring lunch. Without a car, I couldn't go out and get anything. My blood sugar warned me that I'd regret skipping out on lunch and breakfast, so I went to the kitchen to see if there was something I could fix up. Trudging up the steps, I rounded the sharp corners and the curved ones too until I finally reached the kitchen.

If I ever got myself a house, it would be a small one. It was a lot of work keeping up with this place, and running from one end to another for a bag of chips and a Coke wouldn't be worth it. I used to dream of owning a big old house on some property, but now that I knew what it was like, I decided that it wasn't for me.

My parents had a manufactured home on a bit of land. Before he died, my daddy always fancied himself a farmer. They had some chickens and six teacup Dachshunds that would run along the fence and bark at every passing car. Mama had an herb garden and tomato plants, but that was the extent of their farm. The house was the perfect size, though. Not too big, not too small.

I opened the blue-enameled Frigidaire, and my mouth dropped. There was nothing inside. Not a single thing. No milk jug, no carton of eggs, not even ketchup. It was empty, as though no one had used it. It was in working order—there was a chill, and the fridge motor kicked on—but it was spotless.

Did she keep a freezer somewhere else? I hadn't seen anything, and I didn't imagine she was the sort to hide food when she kept her tea in the cupboard. I checked all the other cupboards one by one, and each time, my concern for the woman grew until I debated interrupting her nap. There wasn't a single scrap of food in the house.

It was a rule that no one come to the house, so I knew she didn't do take out. Plus, I would have seen the remains somewhere. I opened the garbage can and found that it, too, was nearly empty. The only things in there were used tea bags and yesterday's sack lunch.

How was she eating? What if she wasn't? My mind went back to my mama before we put her in a nursing home. She was afraid to take showers and stunk of body odor, and she stopped cooking after she lit a dishrag on fire. Mama knew she wasn't right, and it scared her so bad that she stopped taking care of herself. What if Mrs. Swollas was in the same position, only she didn't have a family to look after her?

Mrs. Swollas didn't stink, and she seemed cognizant. Her stride was always determined and her words precise. Her long flowy gowns were unwrinkled, and her hair was never out of place. From her long-manicured fingernails down to the shine on her shoes, nothing about Mrs. Swollas suggested suffered from dementia.

"What are you doing?"

I whirled around with a start. She had a bad habit of appearing right behind me. "You're up."

It was probably just my imagination, but Mrs. Swollas's smile was tinted with menace. She had recovered some from her nap. Her eyes were a little softer and there was a hint of color in her cheeks. "Were you expecting otherwise?"

It was her dry humor, I knew, but it still had me feeling uneasy. Something about this just wasn't right, but how to broach the topic? I didn't want to come off as nosey or prying into business that wasn't my own, but this was my business now, wasn't it? She wouldn't approve of silly questions. "I cleaned the window," I said. "And the laundry is finished."

She gave a nod of approval. "The garbage is satisfactory as well?"

I lifted my foot from the pedal, and the lid of the can resounded with emptiness. "Yeah, just thought I'd check. There isn't much in there."

"Tea, my dear," she said before sitting in her chair.

"Yes, ma'am."

The kettle was on and the cups prepared. My stomach would be grateful for anything in it at this rate.

Swollas... It was a strange name. I had never heard anything like it before. If I didn't know any better, I'd say it was made up. But that was a stupid thought. Why would someone as proud and eccentric as her go and change her name?

"You're brimming with questions," Mrs. Swollas said, folding her fingers neatly on the table before her.

Damn. She could read me better than Greg. I had always wished I were the mysterious sort, the kind that had all the boys falling all over themselves. Dark hair and bright eyes and that cruel smile that had them begging for more. Instead, I was the girl you sat next to on the bus for six months but never bothered to learn her name.

"I bet you were striking as a young woman," I said.

"Am I not striking now?" she asked, taking the cup into her hands.

Come to think of it, she really was. Yeah, she was old, but not in the way I had always seen and expected women to age. It was more like she was out of time. Like some aging heiress or a career ballerina. Age only added grace and sophistication to Mrs. Swollas's face. For most people, age was backpain, diabetes, and cataracts. She had none of these.

"Well, yeah," I said. "But I just mean I wonder what you looked like in your twenties."

"I did not reach my prime until my forties," she explained, taking a sip of her tea. "I was beautiful to be sure, but I had no idea what to do with it. I floundered and chased the man I wanted even when he was engaged to someone else. I allowed others to determine my worth. No, it wasn't until I had a daughter of my own that I realized just what power I had."

A cloud of self-doubt drifted over me then. Wasn't I worth it? Greg could say or do just about anything, and I let him walk right over me. He took my car, took the phone with internet, didn't pay for anything. I told myself it was just because he was going through a bad phase, but we both knew the truth. I could do better, but that didn't mean I deserved it.

"I wish I could do that," I said dismally.

"You remind me so much of my daughter. She was an anxious girl who always second-guessed herself. I thought getting married would make her stronger, but..."

She already mentioned this before. It was replaying in her mind a lot today for some reason. Past regrets had that effect on anyone, but this specific instance was something Mrs. Swollas wanted to speak of but also wanted to avoid reliving. To speak trauma out loud confirmed its impact on your life, but I suspected something else was at play here.

"What was her name?" I asked.

Mrs. Swollas's green eyes widened as if I startled her with a question out of the blue. "Who?"

My heart sunk in my chest. It was just as I feared. Mrs. Swollas wanted to tell me about her daughter, but she couldn't remember what happened. "Your daughter."

The old woman muttered under her breath, caught in the alarm of it all. She shook her head and said, "I think I'm still groggy from that nap. I can't seem to remember."

"Did you still want me to look into a washer and dryer?" I asked. I hoped she didn't forget that one. I was not about to wash everything by hand again.

Mrs. Swollas was still rattled but gave a sullen nod. "My purse is hanging on the coatrack. Take the blue Visa card."

While I was out, I'd buy her some food. At least some protein shakes and some crackers—anything to get her to eat. No doubt her memory and mood were being impacted by not eating. Knowing she had absolutely no food in the house and couldn't remember her daughter's name, I did not want to leave her alone. "Are you sure you don't want me to stay a little longer?"

"It's nearly dark," she said, facing the window. "You know the rule."

I got the impression it wasn't her rule, rather a rule imposed on her, but by who? It wasn't like there was anyone around, not I could picture anyone telling Mrs. Swollas what to do. Still, it felt like she didn't want me to leave.

"Are you sure?"

"Go," she said. Her reflection warped in the glass, and for a moment, it was like she was someone else. In the place of the old woman's reflection was a young girl with elvish features, sharp and cruel. I was so startled, I staggered back. I didn't believe in ghosts, but this place was changing my mind.

I blinked, and she turned away from the window to regard me. "Are you alright?" she asked.

Nope. I felt the blood draining from my face and my fingers were numb and clumsy. I was lightheaded and, for a split-second, I thought I was going to fall over. The dizziness evaporated, and I sighed. "I skipped lunch," I explained.

Mrs. Swollas frowned the way any mother would at the mention of skipping meals. "Really, you're a grown woman. You should know better. Bring food here; I hardly use this kitchen."

So, she was aware of how it appeared? "I was going to ask you," I said. "It took me by surprise that there was no food in here."

"I have a kitchenette in my study," she explained. "It's adjacent to my library where I spend most of my time. It became too bothersome to use and maintain both, so I found myself using just the one."

"Oh, that makes me feel so much better," I said. "For a minute, I was scared that you weren't eating."

Mrs. Swollas dismissed my fears with a wave of her hand. "My appetite has always been peculiar at best, but I ate fowl just this morning. Just enough to keep the cravings at bay."

That was a relief. I had wondered why there was only one kitchen in a house with two wings, but there was a second kitchen just tucked away. Running up and down these stairs took it out of me on most days, so I could understand an elderly woman sticking to a small kitchenette.

"Is there any limit you want me to stick to when buying stuff?" I asked.

Mrs. Swollas thought about it. "It has a limit of forty-five thousand, so try not to spend that much. Otherwise, I fear it won't work."

My lip curled at one corner as I stared at the woman. She had known me all of a few weeks but was handing me a credit card with a high enough amount to outright buy a house. Wasn't she worried about theft? It didn't appear that way. She was sipping her tea without a second thought on the matter. I had assumed her rule of no visitors was a safety precaution, but clearly, money wasn't a concern. It explained my wages.

Mrs. Swollas had little to no concept of the value of money. Back in high school, our history class had a brief section on World War Two. Students asked why anyone would support the Nazi party, but the teacher showed us a picture of a half-starved woman with a wheelbarrow full of money.

German woman buys bread.

Their money basically meant nothing, so people were buying a single loaf of bread for thousands in whatever their currency was at the time. The memory made me feel sick to my stomach. Mrs. Swollas did not leave the house. Never. At least not that I saw. How had she managed all these years without basic knowledge of the world? How did she manage to get into the states?

I was beginning to suspect she was an illegal immigrant who could fly under the radar because she was a white woman. People around here called them illegals or illegal Aliens, but Greg hated those terms. I used to use them until he pitched a fit, and he was right to do so. They never call people like Mrs. Swollas an illegal, but for some reason, it was okay to call a Mexican that.

Maybe the reason she didn't want to go out or have people around the house was because she feared they'd check her immigration status.

Whatever the reason, it was in my best interest to keep my employer a secret or I'd be out of a job.

I clutched the card in my hand like it was a winning lottery ticket. "I think a brand-new washer and dryer is a few thousand."

"Very well. Get what you think is best, but you should leave. There is a car honking on the street."

Shit. I forgot about the driver I had scheduled for taking me home. "I should go."

Mrs. Swollas eyed me with a smirk as she sipped her tea. On her lips was a joke I wasn't in on. I rushed out the door and gave one glance over my shoulder. Whatever Mrs. Swollas thought was so funny, her nasty gargoyle also thought it was funny. Its wicked grin sent me running all the faster toward the car.

5

— • —

I had forgotten all about the fight I had with Greg up until the moment I walked in the door to find a bouquet of red roses in a blue glass vase. I was furious all over again, but he was making omelets, and I was too hungry to argue. He gave me a sheepish glance before sliding a massive cheese and pepperoni omelet on a plate. Wordlessly, I took it from him and fished a fork out of the drawer, shoveling food into my mouth as I sat down.

He had the good sense to wait for me to finish eating before saying anything. I ate quickly and mindlessly until my stomach went queasy. That morning, I had debated all the ways I wanted to punish him, but with my stomach full, I could only think about Mrs. Swollas.

"I'm worried about that woman," I said, taking a sip of wine that had been waiting unbeknownst to me until a moment ago. "I think her mind might be slipping."

Greg leaned back in his chair and crossed his arms. "You don't think she's a danger to herself, do you?"

I shook my head. Honestly, I didn't know. "The house is weird. It's almost like she's a captive in it. Greg, she can't remember her daughter's name."

"Can you get her to a doctor?"

"No. She wouldn't agree to that, and I can't bring one over because of her rules."

"I don't know, Jayme," he said. "If you think she's in trouble, you should do what you think is best for her and damn her rules."

"I think you're right."

Of course he was right. If Mrs. Swollas needed medical attention, I couldn't just turn a blind eye. Job or no job. I could always find another, but if she died on my watch, I would never forgive myself. Still, I didn't want to betray her trust either. "She doesn't act like she has dementia; she's quick and takes good care of herself. But I don't know…"

I couldn't explain it without sounding crazy. The expression on her face when I offered to stay. It was like she didn't want me to leave but had no choice. What was she hiding in that big old house with its locked doors and scary gargoyle guardian perched on the balcony?

Greg took this seriously, and I was grateful. His face stern and brow furrowed. "You said she couldn't remember her daughter's name. You said she died, right? Did she say how?"

"Something to do with her husband."

"I wonder if it's not a dementia thing but more of a trauma issue. Sometimes, people with PTSD have memory issues. It sort of just pops into their head when they don't want it to."

"That sounds more like her," I said. "She mentioned her daughter's death twice today but didn't go into details."

Greg nodded. "She still needs help, but it may not be due to her age. Older generations carry their trauma along with them. They don't want to talk about it or admit they need help."

That was the epitome of Mrs. Swollas. That reminded me. I needed to buy her a washer and dryer. "Can I borrow your laptop?" I asked. "I need to do some work."

"Yeah, sure."

He got up and took his laptop from the living room and placed it in front of me before whisking away the empty plate. If there was a medal for skating on thin ice, Greg would have been an undefeated champion. I was angrier at myself for not doing anything about it than I was at him.

"You doing some research?" he asked.

The credit card remained in my purse. I didn't want him to know she had given it to me. I was just anxious to be using someone else's card, and the amount of money available was troubling. He had so many debts—one swipe of that card would solve some of his problems. He wouldn't do that, though. No one would accept he was H. Swollas, for one, but if she reported it as fraud, it would be too easy to trace back to him.

"Yeah, I told her I would help her find a washer and dryer for the house."

He sat down beside me as if he intended on helping my search. I wanted to tell him to bug-off, but there was no reason to do that. Greg would know more about appliances than I would. Still, I didn't want him asking questions. I hated lying.

"You said she didn't want visitors," he said. "How are you going to get them over there?"

I sighed. The prospect of dragging them in and connecting them myself wasn't something I was thrilled about. Greg nodded and said, "I could help, you know."

"No, you can't come over either."

"Even me, huh?"

Especially you.

The thought took me by surprise. Why would I think something like that? He wasn't a thief. Well, only when it came to the car. It killed me to be so suspicious of him. Guilt wracked my brain over it. We both made our fair share of mistakes. Lars didn't deserve to be embarrassed in front of our families the way he was. He flew people all the way from Germany to attend the wedding.

Our honeymoon to Hawaii was non-refundable. I never did ask what he did with it. Maybe he went by himself. It was unbearable to picture Lars by himself with a lay around his neck, drinking by himself. If his brother went with him it wouldn't have been so bad. Two Germans all laid up at a bar watching pretty girls dancing while drinking Pina Coladas. That made me feel a little better. He moved on, had a bunch of kids. His wife was gorgeous.

My resentment settled. I couldn't beat on Greg for trying to do what he could to save himself. It was the only way he could be with me. "I guess not," I said. "She doesn't trust anyone."

"Hm."

Something in me stirred then. Like a snake rearing its head before it struck. A deep-seated anger or something, but it wasn't like me. At the same time, I couldn't stop the words from coming out of my mouth. "Greg," I said with an air of coolness, "if you take my car without my permission again, I'm going to kick you out."

That wasn't what I had wanted to say at all! What was that about? I was so startled, and so was Greg. He raised his eyebrows, surprised that I made such a threat. "What's gotten into you? You know I'm sorry."

A swell of panic bubbled in my ribs. What the hell was wrong with me? I opened my mouth to apologize, and something else came out. "Sorry isn't enough," I said. "No more excuses. Go back to teaching."

There it was again! I said sorry, but then my mouth kept on running. I shook my head, just as confused by this as he was.

"I didn't say those things."

His face prickled red as he glowered at me. "Who the hell are you to tell me what to do? I already said I was thinking about going back. I think that old lady is a bad influence. Claire used to make ultimatums like this all the time.

"I...didn't say those things."

He was angry and didn't believe me; I didn't believe me either. He was on his feet and walking away. "You know I don't like games."

"Greg," I started, "I don't know where that came from, I swear. It wasn't me. It was like someone else was talking through me."

He stood and strode off. "Well, I guess now that you have a good job, you have it all figured out."

What the hell just happened? I sat there on the couch for several long minutes, waiting for something else to happen, but nothing did. I mouthed words, but they were the words I intended to speak. Was there some kind of mental disorder that made people say things they didn't want to say?

Come to think of it, I wasn't all that upset about what I had said. It was like half of me truly meant it. He did kind of deserve it, even if it wasn't what my brain was trying to say. My body was more tired of his shit than I thought. I had been working myself to the bone these last few weeks, and he was only adding to the stress when he should have been supporting me. Still, if I did something like that again, I'd need to see a doctor.

On the screen, a folder labeled 'Thesis' sat prominently next to a wilted, blue vagina lip. I clicked on it and saw research on how to extend life using plants now extinct due to deforestation. The thesis itself was still a blank page. After all these months, he hadn't done a damn thing.

Before I finished up for the night, I made sure to delete my browser history. The severely infected vagina was still the picture on the screen.

I was surprised he didn't say something, but maybe he hadn't used his laptop at all. He certainly wasn't working on that thesis like he claimed... What else did he do all day?

At least with Greg out of the room, I was able to shop for appliances in peace. Armed with Mrs. Swollas's card, I purchased a washer and dryer and got a rental truck. I decided on a front loader. I preferred top load, but the new ones were so big, I was afraid Mrs. Swollas was liable to fall in.

Imagining her headfirst in a washing machine, cursing and kicking her long skirts in the air, I giggled out loud, and there was a bang from inside the bedroom. Greg was probably throwing a tantrum, assuming that it was him I was laughing at. As if he was the only thing that mattered in my world.

A little string of guilt twanged. It wasn't right to toy with him the way I had, intentional or not. He pissed me off when he took my car and hung up on me, but I got him back and then some. I slid the card back into a small side pocket of my purse before going off to bed.

It was dark in the bedroom. He was pretending to be asleep. "I wasn't laughing at you. I was laughing at the idea of Mrs. Swollas falling into a washing machine."

He responded with silence.

I felt my way through the black bedroom and undressed before feeling for the plastic round button that turned on the cool air. The AC groaned to life, and I crawled under the covers. "Look, I get that you're mad, but I have every right to be, too."

In the darkness, hard conversations were easier to have. There was no face to the voice, no eyes to emphasize the words. Here, things could be said that couldn't be said in the light of day and face-to-face. We could wallow in our hurt and resentment while speaking truths.

"I fucked up again," he said at last. "Claire didn't give me an inch. I don't know where your breaking point is. I guess I found it."

"It didn't occur to you that threatening our livelihood wouldn't have consequences?" I countered. "Greg, I'm doing the best I can here, but you need to let me do it."

Don't drag me down with you was what I wanted to say, but even the darkness couldn't protect him from such a blow.

He was quiet for a long while after that. For a moment, I thought he managed to fall asleep. Greg's voice jolted me awake when he said, "I'll go back to Berry, see if they can't find a place for me."

Relief came crashing down from all around. Claire would insist on alimony, but the divorce would be finalized. His wages would be garnished, but any wages were better than none. And Berry was a short ride away from here. He could ride his bike until we saved up to get him a car, too.

My hand searched among the folds of sheets until I found his. With my hand tightly clasped around his, I said, "The best revenge is the one where you move on, and we can do that together."

Stifled sniffles broke against his pillow. "You're a saint, Jayme. You know that?"

Would Lars think so? I doubted my parents would agree after spending fifteen grand on a wedding I bolted from. Daddy and I didn't talk for a year, and then he up and died, and my Mamma... Well, that was another story. It was more like she left with him, left me with a stranger for a mother.

"I mean it," he doubled down. "You met me at my worst. I don't recognize myself in the mirror half the time, this divorce has me so wrecked. You're right. Claire wins if I keep carrying on like this. It's time to move on."

Was he just saying that because I scared him? He had made promises like this before, but he never followed through. Lars never made promises he couldn't keep, too. In fact, he kept every last one of them. It was me who broke all the promises. I'd never forget his face. The way his eyes teared up when I said yes to his mother's wedding ring. How everyone in that fancy restaurant stood and applauded.

The room was full of lush red carpets and men in suits. Tears welled in women's eyes, but their mascara never ran because their tears could not seep past the waterline. Their perfectly lined lips and sharply tailored outfits remained pristine even after sipping several glasses of white wine.

The only thing amiss was the waiter's expression. Lined and dull as if he had seen one too many proposals like mine. A country girl and the charming older European man, breathless by the conquest of the American romance come true.

The waiter applauded dutifully as Lars slipped the diamond-encrusted ring on my finger, but the waiter and I were thinking the same thing. I didn't belong with Lars, and I did not belong in that restaurant. How could I make Lars understand that? I wasn't meant for him. I couldn't explain it, but even back then, I knew I was meant for some other purpose.

                              #

I woke up somewhere around six in the morning. A hot, sticky wetness was massing in my drawers. I fumbled through the darkness to the bathroom and confirmed that I had indeed started my period. Of course. Why else would I have been acting the way I had been today? A reel of thoughts and actions played in my head as I cleaned myself up. Getting so upset at Mrs. Swollas, the forgetfulness, stirring up shit with Greg, it must have all been my hormones hijacking my mood.

Well, at least my period started. It was better than not starting; otherwise, I'd have even bigger problems. The last thing I needed was to get pregnant. I was on the pill, but I knew I had missed a day or two, mainly because I couldn't pick up my prescription until payday.

I went back to sleep the moment my head hit the pillow. I groaned when the alarm went off what seemed like a few moments later. Greg was already up. His cologne lingered with the toothpaste and the steam from the shower, and the sizzle of bacon came from the kitchen.

Pulling on a pair of sweats, I came out to find that not only had he cooked breakfast, but he made two lunches instead of just the one. Folding my arms in front of me, I leaned against the wall. He was wearing a tie with his slacks and button-up shirt. It wasn't just any tie; it was the amoeba print, his lucky one that paid homage to his profession as a biology teacher. "Hey, handsome."

He grinned at me in a way that had my knees quivering. "Hey yourself."

"I see two lunches," I said.

Greg strode toward me before pulling me roughly toward him. He inhaled against my neck, taking in the smell of my hair before kissing my temple. "I was serious," he said. "I'm going back to Berry, and if they won't take me, I'll go to the next college. Hell, I'll go to high schools if needed, but I don't think it will come to that."

I wanted to take him by the hand and go right back to that bed where we belonged. "You're really doing it?" I asked.

"Yeah," he said. "I'm really going to do it."

We ate breakfast together before we both went our separate ways. He took his bike from out of the storage unit, and I headed to my car, sack lunch in hand. It wasn't until I got to the car that I realized something was missing.

"Jayme!" Greg shouted as he came peddling across the lawn. "You forgot these." The keys dangled from his extended hand toward me. "Won't get far without them."

"Thank you!" I said, clasping the keys.

"You have a good day, all right? Love you."

"You too."

The sun was shining through the tall trees and reflecting off the lowlands. My favorite songs were playing on the radio, and even if they weren't my favorite songs, I sang along as I pulled into Mrs. Swollas's carport. When I came into the house, I set my lunch on the kitchen counter and promptly went to sweeping and vacuuming.

I was more of a maid than an assistant, really, but I wasn't about to tell Mrs. Swollas that. I would tell her about the washer and dryer set I ordered whenever she decided to grace me with her presence. While I was out, I'd get a few groceries just in case she or I forgot a meal. Avoiding the front of the house would be today's objective. I had no desire to see that gargoyle and let it ruin my day.

Mrs. Swollas rounded the corner with a sheet of paper in front of her. Her hair was assorted in a slightly different style, but it had the same cold severity around her face. "I see your car is in your possession today, so I compiled a list of things to get while you're at the store."

"Yeah, I got a washer and dryer ordered," I said. "I just got to go pick up a truck to haul them over."

I took the paper, but didn't bother to glance at it, I was preoccupied with Mrs. Swollas. She looked different somehow. The lines of her face were shallower somehow, and the skin didn't hang in thin strips around her collar like before. "Are you using a new face cream?" I asked.

She padded at her face with a withered hand. "No, same as usual. I did finally get a good night's sleep, though."

Good sleep took years off the woman's face. "Wow," I said. "I wish it had that effect on me."

"You do look a little peckish today," she said in a motherly tone before resting a hand on my forehead. "Are you sure you're up to so much exertion?"

I soaked up that attention like a cactus in the rain. My mama used to fuss over me in a similar manner. Even as an adult, I craved that nurturing. I closed my eyes, and for a brief moment, I was a child in bed, and it was my mother checking my temperature. She'd fuss over me and insist I eat chicken dumpling soup and wash it down with some sweet tea or a Coke.

My eyes flashed open, and in the place of my mother was a frowning, ancient woman with vivid green eyes. "I'm fine," I said. "Aunt Flo is just paying a visit, that's all."

Mrs. Swollas frowned and said, "I see. Best not let this aunt take advantage of your good nature."

"As if I have a choice," I joked.

A bony hand clutched mine. "You always have a choice, my dear."

I was taken aback by Mrs. Swollas's sincerity. The way she looked at me in that moment... Was it someone else she was seeing? I occurred to me that there must have been a language gap because she did not understand that Aunt Flo was not a literal relative. I would have explained it to her, but if I didn't go now, I'd miss the pick-up time for the truck.

"I'll be back soon," I told her.

The old woman recoiled slowly as if remembering herself. She straightened and gave a sullen nod. "Be sure to get the things on that list."

"I will."

As I was leaving the house, that voice came from nowhere again. It was too soft and young to be Mrs. Swollas, but no one else lived here. No one alive, at least. "Hello?"

A gentle laughter ricocheted off the walls, and an unseen wind tugged at my hair. I released a shiver and stepped into the humid heat, but the chill still followed. This place was haunted. I wasn't one to be superstitious, but I could feel it in my bones. At least it wasn't a mean spirit—that, too, was something just based on a feeling rooted deep in my chest. I didn't know who she was or why Mrs. Swollas didn't hear her, but she was most certainly there. If anything, it was comforting to know I had company, even if it was the incorporeal kind.

The truck on the other hand, made me very nervous. No matter how many times I adjusted the mirrors, my vision was still blocked by the cab. Everything was so foreign. The gearshift was a cold, unforgiving plastic. The engine rumbled to life and the truck screeched as I went to accelerate. I was waived down by the associate.

He mouthed the words, "Emergency break."

I pushed down the stick and sighed. "Lord, let me make it in one piece."

Reaching the hardware store wasn't too much of an ordeal; it was a straight shot down the road. It was the freeway I dreaded. The service man named Jose loaded up the appliances. He glanced at the extra-wide dolly and asked, "You're installing this yourself?"

"I'm afraid so."

"We can do it, no problem."

"My employer won't allow strangers into the house," I explained.

The old man nodded with the understanding that, like him, I was just doing my job.

"There are some videos online," he offered before extending a card. "If you have any trouble, just give me a call, and I'll talk you through it. Just ask for Russ."

It was a relief to know I would have a backup plan in case the videos didn't work, and I couldn't decipher the instructions. I wouldn't be able to connect to the internet once I was at the house, but I used the hardware store's WIFI to download them while I shopped. "I need a few more things inside," I told the old man.

He motioned toward the automatic doors. "If you need help finding anything, just holler for Russ."

Judging by the list, I'd be searching for a while. Mrs. Swollas listed brands and not the actual products or their intended purposes, and none of these brands were on the shelves. I had half the salespeople scratching their heads and the other half running around checking their phones when Russ, the old man, came striding my way. He was a head taller than me despite being hunched, and his red vest hung lower than anyone else's on account of his hunch. "I had a feeling I'd be seeing you again," he said.

"Boy, am I glad to see you!"

"Let me see what you have there," Russ's accent was a rural one. So thick that even I had a hard time understanding it. I extended the note to him, and he scowled at it before saying. "Most of these things were taken off the market decades ago."

I wasn't surprised by that. It was probably the last time Mrs. Swollas shopped for herself. The day was getting hot, and pushing through the sliding doors of the store, I was frazzled to the bone. I still had to drive that thing back to Mrs. Swollas, drop off the washer and dryer before returning it and I was running low on time.

"What are these things?"

The old man translated most of the products. Rat poison, glass cleaner, along with paint stripper and a few other things. "This is about as close as I can get it, most of those products were discontinued due to health hazards. If you have any lying around, best get rid of it."

"I will," I promised. The last thing I needed was to have Mrs. Swollas running around using lead-based paint or some other noxious chemical. Despite what she may have thought, she wasn't immortal.

For all my fuss and worry over driving on the freeway, I merged without a hitch and was making good time. I always got anxious about stupid things, only to find that they were just that. I drove that lumbering truck all the way to Mrs. Swollas's home, bobbing on every hill and pothole. The shocks on the truck were good. Better than the Kia, anyway. I wheeled the washer and dryer into the laundry room, down the stairs and everything. I was proud of myself. If I learned anything from today, it was that I could do just about anything by myself if I wanted to. All I needed was a dolly and an instruction manual. Maybe a little encouragement from Russ.

Mrs. Swollas found me in the bottom story of the house panting while I leaned on the dolly. "Goodness, you were quite determined."

"You'll thank me come winter," I said between breaths.

"It's hard to imagine this land covered in snow when the spring is already so warm."

I unhooked the straps and folded them back onto the dolly. "Oh, we can get several feet of snow."

That was when I felt it. My period had broken through the tampon and was making a damn mess. I was so busy that I didn't have time to stop and change it out. Now, hot blood oozed onto my underwear, and my purse was still in the car.

Shit.

There was no sense getting upset about something that had already happened. I was just about to go to the truck and get my purse when Mrs. Swollas went rigid like a plank of wood. Her eyes dilated wide as she inhaled deeply like a bloodhound picking up a scent.

"Jayme," she whispered breathlessly. "Did you cut yourself?"

I remembered her rules, but I didn't think I had injured myself. I gave myself a look over and said, "No."

Mrs. Swollas staggered up the stairs. She clutched the handrails so hard her knuckles went taught and white.

"Should I call an ambulance?" I asked.

"Just go," she growled. "Go, and don't come back until your cycle has finished. You'll be paid regardless."

What in the hell was that all about? Her rule didn't mention menstruation; maybe she forgot that most women did that. Her aversion to blood was far more serious than I realized. It was like she could smell me. Floorboards creaked overhead, and I waited until I heard no sign of her before returning to the truck with the dolly. I really needed to change my tampon, but I didn't want to upset her further.

I stopped at the nearest gas station to take care of the situation in my drawers. With all the exertion, I didn't realize that I had been leaking for quite some time. I peeled my heavily stained panties off and rinsed them in the sink before wringing them dry and putting them in the pocket of my purse. Going commando wasn't something I enjoyed, but I had no choice at the moment.

It was dark when I rolled into the parking lot of my apartment. The moment I was in the door, Greg was on his feet. "You had me worried."

"Sorry I'm late," I said, hanging my purse on the stand.

"I thought you said she didn't want you there after dark."

"She doesn't. I caught a lot of traffic after dropping off the truck," I explained. Sinking into the couch, I told him about my day. Greg withheld his comments, but the tension in his stare said more than enough. Her reaction wasn't just weird; it was scary. The way her hand gripped the banister, it was like she was trying to keep herself from doing something she'd regret later.

"So, I guess I'm going to take a few days paid vacation," I said.

"Jayme," he said at last. "This is just weird. The whole thing."

"I know it."

Pensive and concerned, he inched closer to me. "Roberts said he'd give me my job back," he said at last. "I start next Monday."

The four words I had been waiting a year to hear. "I'm so happy for you."

"I make decent enough money even if Claire gets a cut," he said. "You don't have to stay at this job if you don't want to."

For once in our relationship, it was me who could relax. I could make the breakfasts and lunches. I could fix dinner for when he came home. No more catering to jerks or fighting over the car. We could afford two now. If Mrs. Swollas gave me any more of her shit, I could just walk out and not come back.

Part of me wanted to. I didn't need to drag washers and dryers around, and I didn't need to get yelled at and insulted for not knowing how to handwash laundry. She was crazy with all her rules and creepy gargoyle, and I was the butt of her jokes on many occasions. It wasn't my job to worry about an old woman who was probably demented from too much rat poison and lead-based paint.

Still, the pay was good, and I didn't know if I could trust Greg to keep his job. Up until the divorce, he held the same position for nine years, but that didn't mean he would continue where he left off. What if he got fired or quit? Then I'd be out of a good-paying job, and we'd be back where we started. If we both had good-paying jobs, we could get out of this hellhole for good. Pay off Greg's debts faster and move into an apartment with real AC.

There was also the fact that I cared for Mrs. Swollas. She was strange and sometimes grumpy, but I got the feeling she cared for me, too, on some level. The way she reacted to the Aunt Flo comment today was genuine love, even if it wasn't necessarily for me. She did love, and like it or not, I couldn't deny my desire to win her approval. What would happen to her if I left? She'd be on her own, and it left a sour taste in my mouth just thinking about it.

"I can't leave her alone, Greg," I said at last. "I'm all she has. Besides, if we both have good-paying jobs, we can get a second car."

A smile formed along his sharp jawline. "That would be nice. Just promise me you will walk away if things get too weird."

"I can handle the old bat," I assured.

It was a sensible enough request, but for some reason, I couldn't bring myself to promise anything to him. My father would have named it a flaw of mine. If you don't make promises if you don't break any, and the one promise I had broken was enough damage to last a lifetime.

6

I played house for the next few days while my period raged on. There were no calls from my employer as she was apparently secure that I hadn't ran after the incident. Did she even know my phone number? She was so aloof sometimes I couldn't decide if she was just confident in my return or if she just didn't care. I chose to believe the former.

I took the opportunity to catch up on some laundry and tidy up the apartment. There wasn't much to clean, but I vacuumed for the first time in months. Greg did all right in keeping the place picked up. Admittedly, I was the slob. I left my clothes all over the floor and never did learn how to use an iron. My cosmetics from the dollar store were strewn about the small bathroom counter, and I had left more than a few dishes sitting in the sink.

My shoes had been kicked across the room yesterday and remained on the carpet. Greg always took his shoes off in the entryway. A habit instilled by Claire years ago. There was some dust in the vacuum filter, but not much. So, I smacked that against the garbage can. I got around washing my dishes and putting them away. With the way Greg kept the house, we'd get our full deposit back.

By day three, I was bored. Daytime drama on TV was calling to me. While I always wanted my period to finish as soon as possible, I was desperate for every sign of its end. What if Mrs. Swollas decided she didn't need me or that she'd rather hire someone else? I did not want to be replaced.

I was just about to watch the dramatic reveal of Bethany learning that her child was switched at birth by her evil twin sister when a voice called to me from another room. I jerked so hard I spilled my crackers all over the floor. "Hello?"

Why did I do that? Like I expected her to answer. I bristled, trying to soothe the little hair on my arms back down and suppress the telltale shiver. I had decided Mrs. Swollas's house was haunted, but how could a ghost follow me here? Unless it was just me who was haunted and not the house. It made sense since Swollas never saw or heard anything weird. She could have been lying, but why would she? More like everything weird happened around her, and she was too old and stubborn to notice.

"What do you want from me?" I whispered. There was no answer, but the eerie chill about the apartment and the sensation of being watched remained. Maybe she wanted to tell me but just couldn't for some reason. What if this was the daughter? "Is Mrs. Swollas your Mama?"

I wandered around the house, waiting for something to happen. I checked the knobs of the oven and unlocked the front door in case I needed to bolt. The toilet was running in the bathroom. How had I not noticed? Twitchy fingers lifted the lid to hook the chain to the pump. Porcelain was always so loud. I knew it was just because the tank was hollow, but I was always afraid I'd break it.

The tank simmered before coming to a complete stop while I organized my cosmetics on the counter. Some of this stuff I hadn't used in months, and they were probably bad. I didn't wear makeup to Mrs.

Swollas's house. The last thing I needed was mascara running in my eyes while I was sweating like a nun in a cucumber patch.

I thought about putting a little of it on just to give Greg something to think about. He loved it when I wore bright red lipstick. I only put it on for him. Bringing the stick to my lips, I looked into the mirror. Only it wasn't me staring back. It was someone else. Big, soft brown eyes lined in feathery lashes. A perfect smattering of freckles across the bridge of her nose and cheeks. Her lips were small but pouty, and her hair was a pale yellow that fell smooth and flat around her collarbone.

I screamed, and the lipstick clanked in the sink before rolling around, leaving a line of red. Backing against the wall, I wailed and sank to the linoleum floor. "Why are you doing this to me?" I screamed between sobs. "What do you want from me?"

Just when I had calmed down some, there was a tickle across my foot. Bumping across my toes was a giant wood roach. Well, that did it. I screamed even louder before scrambling to my feet and out of the bathroom. I got in the bed, pulled the covers over my whole body, and cried myself to sleep.

About forty-five minutes later, there was a knock at the door. I opened it to see two police officers standing there. Both were tow-headed men with buzz cuts. They could have been brothers by the looks of them. "We got a noise complaint. Is everything okay?"

"Sorry," I said. "I didn't mean to disturb anyone."

Their eyes flickered inside the apartment in unison. "The caller was more concerned than angry. They say they heard a woman screaming and crying."

Damn those paper-thin walls. "A cockroach crawled across my foot."

"Ma'am, this is the south. You should be used to that by now."

"I know," I said. "I just really hate bugs, especially if they have faces. Never did get used to it."

"Do you mind if we take a look around?"

There was no sense in fighting them. They were just doing their job, making sure no one was holding me hostage or something. I opened the door and allowed them to come in. The apartment was less than seven-hundred square feet. It took all of five minutes for them to check everything.

There was a stomp and an audible crunch, and I winced. The cop came out and said, "Well, that roach won't be troubling you no more. You should call the apartment manager and get them to spray. The trees outside house those nasty buggers."

I thanked them, and they were on their way. Damn right I would be calling the manager. I wasn't lying when I said I hated roaches. Creepy things the size of a thumb getting into everything and shitting everywhere. I shivered and sprayed the house down with bleach water wherever I could.

When Greg came home, he found me with an empty bottle of wine. I didn't tell him about the woman in the mirror, just the cockroach and the police coming. "Jayme, I know you don't like bugs, but you're awfully shook up."

"I'll be fine," I lied. "I just really want to get back to work already."

He eyed me with suspicion. No doubt he knew I was lying, but what could I tell him? He would think I was crazy. I had been acting weird lately. Hearing things that weren't there. Now I was seeing them. Who was that woman in the mirror?

Greg enjoyed having me home while he worked. He was always smiling when he came home and told me about his lectures and how the students reacted to them. "It's like I'm back where I belong," he said over meatloaf. There was a pause, and he set down his fork. "I...uh, saw that picture you put on my laptop."

I had forgotten all about that. The image came to mind of the blue and purple vagina, and my food came falling out of my mouth and back on the plate. My face got all hot, and I laughed. "I hope no one else saw it."

"No," he said. "Thankfully, I didn't have the laptop plugged in. Where did you get an idea like that? It was gross."

I wasn't sorry. I don't even remember what he did, but he probably deserved it. I resumed eating while Greg stared at me.

"You're not even going to say you're sorry?"

"Do you expect me to?" I asked.

He chuckled as he leaned back in his chair. "I know I already said it, but Mrs. Swollas is not a good influence."

As if consorting with an ancient woman would be enough influence to be spiteful? I could do that on my own. It was easier to blame an outside source rather than look at our problems or his own behavior. "You think Mrs. Swollas knows what a blue waffle is?"

Greg frowned at this. "Well, I suppose not. Do you think you still want to work for her after that business with your period?" he asked. "I imagine she had one at some point."

I shrugged. "Not everyone thinks like you do." I used to be so embarrassed of mine that I'd run out of the room any time the TV played a tampon commercial in front of Papa.

"It's natural biology. Healthy, even. You said she had a daughter. I just can't imagine why. A woman of all people should understand these things."

"Not everyone is as comfortable with biological things as you are," I reminded him. He of all people should know that. Different beliefs and superstitions still gripped modern day cultures; why should an old woman from an unknown land be any different?

His expression soured as he ate his green beans. "It's perfectly natural. To treat it otherwise is just bizarre."

I knew just how to counter his argument. "Yes, but cultural aspects might be at play here."

Stabbing at the chunk of bacon in his beans, he begrudgingly agreed. "I suppose, but still. I just don't like it. She's paying you so much money just to clean the house. It's weird, all of it."

"Jealous?" I teased.

His shoulders tensed, and he tried to deny it before letting out a sigh. "Maybe a little. I went to school for five years to get paid a decent wage only to have a—you run right up next to me."

A girl. That was what he wanted to say but caught himself. "I thought you were a feminist, Greg."

"I am," he said. "It's not about your gender; it's about your education. It's just unfair."

"So I should quit just to make you feel better?"

"I didn't say that. Look, I'm just worried. The whole thing stinks to high hell to me. It's creepy—you mentioned that gargoyle, too."

We were on the cusp of another fight. Part of me wanted to provoke it, to keep it going. That venomous snake that liked to snap at Greg was coiling and rattling its tail. If I didn't cool the situation, I might lose control again.

"I was going to ask you about that," I said. "What cultures revere gargoyles?"

Learning about the gargoyle might be the key to understanding Mrs. Swollas. Greg pondered that for a moment, and tension eased in my chest. There would be no argument tonight. I was still shaken up by the woman in the mirror that was all.

"It's like the European version of a dragon. Mostly, the Catholic church used them to signify evil."

"So, no cultures in Europe revered them?"

"Not any of the Christian ones," he said. "Mostly, they were just ornate drainpipes."

I had hoped for more significance than that. The one Mrs. Swollas had was not for a drainpipe, and it didn't resemble anything perched on cathedrals. This thing was something older, something that existed before Christianity. "Maybe I'll get a picture of it to show you."

"Some believed they warded off evil," he suggested. "Maybe that's why she's so keen on hanging on to it."

That made sense. Mrs. Swollas was a practical sort of woman but there was an air of suspicion about her. If this gargoyle served to protect her from evil, maybe that was the connection. "You know I don't believe in the supernatural," I started.

Greg stopped chewing and raised his eyebrows. It made me giggle.

"It's just that something is weird about that house. I can't help but feel like she's trying to protect me from it."

"So, you feel like she's trying to protect you," Greg said at length.

"I guess," I said, waving my hands in the air. "I don't know, maybe I'm just being stupid."

"Well, whatever it means, it sounds like she has your best interests at heart. Regardless of the house or the gargoyle, it sounds like, deep down, the woman is fond of you. If I'm not mistaken, you're fond of her too."

I sighed. Greg was insightful and wise, as always. "She's not everyone's cup of sweet tea, but I really think she does care about me. She trusts me, too."

Tension pulled at my insides like a cord. I didn't mean to say that. Greg picked up on it. "Of course she trusts you," he said. "You're a trustworthy person."

The cord went lax, and remorse took its place. Why was I so afraid to tell him such things? His only crimes consisted of taking my car a few times and getting dumped by a socialite. Still, the question I hadn't dared ask came spilling out.

"Why did Claire divorce you the way she did?"

His fork went still in his hand as he studied my face. "Why do you ask now?"

We had been together for over a year. Never once did I ask why they broke up or why she was grabbing for his balls in the divorce. I had just assumed that she was money-hungry until now. But Claire had money. She was just doing it to be spiteful. He must have done something to make this divorce an act of revenge.

I never thought about it before, but now it sat like a brick on my shoulder. Greg told me she was bad, and I just accepted it, but that couldn't be everything. Why didn't I ever stop to ask why she was acting so hateful? It was probably because I envied her. The woman didn't have to work a day in her life, and I hated her for it. My hatred and the strife of our financial situation kept me blind to other reasons for their divorce. Greg didn't lie, but he took advantage of the assumptions others made.

I shrugged and poked at my meatloaf. "We never talked about it."

We never talked about it because Greg had a knack for instilling me with the same level of hatred for his ex-wife as he had. I had walked every trial and tribulation with him, but why was Claire so intent on making him miserable? There had to be a motive on her end. One that was big enough to make him quit his job to evade her demands.

"We were young when we got married," he said at last. "I asked her to marry me to make her parents happy, and she married me to spite her parents. I was okay with that for many years, but at some point, you need to love the person you got, right?"

"She didn't love you?" I asked, instantly regretting the question.

"Claire did love me," he said with a sigh. "That's why she got so angry, you see. Somewhere along the way, she fell madly in love with me, but I was always looking for a way out. The final straw broke when she wanted kids and I didn't."

"So, you told her no?" My voice was weak, and he was refusing to look at me.

"I got a vasectomy years ago."

I was utterly dumbstruck. All this time, I had been scrounging for money to buy birth control. He knew I was worried about it and never told me. We could have saved that thirty bucks a month. All the nights I fussed over getting pregnant. He always assured me we'd be fine, but why not tell me? "This is news to me."

"I should have told you. I should have told both of you." Greg bowed his head. "I let her believe it was her and not me. It went on for years. She tried all sorts of things to get pregnant, and nothing worked. Never once did anyone consider that it had to do with me until she started seeing a specialist."

What a horrid lie. No wonder she was so angry. I didn't want to get pregnant, but the betrayal stung me as well. Claire spent years thinking it was her fault she couldn't have a baby just to find her husband had gone behind her back and had a vasectomy. I wanted to slap him. Kids were never something I had wanted, but this was outright deceitful and cruel. It seemed there was no avoiding an argument tonight. I just hoped I wouldn't lose control like I did last time.

Rather than face my judgment, he got up and did the dishes, signifying that he did not want to hear my opinion on the matter. I couldn't let it go, not this time. That urge to fight reared and took the place of the woman who would have rather just avoided the confrontation.

"Greg," I said, standing up, "why didn't you just tell her you didn't want kids? Why not tell me?"

Why let her carry on like that? Or me, for that matter. One of my cousins had conception issues, and it drove her to therapy. I couldn't imagine what Claire was thinking at the time.

The dishes clanked in the sink before he turned to me and said, "Now you know why she wants alimony," he said. "She wants me to repay all the money and time she spent trying to conceive with a guy who was shooting blanks."

Specialists and IVF were expensive. How far along did he go with the charade before he was caught? Enough for a judge to warrant reparations. She wasn't trying to punish him. Claire wanted her money back. Her parents probably wanted their money back, too, which is why whole legions of attorneys were after him.

"I tried to tell her, but she just wouldn't take no for an answer. I didn't tell you because I was afraid it would be a deal breaker for us, too."

He had tried to tell her, but she didn't want to listen. Marriage was complicated, and I understood that. Spending years with someone, weaving in and out of another person's life and goals, was bound to meet conflicts. Had she talked right over him? Insisted that he was ready to be a father when he told her otherwise? She must have. How else would she have racked up such a huge bill without any debate on whether it was her who was unable to conceive?

Greg made a mistake, and what he did was wrong, but how long had she rolled over everyone in her quest for conception. "Greg," I said quietly. "When did you finally tell the truth?"

His arms fell to his sides. The sleeves rolled up to his elbows were laden with veins and muscle. "I tried to tell her a few times, but it was like she just didn't care what I had to say in the matter. Like I was just the sperm doner. When the doctors asked to test my sperm, she would always insist her family history was to blame. Finally, I just blurted it out in front of a panel of specialists her mother flew in from all over the states."

My upper lip curled in disgust. "Why wouldn't she listen?"

His shoulders lurched. "She didn't have to. Mommy and Daddy would pay the bill. It was only after my little announcement that they got mad at her and demanded she pay them back. That meant I had to pay her back. So here I am, fucking up your life too."

I embraced him in a bear hug. "You didn't fuck up things with me," I promised. "We're okay."

He leaned his head against mine and sighed. "I was so afraid to tell you. Thought you'd walk out for good."

"No." I wouldn't leave him for something like that. They say love conquers all, and I believed it. I believed it with my whole heart. Love wasn't easy and simple; you had to work through the bad to get to the good. "You were with the wrong person, and she refused to accept that."

He held me as his chest heaved while he silently cried. I couldn't be the woman Lars needed, but I could show Greg that there was more to life than just surviving. He didn't come into this relationship with demands and expectations, and that was all I needed. "How much does she want?" I asked.

"Twenty-three grand."

The number was enough to send my knees wobbling. Where would we find that kind of money? There was only one answer. "Well, she will have to garnish it from your wages for the next twenty years, but it won't change what happened."

"But you're really okay with that? I can never have kids."

I didn't exactly have plans, life goals, or visions of how my future looked. When other little girls were playing pageants and wedding days, I never did. When I agreed to marry Lars, I did it because I was in my late twenties and thought it was expected of me. Expectations hounded me at every turn, but I never had a real answer for them. I was meant for something, something important. I knew that much, but when it came time to rationalize or explain it to others, I had nothing.

As I stood there in the kitchen of the studio apartment, clutching Greg. I needed to put away these foolish desires for some great and important destiny. It screwed everything up with Lars, and if I wasn't careful, I'd lose Greg to it too. Maybe I was manifesting some haunting that wasn't there because I was trying to sabotage this relationship too.

7

—·—

"Is there a reason you're rubbing dirty water all over the floor?" Mrs. Swollas asked, hanging over the banister.

I stopped mopping and rolled my eyes. "How would you have me do it, Mrs. Swollas?"

When I returned to work, the old woman acted as if she hadn't sent me home for starting my period. She set me to work on the floors, and only when I was done with that could I install the washer and dryer still sitting in their plastic downstairs.

"This won't clean the grout," she lectured.

"What do you want me to do?" I asked. "Scrub it on hands and knees?"

I shouldn't have asked. Not long after the question, I had a bristle brush in both hands and was scrubbing the grout with the woman standing over me. "If you had gotten the things I had asked for, this wouldn't be a problem."

"They don't make the things you asked for," I said. "All of them are discontinued as health hazards."

"Bah!" she scoffed. "I've never been sick a day in my life."

Oh, I believed it. My knees ached in rebellion as I pressed into the ceramic tiles. I was too old for this. I needed some knee pads or something. I made do with a folded towel under my knees, which provided no end of amusement for Mrs. Swollas.

"You know, I was an old lady scrubbing the floors just as you are now, and I never needed to baby my body in such a way."

"Was that in the first World War or the second?" I asked. It was sarcastic and mean considering she was a refugee from a war-torn country, but damn she was bitter. Maybe she was a Nazi who fled war crimes that decided to plant herself in America. She couldn't have been the first.

"I have no idea what you're talking about. What world war, and why was there a second? One bloody battle wasn't sufficient?" she asked.

I stopped scrubbing to check if she was serious. Somewhere in there, she had lost interest in banter and genuinely wanted to know. Her head was tilted in anticipation of an answer. "You know," I said, "the Nazis tried to kill all the Jews and take over the world. We stopped them."

Mrs. Swollas's eyes were blank of any recognition. Had she missed out on the biggest war of the nineteenth century? I thought, being from Europe, she would have known firsthand, but maybe it was called something else over there. Well, there went my Nazi theory.

"I haven't the slightest clue what you're going on about," she said. "What are Nazis, and why would they want to kill the Jewish?"

How could she not know?

"Mrs. Swollas, where are you from?" *Where have you been?*

I wanted to know so badly. It was a question that nagged at me late at night when I was supposed to be asleep. Whenever I watched TV, my ears pricked at every exotic accent as if my brain was seeking the answers even on an unconscious level.

"Not from such a horrid place, I can assure you. And people called my family monsters!"

Okay. So, she wasn't from Europe per se. Maybe she was from Australia? That didn't match her accent, though. I didn't know many Australians or New Zealanders, but her accent was not it. She was no Crocodile Dun Dee or Steve Irwin. Her accent had a Swedish flair but was more subtle.

Was she from Iceland or Greenland? I could never remember the difference. I'd google their stance on World War Two if I had internet in this damned house. She may have been too young to remember it. Looking at her now, it was hard to imagine she was that young. She had to have been in her seventies or eighties.

"Well," I said, throwing a brush into the bucket. "There was war, and a lot of people died."

I gave her my lacking rundown of the Holocaust. The disgust on her face was visible from the stairwell. She stood there, her fists balled as if she wanted to punch someone. "A lot of people were murdered. Such a waste. And you still think humanity is worth it? Maybe it would be better if someone came along and devoured it all."

It was an oddly specific description of how the world could end. Most went with meteors or zombies. The duplicity of this woman was fascinating. One half of her thought the world would be better off without people in it, and the other was shaking with anger when she learned that millions of people had died.

"Well, I think I was speaking more about myself. I've made some mistakes, but I'm trying to be better. Germany made a big mistake, but they are a really good country now, from what I understand."

"I see," she said quietly.

"Why did people call your kin monsters?" I asked.

"Where I come from, worshiping the old gods was a crime beyond death. They were banished because of me. Humans are vain, stupid creatures."

Her story was coming together now. Religious persecution wasn't uncommon. She was sent to some island without a name. No wonder she hated people so much. I wanted to remind her that she too was human and capable of error, but I suspected she was speaking on a philosophical level.

"Greg says that we have such great capacity but lack the respect and wisdom to use it."

"Men always sound wise in theory, dear," she said in a patronizing tone. "The truth is that given the option, the very same men who say such things will do even worse crimes given half a chance."

She was probably right. Greg withheld one detail and caused twenty-three thousand dollars worth of damage. What would he do with actual power? I shook my head. It wasn't fair to judge him on something I didn't witness firsthand. There was no amount of scrubbing that would remove these grout stains. "Mrs. Swollas," I said. "You might need these floors to be regrouted."

Her mouth tightened. "Yes, I feared as much. Tea?"

If she feared as much, then why the hell make me scrub? The money was worth it, I reminded myself as I stood. My knees stung as I eased into a natural position. A creature of habit, Mrs. Swollas took to her chair and waited for her scalding hot tea.

"This house will need a renovation if you intend to sell it." I slid into the seat opposite of her. "A new coat of paint, some new grout, updated appliances."

"You haven't seen all the rooms," she said. "I keep them locked for a reason."

I hadn't given much thought to why those doors were locked; I
assumed she had valuables and cherished keepsakes or even another
nasty gargoyle in those rooms. "Is it mold?" I asked. The tea was more
acidic than usual and made my tongue all dry.

"Mold," Mrs. Swollas agreed. "Floors so rotted a person is liable to
fall through them, among other dangers."

"Mrs. Swollas," I started. "I know you don't want people in the
house, but if you want this place fixed up, we're going to need to hire
people."

She sipped her tea with thin, tight lips. "It won't matter soon. Just
so long as the rules are followed."

Mrs. Swollas didn't plan on selling the house. She planned on dying
in it. Why bring me in, then? Maybe she just wanted some company
before she joined her nameless daughter. I didn't want to press the
issue further. Mrs. Swollas was in a decent mood today, and I was
intent on keeping it that way. "Oh," I said. "Did you want to see how
the washer works?"

The old lady frowned. "The what?"

An unsettling stillness came over me. Had she forgotten already?
Maybe she didn't have what Mama had, but there was clear evidence
of memory problems. It could have been trauma, as Greg suggested,
or even just age, but something was amiss. Mama was the one who
decided to go into assisted living, but we all agreed on it as a family. I
was the only person Mrs. Swollas had.

If I left, she would keep carrying on like she had. Sure, she was
grumpy and weird, but she was wise and cared about me. She trusted
me, and I trusted her as well, though I couldn't say why. Something in
me wanted her approval so badly. To crack that hard exterior and find
kinship with the vulnerable woman inside. If she needed someone to

hold her hand in the end, then damn it all, I was going to be there for her.

"Mrs. Swollas, I never asked. What is your first name?"

"I never told you?"

I shook my head. Even the credit card did not reveal it. Mrs. H. Swollas was all it said. The lady raised her brows in surprise and shrugged. "My first name is Helicant."

An unusual name with no origin I was familiar with. "That's an interesting name, I like it."

"Interesting is a word that serves no purpose."

I didn't know how to respond to that. One of Mrs. Swollas's quirks. I had to squeeze as much information out of her before she stormed off, and her opinion on a word was just going to waste my time. The episode in the bathroom yesterday was still reeling in my mind. "What kind of person was your daughter?"

Her fingers danced across the lip of her teacup as she thought about it. "She was a lot like you, really. She was wild as a little girl, but she grew into a kind, sensitive girl. Incredibly lonely, full of fears and anxieties. I suppose that was why she was so gentle."

The presence and the voice I had been hearing around the house didn't strike me as evil. Then again, it wasn't all that nice to startle me in the mirror like that. I wanted to know if the daughter was the one haunting me, but how to go about it? "She didn't play practical jokes?"

"Maybe she would have if she had someone to joke with," Mrs. Swollas said. "It was just her and I, you see, and she was timid. She was witty but more bookish than anything. She spoke several languages."

"English?" I asked.

"Of sorts. Nothing you would recognize, however. It was old English we spoke on the island."

So, she wouldn't be able to speak to me even if she wanted to.

Mrs. Swollas tilted her head to regard me. "Is there something you're not telling me?"

I opened my mouth to tell her everything, but only one word came out: "No."

The frown on her face was sharp and scathing. She knew I was lying. I had intended to tell her everything, but it was like my lips wouldn't cooperate. It was like my body was being put on autopilot, and I didn't like it one bit.

"Well, in any case, that grout is not going to finish scrubbing itself."

"Yes, ma'am."

Defeated and frustrated, I went at the floors with a renewed vigor. I kept saying things I didn't mean and wasn't able to say the things I wanted to say. Maybe I needed to see a doctor. People in their thirties didn't get dementia, did they? I'd check on my phone, except there was no internet. Whatever was going on, it wasn't natural.

It had to do with the lady in the mirror and the voice I kept hearing. Whoever she was, she didn't want Mrs. Swollas involved. Could it really be the ghost of the daughter? I was no expert on ghosts, but they couldn't control you. They just floated around and scared the bejesus out of you. The urge to investigate the locked rooms was becoming hard to ignore. A nagging every time I passed that hallway. Every time Mrs. Swollas went off to do her 'work.' Something told me I would find answers in those rooms, but I'd need to break her rules and risk my job to do it.

8

The Southern spring was ramping up to another sweltering summer. The AC blared in the car as I drove home Friday afternoon, hesitant to leave Mrs. Swollas, but Greg had insisted.

"I suspect your lover has a surprise in store for you," Mrs. Swollas said. "Go on, dear. I'll be fine."

She was right; he had something up his sleeve. He got his paycheck at the first of the month for the first time in a long time. We agreed to split all the bills and paid them in full right then and there. No late fees, no bouncing checks, and money left over. He had a divorce hearing coming up the following Monday, and even that couldn't dampen his spirits as of late.

"Are you sure you're going to be okay?" I asked.

"Goodness," Mrs. Swollas scoffed. "It's just one afternoon. You act as if you don't want him to surprise you."

That was more accurate than she realized. Greg often surprised me. I should be used to it by now. He would come home with roses accompanied with unpaid bills, hugs from behind followed by a request to borrow money, and seldom did one come without the other. Whatever good surprise he had was often accompanied by a bad one, and I wasn't sure I could take another bad one.

The front door hit against something as I opened it. I craned my head in to find my rollaway luggage. "Greg?" I called.

"I'm in here!" he called from the bedroom.

He had clothes laid out and an open suitcase. "You're home earlier than I expected, so surprise!" he said with a shirt on a hanger in one hand and a pair of boxers in the other. "We're going on a trip."

Unwanted excitement rippled through me. What was the catch? I folded my arms over my chest, bracing myself for the other shoe to drop. "Where?" I asked.

He turned to me and smiled with mischief in his eyes. "Gatlinburg."

I hadn't been there since I was a kid. I told him I wanted to go back one of these days, but we never could afford it until now. I couldn't help but smile, and he grinned, knowing he did good. "I booked the hotel and everything," he explained. "All on me."

It was a four-hour drive across several state lines. We made it to Chattanooga when the temperature gauge on my dash rushed to the red marker. Seized by panic, I dashed across all five lanes of the interstate toward the nearest exit. Greg was shouting, but I didn't hear him. Vines of smoke crawled out from underneath the hood as we got onto the onramp.

Greg turned on the caution lights as the Kia rattled to a crawl, but not before I put it in neutral and guided it a few feet from a gas station. This wasn't my first rodeo, but the fear of losing our only car had me gripped with fear as the dollar signs stacked in my mind. Towing fees, mechanic fees, possibly a new car that I couldn't afford quite yet. It was a downward spiral back to poverty and all for what? A stupid trip to Gatlinburg. God forbid we wanted to pretend we were financially stable for a moment.

"Don't worry," Greg said as he got out of the car. "It will be fine."

I popped the hood, and he took a quick look before going into the gas station. Not even five minutes later, he was back. His face was grim, but in his hand was a jug of radiator coolant. "The coolant was gone. I think there's a leak, but there is a mechanic just a mile down the road. I think we can make it."

We did make it. So, at least we didn't have to pay the towing fee. I drummed my fingers on the arm of the mechanic's pleather chair in the waiting room. My stomach churned from nerves. The smell of old car oil didn't help the situation.

My anxiety was sky-high when a familiar voice sang. I glanced around the room. No one else heard it but me. If it were a ghost, wouldn't everyone hear it? If Greg and the trucker reading a magazine didn't hear it, that explained why Mrs. Swollas couldn't either. It was just in my head. Maybe I was developing some kind of stress-induced psychosis. That happened sometimes. I'd need to see a doctor real quick.

The song and my thoughts halted as a man in a grey jumpsuit made his way to the lobby. I stood as the mechanic came in like a family member awaiting news of a dying patient.

"Your cap was broken," he said, wiping a wrench with a dirty rag. "I just put a new one on and refilled your radiator fluid."

We drove away cackling. The radiator cap was eight dollars, and the fluid was forty. It was a roll of the dice where we came out on top for once. A sign that things would be all right. Voices in my head or not, we were going to be fine. The rest of the drive consisted of singing at the top of our lungs. We sang the lyrics we could remember and ad-libbed the rest.

"Why are you so much better at lip-syncing than me?" he asked.

It was an old trick I learned in choir back in middle school. I could sing well enough, but whenever I got a little too loud, the old bat of a teacher would scowl at me. It got to a point where I got so fed up that I wanted to quit. Daddy wouldn't let me, so I learned that if I just mouthed the word *watermelon,* it almost always looked like I knew what I was singing.

Part of me wanted to share the trick with Greg, but for once, I wanted to be good at something. He had a master's degree. He was an honor student. Before his dad up and left, his family had enough money to send him to Europe for his senior year of high school. The furthest I had ever gone was to West Virginia for a funeral. Just once, I wanted to have something that he didn't.

"I don't know. Probably just something I picked up from choir."

Gatlinburg was a tourist town, but still magical nonetheless. The main street was lined with shops that had t-shirts and shot glasses with the name printed on them. The miniature space needle stood four stories high, and Ripley's Believe It Or Not had a line that rounded the alley. Throngs of people stood along the corners, smoking cigarettes and talking amongst themselves.

I glanced at Greg as he drove down the main strip, playing with my hands in my lap. This was something we had talked about for so long, and now, we were doing it. I wanted to squeal with excitement as we rolled up to the motel. He checked us in and, keys in hand, Greg led me to a second-story room marked three-twenty-four.

It was a standard hotel room. One queen-sized bed with a small sitting area. The toilet and tub were behind a door, and a sink sat two feet from the front door. "Not much of a suite," he commented, dragging our suitcases in. I pulled open the curtains and took in the view—a back alley and a row of dumpsters.

"It's perfect," I told him. "It's not like we will be here much."

"Or we could spend all weekend here," he said with an impish grin.

I giggled, and we unpacked our bags. He brought so much stuff that most of it remained in the suitcase. Greg didn't know what I would want, so he packed half my wardrobe, and the other half were makeup and hair accessories I didn't use, but I gave him credit for trying. It was sweet that he packed my suitcase with the full intention of whisking me away on a romantic weekend.

"What do you say we get something to eat?" he said.

My stomach was still queasy from travel and the car hiccup, but food was what I needed now. "I'm hungry."

"I was hoping you'd say that. I got a reservation at that fancy restaurant a few blocks from here."

My heart soared as we walked to the restaurant, the humidity swelling the waves of my hair and making my skin tacky to the touch. Despite the twenty-year difference, Gatlinburg was unchanged in my mind. The same sense of lightheartedness filled me now as it did then. We were on a weekend vacation, just the two of us.

Greg clasped my hand, making it known that we were a couple. There were a few glances at us. A happy couple on a getaway. The restaurant had several stories, and we got a window seat where we could overlook the Smoky Mountains.

"This is perfect," I whispered as I pulled my chair toward the table.

Greg was less enthused. "I asked for a good seat."

It was a good seat. I glanced around and shrugged. "It is good."

"We're sandwiched in pretty tight," he said.

That was true. We were at a small table squished between two four-seat tables, and both were busy, but who cared? It occurred to me that Greg had expected far more of this venture than I did. He wanted perfection. I grasped his hands in mine. "I'm just so happy to be here. With you."

The tension in his shoulders relaxed, and he sighed. "I'm sorry. I just wanted it to be special, you know?"

We ate oysters and drank a thirty-five-dollar bottle of wine. Greg tipped the waiter in cash for half of what our bill wracked up to. He was always so generous to waiters. He was one in college and never forgot how rude people could be. Light and fuzzy from the wine, I suppressed a smile when the waiter thanked us for the generous tip. I winked at Greg, and he nearly dropped his napkin onto the plate.

It was dusk when we walked the strip. He got me pink and blue cotton candy. It was so sweet it made my teeth hurt, but I ate it anyway. We talked about little things, mostly; he asked me if I wanted to "go here" or "do that." We visited the Ripley's Believe It Or Not Museum. It reminded me more of a circus sideshow than anything, but I found it all fascinating.

Greg had a particular interest in it since he was a biology professor and loved to explain all the exhibits. Giant puffer fish with teeth that ate shells and shrunken heads that were culturally still relevant in some secluded societies. "Some of these people practice cannibalism," Greg explained.

I tilted my head as I regarded the Asmat corpse. "They slept on the skulls of their enemies," I read out loud.

"Bizarre, isn't it?" Greg said, stroking my lower back.

The skull had some sort of nose bridge and a bone that went through the bridge of the nose just under the eye sockets. Take that away, and he was just a man. "You once said psychological warfare was the most effective tool."

"It's true," Greg agreed. "Still, seeing it in person, it's just more real."

Asmat may or may have eaten human flesh in ritual. He probably slept on the skulls of his enemy, but who wouldn't if it meant keeping invaders away from his home and loved ones? I'd sleep on a pile of bones, too, if it meant keeping all I loved safe. "We do what we must," I countered.

Greg's stare didn't go unnoticed, but I ignored it. "If it came between putting Claire in an Iron Maiden or letting her get away with her bullshit, which would you have me do?"

He blinked. I shouldn't have said that, so I laughed. "I'm sorry, I don't know where that came from," I said. "Probably the wine gone to my head."

"I think that woman is rubbing off on you," he muttered under his breath.

I roped my arm around his. "I think I'm just anxious about the arraignment."

"Me too," he admitted.

We hadn't spoken of it except in passing. It loomed on our calendar in Greg's scrawling handwriting, and each day, I stared at it. He tensed at the mention of it. "I talked to my lawyer about accepting her terms," he said. "He said that they would only take ten to twenty percent of my wages each check."

"That's still a lot."

Greg nodded, and we stepped up the black-painted steps to the next exhibit. "It's not as much as she wanted," he quipped. "The attorney said she threw a fit when she learned that."

Of course she did. Claire had ruled his life with an iron fist for years. The prospect of being unable to control his life outside of their divorce was an insult to her. "Maybe if you agree to let her pick out your ties for the next five years, she will feel better."

Greg burst into laughter. "I haven't even mentioned us yet," he said. "I'm waiting until after everything is said and done before I drop that nugget."

How would Claire react to knowing we were together? I hadn't even met her before. We went to different high schools, but I knew of her. Greg didn't keep pictures of her; he threw those out before we moved in together. I remembered seeing her in the paper when they announced the prom kings and queens across the county. She had dark hair and a perfect, pinched little nose. She was on the cheer squad, too, if I remembered the article correctly. But her husband was with me, a Coosa Valley girl. And my football team smashed hers every time. She'd be irate on many levels, to be sure.

It was fully dark now, and the buildings were all lit up like Christmas trees. Lights streamed from one side of the street to the other in the place of the hanging planters full of blooms. Swept away with the romance of it all, I leaned my head against Greg's shoulder.

"This is really beautiful."

He nuzzled against my head in response. Everything was going to be all right. He would be a free man soon enough. Though, if she didn't know about me, it begged the question of where he was living all this time. "Where does she think you've been all this time?" I asked. "Under a rock?"

Greg smiled. "She thinks I'm living with my mama."

I looked up at him and laughed. His mother lived in a tiny apartment above a coffee shop in Rome. It was a senior living apartment, and nobody under sixty-five was permitted to reside there. "Where? On her sofa?"

"I don't know," he said with a shrug. "She was all pissed off at me a few months back and blurted it out. I just never corrected her."

It was probably a good thing he hadn't. If Claire had any idea he was seeing someone else, she would make the divorce that much more painful. Never mind she supposedly had a fiancé of her own. Still, twenty-three thousand dollars would take years to pay off.

We went back to our hotel room and slept together. It was sultry and passionate—the way good sex should be. When we were spent, I fell asleep to him tracing circles on my bare back. As I drifted off to sleep, he pressed his face against my ear and whispered, "I love you."

I smiled and murmured a response, but it came out more like a grunt. I'd tell him later.

The next morning, we had sex again before taking a long shower together and eating brunch at the diner next door. I ate waffles doused in maple syrup, and he had biscuits and gravy. We walked the strip and window-shopped before being the only two adults without children to run around the arcade without kids.

Skeeball was a personal favorite of mine. I wasn't very good at it, I never could hit the 1000-point holes, but I enjoyed it all the same. Greg eyed the holes and treated it like some professional bowling tournament. He hit his target nearly every time, but when he missed, he'd cuss under his breath and stomp around. It was awfully childish. Even the kids stared at him.

"Let's try a different game," I said. Taking his arm, I led him away from the skeeball before he broke the damn thing, and we settled on the coin slots.

I was dropping aluminum coins into the slots when a smash rattled the whole thing. I leaned over to find Greg was angry at this machine, too. What had gotten into him? The girl at the counter was eyeing him with one hand on the phone. At any moment, she'd call security or the police. "Greg!" I whispered. "What's gotten into you?"

He was all red in the face, like he had gotten too much sun. "Sorry. There was a coin just sitting on the edge."

Clearly, the arcade was not a good place for Greg. "Come on. Let's cash in these tickets and get out of here."

"Not yet," he said. "Just give me a few more minutes. Stay here." The intensity on his face was scary. Who got so worked up over an arcade?

I really hoped he wasn't doing anything stupid, but I shrugged and went back to skeeball. I played four rounds before people began making a commotion behind me. Turning around, I saw a giant stuffed horn parting the kids as it made its way toward me.

Dumbstruck, I could only watch as a giant Narwal emerged from the crowd with Greg underneath it. Everyone was clapping and whistling as Greg presented me with a six-foot stuffed animal in the likeness of a Narwal. "I saw this at the counter, and I really wanted to get it for you. I know how much you like these."

"Is that why you were getting so testy with the machines?"

I petted the stuffed animal. It really was cute, but big. How would we get that thing in the car? I supposed we could strap it to the top and have our friend sailing down the interstate.

"I had to get it for you."

"That's sweet," I said, planting a kiss on his lips. "Let's take this thing to the hotel room."

I named the thing Randy, and it took up occupancy at the end of the bed. We took pictures of it while resting in the room for a little while to get out of the heat. My stomach began to grumble. We just ate, but I was hungry again. Must have been all the walking around.

"What's for lunch?" I asked, rolling onto the Narwal.

"Let's just get something quick," Greg said. "I have tickets for the sky bridge."

I gasped before sitting up. "The sky bridge!"

"Yeah," he laughed. "But we need to hurry."

I settled on some Krystal burgers on the way to the bridge. I had heard of it but never got to go myself. My brothers were afraid of heights, so it was always off the agenda. We had to take a lift like skiers did to get to the top. I clung to Greg with one hand and the railing with the other. Greg was smiling, but he was rigid, and the forming sweat was glistening across his face.

"You're afraid of heights, aren't you?"

His smile was still plastered on his face, but his eyes were telling a different tale. "I knew you wanted to come here."

Good Lord. He was petrified but insisted on coming up here just for me. "You didn't have to do that," I said. "I could have gone by myself or with some girlfriends."

"You don't exactly have girlfriends," Greg pointed out. "Unless you counted Mrs. Swollas."

I elbowed him, and when he was nudged, he yelped before swallowing his cry. I felt sorry for him. Here he was, scared shitless, and I was knocking him around on a skylift hauling us up the mountain.

Greg had a point, too. I didn't have any friends. I used to have lots of them at some point. Everyone grew up and moved on. Most had got married and had kids.

It wasn't that I hadn't tried to be a part of their lives, but the common interests just sort of drifted. They were talking about babies and pre-schools, then elementary schools, PTA meetings, and shit their kids did. I couldn't relate. I attended every one of their baby showers and had half a dozen bridesmaid dresses. We'd have a rare girl's night out here and there, then it was just pictures on social media. I went from being everyone's confidant to being updated on a public post along with old coworkers and obscure relatives.

"Hey," Greg said softly. "I didn't mean anything by that."

I gave him a fake smile, and the skylift lurched to a stop. "We're here!" I said as cheerily as I could. It was easy to shrug off the thoughts up there, surrounded by clouds and dense forests painted the landscape in greens and browns. Whisps of clouds emerged from the forests that clawed at the sky with curling fingers of mist. I'd pack away the worries and fears with my luggage and deal with them when I got home.

The arc over the bridge was painted in big, bold letters, and the bridge spanned into the setting sun. I grinned at Greg, taking his hand, I hurried to the bridge. Phone in hand, I took panorama photos at every angle. For all his fear on the lift, Greg had recovered, and he was calm standing over the mist. "Mrs. Swollas will love these," I said.

I don't know why she was always on my mind. Maybe Greg had a point. She was my only friend. Other people would be posting pictures on social media or showing their family, but I wanted to show these pictures to a hermit who freaked out at the scent of blood. I looked up at Greg for reassurance. We were more than just lovers; we were friends, too.

His arm wrapped around my waist as he pulled me in closer. "It don't get much better than this."

We couldn't linger too long as the park was closing. I buttoned up my coat as we made our way to the other side of the bridge to the awaiting lift. We drove back to the hotel room with a bottle of wine and some Checkers. We ate on the hotel bed from greasy paper bags while watching local news, laughing at the way they reported news.

"People were murdered, there was an armed robbery, but look, ducks!" Greg said in his best news reporter voice. "And now, the weather."

"Hot as hell, followed by... more heat and humidity," I added.

"I suppose the weather updates have more uses in other seasons." Greg searched his basket of waffle fries for the crunchiest ones. "It's nice to know if it's going to shit down so much rain that it stops four lanes of freeway."

"True," I said. Settling into the fluffy white comforter. "We should get one of these."

"I think they got them at the mall."

He was talking about Macy's. It was expensive, but then again, we could afford a few minor luxuries now. "This was really great, Greg. Thank you."

It's always hard to sleep in a new place the first night. The anticipation of waking up disoriented never lets me sleep. The second night is better. It's like my body just adjusts to the new bed and surroundings. The promise of being back in my own bed the next day was also soothing. With all the walking and eating, ski lifts, and Narwals, I drifted into an easy sleep. At least I thought it was until the dreams came.

I dreamt I was in a hedge maze. The bushes were so tall, and I was lost. Gasping in panic, I ran into dead end after dead end. Was there no way out? I didn't know this place, and I shivered from the cold. A man called out to me, but his voice made my skin crawl. He was not safe. I'd rather freeze to death than be caught by him.

This wasn't real, I reminded myself. It was a dream, and I screamed for Greg in the hopes that the body lying in bed beside him was also shouting his name. Sniffing back the tears, I held myself and stared at the bleak overcast sky. My nightshirt was damp to the touch, and I was barefoot. The wet grass was itchy on my skin. It was a dream, but it felt so real.

A flash of pale blonde hair rushed past a green corridor. "Hey," my voice cracked. "Can you help me?"

Was she running from the man who called for her? I thought he was calling for me, but I couldn't understand the words he spoke. It might have been that he was searching for her. "Stay away from that man," I told her. "I don't know why, but I think he means to hurt you."

He called again, but this time, it was a desperate plea. His voice was full of genuine fear, but I didn't trust him all the same. I went after the woman, following in the direction I had thought she'd gone, but the maze was disorienting and playing tricks on my mind.

"Where are you?" I whispered.

The rustling of skirts came from straight ahead. I chased after it when something large swooped overhead. It was too big to be a bird, but I wasn't about to stop and ponder as to what it was. The maze opened into a square clearing with a water fountain in the center. Instead of water, putrid green sludge erupted from the top and overfilled the pool below. A sweet rot mixed with ocean water filled my nostrils, and I gagged.

Come on, Greg. Wake me up.

There was a dead tree and a swing tied to a low branch. I stepped around the slime on the ground and touched the swing. The rope was rough and scratchy, and the wooden seat warped from damp and time. I was somewhere near the ocean. Occasional wafts of seawater blew over the tall hedges that incarcerated me.

It was getting dark now, and I had nowhere to go.

The swing started to move on its own. So slow at first that I assumed it was the wind, but the ropes were taut as if they were bearing some unseen weight. It swung faster and faster. I stepped away from the possessed swing and stepped in some of the sludge. Nastier than any Southern swamp, it was warm and sticky. Cringing, I wiped my bare foot against a patch of grass.

The swing moved back and forth slowly, and a giggle came from all around and nowhere at the same time. I didn't want to be here, but I couldn't escape. I closed my eyes, clicked my heels three times, and began chanting, "There's no place like home." It was stupid, but I couldn't think of anything else to do.

There was a presence around me, like someone was watching me. I refused to open my eyes. The next time I opened them, I'd be back in the hotel room with Greg. I would be safe, and this would all be a distant dream. I just hoped that whatever was watching me wasn't hungry.

Familiar whispers traced the back of my neck and against my hair. "I don't understand what you're saying," I told them, but they didn't stop.

Pain was sharp and sudden against the flesh of my underarm. It was a pinch. I hollered, and my eyes opened with surprise, but when I sat up, I was in bed. I felt my nightshirt. It was wet with sweat, and the AC was freezing it. Teeth chattering, I clambered out of bed and pulled it off. Greg stirred in the bed.

"You okay?" he mumbled.

"I think I have a fever."

Greg sat up and reached for me in the darkness. He pressed a hand against my forehead. "You're burning up," he said. Groping for my nightshirt, he said, "It's damp."

Before I could redress, he was up. Soft yellow light from the desk lamp stung my eyes, and I couldn't stop myself from shaking. All drowsiness had left Greg. He hugged me tight for a moment before asking if I could take a shower. I nodded, and he helped me into the bathroom.

"I'll be right back," he said. "I'm going to see if the front desk has any fever reducer."

The cold water was blissful. I was so hot, the steam rose off my skin. I was still in the shower when Greg returned. He had several bottles of water and a single-serve packet of painkillers. He checked my temperature again and frowned at the results. "I think the shift in altitude made you sick."

"I can't be sick. I have work on Monday."

"I don't think it will last long," he assured me. I took the pills and drank two bottles of water before crawling back into bed. The heat was leaving my body; I was keenly aware of my temperature dropping as I drifted back to sleep. I couldn't recall a thing from that strange dream, though it probably wasn't that strange. Otherwise, I would have remembered.

9

— · —

I returned to work on Monday. Just as Greg had theorized, my fever was a result of altitude sickness and nothing more. Mrs. Swollas was in her forest green gown that had just enough ruffle to add a stylish flair without being considered impractical. On her collar, a massive ruby cut into an emerald shape surrounded by tiny diamonds. It was a natural ruby. I could tell by the natural dimness of the gemstone that the newer ones didn't possess.

"That's a beautiful brooch," I commented over tea.

She fingered it gently and nodded. "An old family heirloom."

A family she seldom spoke of and scarcely remembered. Yet she was proud of it all the same. "I'm going to the store today. Do you want me to pick you up anything?"

"I should be fine, I think."

She caught my frown and sighed. "Though you will need to show me how that machine works."

I had hoped Mrs. Swollas would request groceries or anything, but once again, she declined. She said she had a kitchenette in her study, but I was starting to believe she was lying. There was no evidence. The only trash that went out to the garbage can was the bags I took out every Tuesday. No cans, no food wrappers, not even bones or uneaten leftovers. I had seen videos of people who made it a point to reduce their waste to practically nothing, but even then, I was left scratching my head, wondering how they managed.

My grandma was a product of the Great Depression. Not a scrap went to waste, especially not in the south where poverty was at its worst. I supposed she did a great deal of composting. There was a large wooden box by the planter beds with a wooden cover. It smelled like compost, but I was always told to not put proteins in the compost. Maybe she fed the bones to her Gargoyle.

At Mrs. Swollas's behest, I rounded up the linens. Still clean and unused from the last washing, but she wanted them washed regardless. I separated out the fitted sheets and dropped them into the washer. The old woman scowled at the buttons and knobs as if they were a foreign language and pulled out a laundry sheet.

"I know how you dislike waste, so I got these," I explained. "One sheet is enough to clean a load of laundry, and the package can be composted."

She gave a stiff nod and folded her hands in front of her.

I pressed the start button, and the machine did the rest. "It senses the weight of the items you're washing and uses just enough to clean them."

The washer locked and gently hummed as it worked. Mrs. Swollas was taken aback by it all. "That's it?" she asked. "With all those buttons, I would have thought there was more to it."

"It's so you can manually set it for different clothing. Delicates, bleaching, dark clothing, really dirty stuff. If you had a phone, you could turn it on with that too."

I expected her to scoff at the notion, but Mrs. Swollas stared at the machine. "The world has changed," she said with realization. "I fear I am struggling to keep up with it."

She was old then. Older than I had ever seen her. Her back slouched uncharacteristically, and her hands trembled. The white streaks in her hair were less pronounced as it melded with the once-black hair that had lost all its previous luster. Even the brightness in her green eyes had faded.

"It's nothing to be upset about," I told her. "I feel the same way when I can't figure out the WIFI."

"I don't even know what WIFI is."

I moved to touch her. I don't know why. I wanted to hug her, console her, and lead her from the laundry. Mrs. Swollas backed away and pinched the bridge of her nose. "I feel a headache coming on. I'm going to rest. Go to the store and get things you think are needed."

She rushed from the room and bustled up the stairs, leaving me in the makeshift laundry room. Poor Mrs. Swollas. The world was a scary place when you didn't feel like you belonged. This was why she didn't want anyone coming to the house and why she never left. She couldn't drive, didn't understand anything about the world, and I suspected she couldn't read English though she could speak it. Imagine trying to navigate a grocery store not being able to read a lick, especially when nothing is familiar.

Well, I wasn't about to leave her to eat home-pickled vegetables or whatever it was she had stashed away. I could pick up a few things and let her try them. If she liked it, I could buy more of it. Maybe even take her with one of these days so that she could get familiar with it.

The machine stopped humming and sloshing water had taken its place. I was about to go upstairs when a sigh came from behind me. I turned to find the hallway empty. Not content with letting it go, I opened the door closest to me to find an empty room. I slammed the door shut, wanting to make my presence known, and proceeded to the next room.

This door was also unlocked, and the room was totally empty. Mrs. Swollas didn't use the first story on this side of the house, so nothing should have been sighing at all. I moved to check the last bedroom on the left when the door drifted open on its own accord.

I sucked in a breath and tensed. If someone was in here, I was going to kick their ass. Squatters were common, and most who encountered this place would assume it was uninhabited. With one hand, I smashed the door open all the way but stopped short of entering. It was just another empty room. This one faced inward and didn't have a window. It was just a blank slate of white walls and yellow hardwood floors.

It was just my imagination. This level of the house always gave me the creeps. It was empty and narrow and abandoned by Mrs. Swollas entirely. Shaking off the jitters, I turned to leave when an unwarranted breeze sent my jacket and hair swaying. The scent of seawater intermingled with something else, something rotten. Had something crawled in here and died? The ocean was several states away, but maybe it was a lingering from the swamp or the signs of a bad pipe. It reminded me of something, but no matter how hard I reached to remember, it was lost to me.

#

Of all the shopping carts at the Piggly Wiggly, I got the one with a wheel that squeaked. It announced my presence down every aisle and locked up at the deli. Most of the things I bought were for Mrs. Swollas. I picked up some bread in one of those paper bags, some protein shakes the old people buy, jam, butter, and some orange juice. Who didn't like orange juice?

I grabbed a sandwich for myself, but I paid separately for that. Greg had an early meeting, and since he started working, he didn't always have time to make lunches. He always made me breakfast, though.

Even if he was running late, he'd still manage to put a waffle in the toaster for me. He was always so considerate like that.

The hardware store was too far of a trip to make on laundry day, but I needed to get grout and caulking for the house. One of the banisters was loose, so I'd need to get some screws or wood glue. They recognized me at the hardware store. No doubt from the last time I visited, asking for biohazards.

"What can I do for you?" Russ asked, his accent so thick that I wanted to say he was from Louisiana. It had more of a low drum sound about it.

"Just a few odds and ends," I said.

He led me down the aisles and filled my basket. "You a new home-owner in these parts?" he asked.

"No, I work for an old lady, helping her keep her house together."

He nodded absently while eyeing the screws. "What do you need these for?"

"Loose banister. One of those big loopy kinds."

He gave me a mocking frown. "In these parts?"

"It's a Shingle-style home," I said, repeating what Mrs. Swollas said to me.

The man stopped in his tracks and turned to face me. "There's only one house like that around here. Did Montgomery sell it?"

I had no idea who that was. Mrs. Swollas said she had bought it recently, so I supposed it was true. "I guess so."

"Whatever happened to him? Last I saw, he took in a young woman," he stared wistfully into the distance. "She was a beauty. Long black hair and the brightest green eyes. Like a little porcelain doll, she was."

He couldn't be talking about Mrs. Swollas. "How long ago was this?" I asked.

The man went back to thumbing through screws. "Oh, about three years ago," he said. "Montgomery never recovered from being drafted in the war. He seldom left his house, but he sent the town all a flutter when he picked up that beautiful young woman from the train station."

I was speechless. There was no way that girl could be Mrs. Swollas. The daughter must have come for a visit before she died. Still, Mrs. Swollas never mentioned her daughter coming to town. Maybe there was more to her relationship with the former owner than she wanted to share.

When I got back to the house, I put away the groceries and hung up the sheets while another load was washing. As I got the last few items pinned, Mrs. Swollas emerged. She was examining the clothes hampers. "I thought the dryer did this," she said, motioning to the sheets billowing in the breeze.

"Yeah, but you can't beat the smell of air-dried things," I said. "Come winter, when it's too cold, the dryer will come in handy."

"It's good that some things never change, at least."

"I brought home some things from the store," I said, hoping to pull her out of the slump. "Some bread, butter, jams, shakes. If you like them, just let me know, and I'll get you more."

"Thank you, my dear," she said. "But I'm afraid my tastes are rather slight for such things."

'You need to eat,' I wanted to say. She was so thin and small that it worried me. I couldn't make her eat. Some people were just built like that, and that was fine, but I wasn't satisfied with the answers she gave. "I'm not an expert," I said. "But you need all the nutrition you can get. Proteins, calcium, things to keep you strong."

"Strong for what?" she asked sharply. "Strong for a world I can't navigate? I've lived too long as it is. I have nothing to live for."

Was she intentionally starving herself to death? I shook my head and blinked back the tears. "Mrs. Swollas," I said as sternly as my crackling voice would allow. "If you don't eat, I'm going to call a doctor."

She laughed silently at my threat. "That should be exciting."

Was she calling my bluff? I would do it. I hated the idea of losing her trust or even this job, but if she was on the verge of death, I couldn't stand by and watch either. "You can fire me if you want, but I won't let you go out like that."

Mrs. Swollas observed me for a moment, her green eyes reassessing me. "You have more backbone than I thought. Tell me, when you ran in the wrong direction on that red, tattered runner, did you look him in the eyes first?"

My heart plummeted so fast into my stomach it could have been a brick. How did she know? I stepped back, flinching at the question. Mrs. Swollas tilted her head. "Well, did you?"

I muttered something about needing to leave and bolted toward the car. I got halfway there when I realized I didn't have my purse. I'd need to go back inside. My heart was pounding, and I didn't want to go back in there. Mrs. Swollas was calling my name, but it was the Gargoyle that stood on high and judged me. Those horrible, stony eyes, crazed and vacant at the same time, were staring at me.

"Jayme," Mrs. Swollas's voice came from right beside me. I jumped and let out a yelp while she remained entirely composed. "I'm sorry. I shouldn't have done that."

"How did you get right here?"

Her smile was slight and bitter. "There is much you do not understand, and it wasn't fair that I tried to show you in such a way."

There she was, talking nonsense again. She must have dug up dirt on me before she hired me. A kind of safeguard in case I did something wrong. I didn't know how she managed to sneak up on me outside, but she did it often enough in the house. I was so upset I wasn't paying attention.

"So, you know about Lars," I said. My guard was back up, and I was prepared for the judgmental conversation that often followed.

"Come," she said. "Let's talk over tea."

This time, she made the tea while I sat at the table. The kettle bubbled and threatened to let out a wail, but she was ready for it. How was I going to explain my failed wedding to her without sounding like the total asshole I was? The scent of the tea broke through the steam, and Mrs. Swollas placed a cup in front of me before she seated herself.

"So," she said. "I take it that failed wedding is a source of shame for you."

How else should I have felt about it? "My parents paid so much money," I said. "They were furious with me."

"And the groom?"

Poor Lars. My eyes fell to my cup. "He was heartbroken."

"He was older," Mrs. Swollas said. "Perhaps he was too old."

I shook my head. My brothers came to the same conclusion. Tommy and Bradley both blamed my parents for not speaking up about the fact that Lars was closer to Mama's age than he was to mine. That wasn't why, but they wanted to shelter me from Daddy's disappointment. "That wasn't it."

Mrs. Swollas was watching me. Her eyes scanned my face, and she nodded. "What went through your mind at that moment?"

"I just kept thinking that it was all wrong for me. The further down the aisle I got, the more it screamed in my head. It got so loud, I just couldn't take it anymore. I ran in that damn wedding dress halfway across town and ended up in a back alley."

"Did you cry?"

My eyes met hers. "I laughed."

I had never told anyone that before. It would have been one thing if I cried, told everyone I had a panic attack. They would understand that. The wedding could go on in a smaller ceremony or even a court-house. Everyone would understand. It would have been a funny story we told our children, but there would be no children, and I refused to go back. Not after what I did.

"Maybe it's crazy," I started. "But I feel like there's something else or someone else, I don't know. It's like I'm meant for someone, but I haven't found them yet."

"Lars was not your someone," Mrs. Swollas agreed.

"He was a good man. They don't get much better than that. But I don't want better."

Mrs. Swollas's face softened. "I, too, have a confession to make. Perhaps it will relieve this guilt you have so unjustly held on to. I pushed my daughter to marry. I've told you as much."

She said it was what ultimately killed her daughter. I would have died a slow death if I went through with it, but I could only guess that what happened to Mrs. Swollas's daughter was not a slow death. Was she finally going to tell me what happened?

"Yes."

"I told her she wasn't strong enough to survive without a man. That it had to be the man I chose for her. He changed after they married. He hid his perversions so well, even from me. By the time I sensed something was amiss, I was too late. The house was engulfed with flames, my entire family inside."

My stomach lurched, and I swallowed the urge to vomit. I clamped my hands over my mouth. Mrs. Swollas was not a fan of emotional outbursts. "He killed them all?"

Her green eyes met mine. "No, she did. She did what she had to. The consequences of unleashing our family onto the world would have been devastating. She knew that and did what I never could. She ended it. Now here I sit, afraid and alone. Hastening my demise in any way I can."

In her strange way, Mrs. Swollas was trying to comfort me. She was trying to tell me that if my parents could talk about it now, they would tell me they understood and that I did the right thing for me. But something else was reeling in my mind.

I once saw a horror film about a ship full of lepers that was intentionally crashed into rocks. Not all types of leprosy were contagious, but they were often shunned all the same. The reason Mrs. Swollas didn't know where she came from was because it didn't have a name.

"Were they lepers?" I asked.

Mrs. Swollas laughed and wiped the tears forming in her eyes. "You're a clever girl, always seeking answers."

"How did you meet Mr. Montgomery?"

She frowned at that. A morsel of information I had collected about her life that she had not served. "How do you know about him?"

"The man at the hardware store told me," I said. "He said a pretty girl came to town three years ago. I assumed he was talking about your daughter."

Mrs. Swollas bit her lip. I imagined that if she was a cat, the hair on her back would have been raised.

"It wasn't your daughter, was it?" I asked.

The old woman shook her head.

If it wasn't the daughter, who was it? Who else would have long black hair and bright green eyes with a doll's face? She smiled at me gently then. Something about her smile made me feel all warm and bubbly inside, but the streams of gold filtering through the windows reminded me that the sun was waning.

Mrs. Swollas noticed too. "You should leave. No doubt Greg will be missing you."

It was one of the rules; I couldn't stay past sunset. Greg would start calling if I didn't come home anyhow. The last thing I needed was for him to make a fuss. I'd be back tomorrow, I told myself as I peeled out of the driveway and back to the apartment, leaving home behind.

10

"I don't know, Jayme," Greg said as the bacon sizzled in the pan. "This whole thing is getting weirder and weirder."

I was three glasses into the Pino Grigio and melting into the couch. The local news was blathering on about the decline in wildlife around the area. "It explains the full coverage gowns," I said. "If she has leprosy, it may be somewhere under those dresses. All I can see are her hands and her face."

"Did it ever occur to you that she's lying?" he asked.

Maybe she was. Mrs. Swollas didn't exactly confirm my leprosy theory, but she didn't deny it either. "She probably came here for treatment and just never went back."

"Like she's an undocumented immigrant?"

"Explains why she wants to fly so low under the radar." Greg pressed his lips together as if he were trying to recall something. "Hey, do you remember a few years back about that island off the coast of Iceland?"

How could anyone forget? There were so many wild theories about how the island suddenly appeared, but scientists proved that it had always been there; it was just so small that most people didn't know of it.

"The Brigadoon Island," I mused.

"You don't think she came from that island, do you?"

The journalist on TV was walking through the woods, holding his mic up to his face and ducking branches like he was on some nature documentary. "It's too graphic to show on live broadcasting, but this is the third deer I've encountered. It's been killed by some wild animal, but not eaten."

"Maybe," I said, renewing my interest in the news. "That would explain her not knowing the name of the country she came from and the funky accent."

My tongue was thick in my mouth from the wine, and I was ready for that bacon. Greg and I loved breakfast for dinner. We ate breakfast for breakfast too, but something about having bacon, eggs, and pancakes for dinner just hit the spot. Greg came out with a plate, and we ate at the coffee table.

"They've been going on about this for days," Greg said, biting into his bacon. "They think it's some massive bobcat or wolves. They're going to push a mandate to keep people out of the woods for a while."

I snorted. "Good luck with that. Hunters and Moonshiners won't listen to that."

"Might be a few people start going missing too."

Well, you can't fix stupid. Though, the more I watched, the more familiar the woods became. I lost interest when the commercials came on. Dipping bacon into the maple syrup created the perfect salty and sweet combination. I moaned a little bit when I took that first bite, and Greg snickered. "Getting me all excited now," he teased.

"Good."

His eyes lingered on my lips while I licked away the syrup. I wanted him to stare. Trying to play it cool, he tried to take a bite of his eggs only for them to roll off the fork that he still put in his mouth. The eggs fell to the floor, and he frowned, realizing the mishap.

We broke into giggles, but the tension remained between us all the same. It was like a pull, urging me into his arms, egg breath be damned. We were halfway undressed as the news urged people to stay out of the Chattanooga woods.

Greg paused for a moment and said, "Hey, isn't that around where you work?"

Panting and halfway through slipping out of my bra, I bit back the pang of frustration at the sudden halt in our activities. "So?"

"Don't you think it's a little scary? What if something happens to you or her out there, and you have no way to get ahold of anyone."

Well, that killed the mood.

I sat up and said, "We don't go wandering in the woods."

"No, but whatever is out there is just killing for fun. What if it gets brave and hides under your car or something? It's probably rabid."

I was a thirty-three-year-old woman. I had survived this long without being taken out by wild animals; I didn't think one would get me now. "I park in a carport, and the door is three feet away."

Greg sat up and rubbed his head. "Yeah, I know. It's not that I don't trust you. It makes me nervous not knowing where you work, but now that there's wild animals on a killing spree circling the place...I just don't like it."

"What do you want?" I already knew what he wanted. He wanted me to break Mrs. Swollas's rule and tell him where she lived. His reasoning was sound enough, but this wasn't the first time he tried to learn where I worked. It made his concern appear false and itch with ulterior motive.

Greg shrugged. "I know she doesn't want anyone coming to the house, but can you just tell me the general area? If I need to call the police or an ambulance—"

"If anything happened, I could do the same."

"But what if you're not able to?" he said. "What am I supposed to say when you don't come home? It could take days for them to find you."

Something inside me seethed and barred its teeth. He had no right to try and manipulate me in the guise of my own good. I wasn't some wayward woman who couldn't defend herself from monsters. I was not the damsel in distress that needed rescuing.

When I got a flat tire, I was the one who fixed it. I was the one who paid the bills and fixed the vacuum multiple times because Greg couldn't figure it out. I survived hardship and hunger that Greg couldn't dream of and came out like nothing ever happened.

I survived him... I shook my head. What was I going on about?

"If I don't come home, assume it's because I don't want to."

Greg's face dropped. He was speechless. Swallowing back tears, he sat there dumbstruck while I snatched my clothes up off the floor and strode off towards the shower. Greg remained on the couch for the rest of the night.

#

The next day at work, I brought up the news to Mrs. Swollas while I polished the wooden staircase with a rag and wood polish. The scent was overwhelming. I wanted to tell her that since the wood was painted, there was no point in polishing it like this, but she paid me too much to complain.

"So, I guess there is some rabid animal making a mess out in the woods around here," I yelled.

"You don't need to shout," Mrs. Swollas said from right behind me.

It startled me, and she rolled her eyes. "I thought you were in the kitchen," I explained.

"So, there are wild, rabid animals in the woods," she said. "Are there no surprises left in the world?"

The sarcasm wasn't lost on me, and her dry humor was more than a little funny. "It's not that they are wild or rabid that has everyone spooked," I explained. "It's the fact that whatever it is, it's killing animals but not eating them."

"Hm." She frowned at that. "We had a similar occurrence where I came from. It was a great big wolf that killed for the pleasure of it."

Hearing the ancient woman say *pleasure* made me cringe. "Greg and I got into a fight about it last night."

Mrs. Swollas nodded. "He wants to know where I live. It irks him that you go somewhere out of his reach each day."

"He's not a controlling guy at all," I half-heartedly defended. "But yeah, he is determined to know where I work."

"And you won't tell him?"

I stopped my futile polishing. "You told me not to tell anyone where you live."

"Perhaps you do not want him to know?"

Damn. She could see right through me, the old witch. She smiled slyly, as if she could read my mind. I shook my head in denial, trying to form an excuse, but it was useless. "I don't know why," I said. "I just don't trust him sometimes."

I had every right to be suspicious of him in the past. He always took more than he gave, but once he got his job back, everything had changed. He was a different person now. Still, I learned enough to know that when Greg was desperate, he would do whatever it took to survive. We were different in that regard. He let hardship change who he was, and I remained steadfast.

"Trust your intuition," Mrs. Swollas said before abruptly leaving the room.

Well, okay then. Leave it to Mrs. Swollas to say something so sweet after she verbally backhanded me with truths I wasn't prepared for, only to disappear once again. Where did she always run off to anyhow? I pulled myself up to my feet and went in the direction she'd gone. She had to have gone across the sky bridge, but after that, she could have gone up to her bedroom or down to the first floor—I couldn't say which.

So, I went back to what I was doing. There were a lot of stairs and only one of me. I didn't see the old woman again until lunch. She sat in her seat precisely at twelve-thirty, waiting for tea in her chair and looking out into the woods outside her home. When I placed her tea before her, she took several sips of scalding hot beverage. I knew better than to drink when she did; I waited for nearly ten minutes before trying to drink myself. She must have burnt all her tastebuds off years ago.

I had just reached the top of the stairs when a voice, high like a whistle, drifted through the hallways. "Hello?"

There was no one there. The third story could not be reached except for the stairs, and I was on them. The voice wavered in and out as if it were wandering through the rooms. There were only two up here. One was the room Mrs. Swollas brought me to when we had our first interview, and the other was just a bathroom.

The voice softened to a whisper when I checked the formal living room. The stained glass reflected a spectrum of blues, yellows, and reds across the walls and sofas. Someone was here. I could feel her. She was mischievous but not cruel. Gentle but determined. "What do you want from me?" I asked.

Ghosts weren't real, and if they were, they didn't travel across leagues of oceans to haunt their mother's overpaid housekeeper. I made for the door when the rush of ocean waves splashed behind me. The salty water air filled my lungs and dappled my tongue.

All at once, everything stopped. I was standing alone in an empty room illuminated by sunlight filtering through tinted glass. Dust particles trickled to the shag carpets. My upper arm burned in one spot. I slid my arm out of the sleeve and investigated. The burning subsided as I pulled the underside of my arm upward, revealing a nasty bruise.

#

"What did your daughter look like?" I asked.

"Goodness, that came out of nowhere," Mrs. Swollas said.

I supposed it had, but I wanted to know if the image of the girl in my mind matched the long-deceased girl. After what happened in the living room, it was well past time that I got answers. "Was she blonde?"

Mrs. Swollas set her tea down. "Why yes, though I suppose that was an easy enough guess."

It wasn't a guess. "She had dark brown eyes and brown freckles."

The old woman's hand trembled as she gripped her teacup, but she said nothing. Her eyes lined with curiosity and fear, but I couldn't stop. "She was taller than you. She wore a black lace gown."

Mrs. Swollas's eyes narrowed. "How do you know all that?"

"I saw her in the mirror in my apartment," I said, shrugging off my button-up shirt and exposing my arms. I held up one arm, revealing a mean purple bruise on my bicep. "I can't remember how I got this, but I think she did it."

Who was telling Mrs. Swollas this? My words were foreign to me, and I honestly had no recollection of the dream until I said it. Yes, there was a dream. The night I had the fever in Gatlinburg. "There was a green maze and a swing."

"Beside a fountain," Mrs. Swollas finished. She shook her head in disbelief. "How..."

Something connected us. It was more than just a job or my need for maternal approval. But what? "Sometimes, I say things to Greg. Things that I would never say."

"Like how you said them just now?" Mrs. Swollas asked. Her green eyes pierced into my psyche, searching for something that slipped just out of reach.

"You won't find her there," I said.

"My dear, are you all right?"

No, I was not all right. Not at all. Last night, I threatened to ghost Greg, and he hadn't spoken to me since. Half of me didn't trust him, while the other half desperately needed to. This wasn't like me. I wasn't some alluring, mysterious woman who spoke cryptically about dead daughters I had never encountered. I was Jayme. Sweet, kind Jayme who had two older brothers who gained a reputation for protecting their baby sister.

"I don't know what's happening to me," I whispered. "I hear things sometimes. Things that aren't there. Sometimes the words that come out of my mouth aren't mine."

Mrs. Swollas took my hand and squeezed it. "I want you to go home and rest for today. Don't be alarmed, but I won't be here for the next few days. You are to resume your duties as if I were here. I expect this place to be in proper order when I return."

"Where are you going?" This was such short notice. Why didn't she tell me sooner? Was everything okay?

"There are some accounts I must see to. I need to consolidate some assets for future investments."

I wasn't entirely following, but it sounded like she was cashing out to put her chips in one basket. Did that mean she was finally going to renovate the house, or was there something else she wanted to focus on? "How long will you be gone?" I asked.

"Just a few days!" Mrs. Swollas said. She stood up, and the chair scraped against the tile. "Now go."

I was practically shoved out of the house. All she needed was a broom, and it would have looked like she was kicking out a stray cat. I drove away, rushed and confused. The last half hour was surreal, and I wasn't entirely certain they were my doing. "What was in that tea?" I asked myself out loud.

When I got home, I slid my coat off and hung my purse before plopping on the couch. Greg was still at work, so I had some time to myself for a change. The urge to be productive was overridden by lethargy. There I was, with the time to do something useful, and I had no energy to do it. It left me feeling guilty. How did Greg put up with this for so long?

I was still in the same spot when Greg got in. His eyes went wide with surprise before he remembered that he was still pissed at me. It was a good time to apologize and make up, but what did I have to apologize for? I was being honest and nothing more. Still, if I didn't placate him somehow, he would stew about it. It would create a string of spats for the next several weeks.

And that matters because?

No. That wasn't me. That was someone else. I cared about Greg and didn't deliberately hurt people. "Greg," I called.

He was in the kitchen, sulking.

"Greg, about yesterday..."

There was a clank of a dish in the sink, and he came around the partition between the kitchen and living room. With his hands in his pockets, he waited for me to say what I had to say. Part of me resisted, but I was in control and responsible for my actions.

"I'm sorry," I said. The words threatened to choke in my mouth. "I don't know what came over me."

"I know," Greg said. "It's that woman. Ever since you started this job, you've been different. It's like I don't even know you sometimes."

"I know it," I said. "I don't think it's her doing, though."

He frowned, not wanting to argue the point but joining me on the couch. "What is it then?"

How could I explain it? I was developing a split personality, and my other half hated him? That's what it felt like, but it wasn't something I was willing to share. "I think Mrs. Swollas reminds me a lot of my mother," I said. "I haven't seen her in six months. Here I am, taking care of a woman with a similar illness when I don't even check in on my mama."

It was something that had been milling around in my head—that was true.

Greg leaned in and took my hand. "What's stopping you from seeing her, then?"

"You're right," I forced a smile. "I'll go see her this weekend."

While we had made up, all was not forgiven. Greg was sullen and tight-lipped for the rest of the afternoon. He told me a little about work, but it was strained and awkward. I cut him deeper than I realized. It would take time before we were okay again, just so long as I didn't say anything else stupid.

To avoid the tension in the tiny apartment, I did research on Brigadoon Island. Most of the articles related to how the island was discovered. Just one day, an island appeared a few hours off the coast of Iceland. Scientists think that it was probably mistaken as an iceberg since it was the size of one, but that wasn't the part I was interested in.

I clarified my search to "inhabitants on Brigadoon Island" and was linked to references to a ghost hunter, but all his videos were taken down. I searched for pictures, and there were images of the island, but nothing magical, just a bunch of sheep. A farmer took up residence when the island was declared a providence of Iceland, and that was it.

Frustration intermingled with the tension from staring at a screen for too long made my eyes fuzzy. I needed glasses, I knew that, but I just hadn't gotten around to it. Maybe I'd make an appointment for vision and dental the next time Aunt Flo made a visit. Lord knew I needed both checked out. Before I closed the browser, an image caught my eye. It was a great big pile of debris from a fire. It was a panoramic view of the remains after a great fire. Could this have been the fire Mrs. Swollas's daughter died in?

11

— · —

I t was strange working in the house with Mrs. Swollas gone. It was always quiet, but with her gone, I was acutely aware of the silence. I dropped a teacup in the sink and flinched at how far the sound carried. When I ran water, it echoed along the barren walls. I swear I could hear each bristle on the brush scrapping against the floors and countertops.

I threw the brush on the floor, and it clanged so loud I thought the tile was going to break. Unable to handle the quiet anymore, I went to the carport. There was a radio out there on the shelving. The radio was a box boxy thing from well before my time, but it would serve.

Mrs. Swollas took care of the other wing of the house for the most part. I never really went to that side of the house. Using a cloth wrapped around the end of a mop, I cleaned the windows of the sky bridge. Working from one end to the other, growing more aware by the minute that I was inching toward Mrs. Swollas's private domain. These windows needed to be cleaned from the outside, but she'd never hire a window washer.

If she really was just setting up to die and the house didn't matter, why worry about her investments? Nothing made sense anymore.

I stepped over the threshold to the front wing of the house. For a moment, I half expected Mrs. Swollas to come out of nowhere and demand I clean the light fixtures, but she was not here.

While I swept, I looked around the hallway before attempting to open any of the doors. She still isn't here, I reminded myself. Most of the doors were locked, but I secretly hoped one wasn't. She said it was because the rooms were in disrepair, but I wanted to see this study and kitchenette. She couldn't have been lying about it; otherwise, how could she still be alive? The food I had bought from the Piggly Wiggly remained untouched.

I grew bolder and more insistent with jiggling the doorknobs. The metal fixtures rattled so loud, I broke into a cold sweat. She's not here, I told myself. This was breaking one of her rules, but I had to. What if she wasn't eating at all and truly trying to kill herself? Unlike the other doors, a lighter, tin jingle accompanied the sounds of my attempted break-in.

I gave up, losing my courage and my energy. I picked up my mop and broom to leave in defeat when that tinny rattle sounded from the door. Too scared to scream, I fell back against the wall. A glimmer of something gold rattled at the top of the door frame. It was a piece of metal shaking on its own. Dropping the mop and broom, I fled the hallway, tripping up the stairs on my way out.

I landed on my knees and elbows. Wood crashed against bone, and everything hurt before going tingly and numb. I was flipped over as all the doorknobs were now shaking and jolting on their own. I whimpered and reverse crab walked a few steps when some invisible force grabbed hold of my ankle. It dragged me back down to the hallway. I screamed and grabbed for anything, the railing, but it had a stranglehold on my ankle with an icy grip.

I was screaming for help, for God, for anyone to come, but there was no one out here. And then everything stopped. The house was silent once again. I was lying against the bottom step, panting and crying for several minutes. The whispers, the urges to say things I didn't mean, the doors opening, and the weird dreams. I wasn't losing my mind. I wasn't imagining this.

"Fuck this shit," I muttered. Scrambling up the stairs, I grabbed my purse and coat before fleeing that damned house. I paced back and forth in the yard, searching for a signal. My fingers shook so bad, they jerked across the screen as I dialed Greg.

Please don't be in the middle of a lecture. Please.

"Hello?"

I jumped as I shouted into the phone, "Oh my God, Greg!"

"What's wrong?"

I instantly went into a ramble, and he had to get me to calm down and start over. I started from the beginning, explaining everything I could. Greg listened as well as he could with the reception being so bad. "So, you think Mrs. Swollas is haunting you?"

"No, I think it's her dead daughter. I've been having dreams about this girl, and I told Mrs. Swollas what she looked like, and I just knew it was her daughter. I think she knows it too, but she's acting like she doesn't."

"Jayme, this is crazy."

"I know," I said. "It's crazy and weird, but I swear, Greg, something is happening to me, and it has to do with Swollas's dead daughter."

"What do you think this ghost wants?" Greg asked.

"I don't know. Maybe she wants me to help Mrs. Swollas. I don't know anything about her, but she wanted me to go into that room."

"You didn't, right?"

"No, I was scared shitless. I'm going home right now."

"Good, you do that," he said. "Don't go back into that house alone."

That was totally out of the question—I worked there. But now wasn't the time to argue with him. "I'll see you at home."

I hung up before he could say goodbye. Before he could say anything that I couldn't say back.

Shoving the phone into the bottom of my purse, I turned and found my old friend, the Gargoyle, staring at me. I flipped his nastiness the bird before getting in the car and driving home. I was nearly home when something occurred to me.

The Gargoyle's wings weren't spread out like before. His wings were tucked behind his back.

12

—•—

Greg would still be at work if I went home then and there. I didn't want to be alone. Not after what I had encountered in Mrs. Swollas's house. How could I even begin to explain it? The house wasn't haunted, I was. When the old lady returned, I'd tell her about it. She might think I'm crazy too, but if anyone had insight on this ghost, it would be Mrs. Swollas, as bad as her memory was.

I drove down the highway, uncertain of where I was going. It wasn't until I pulled up to the delicately manicured apartment complex that I realized I went to the person I always ran to when I was in trouble. Or rather, who I used to run to before Lars. Women in pale blue uniforms were smoking under the shade of the tall building. They watched me park with noted interest.

"Can we help you, ma'am?" one said when I made my way to the building.

"I'm here to visit my mother, Mrs. Agnes Coleman."

Their eyes lit with some recognition as well as curiosity. "She's been getting a few visitors lately," the woman said, holding the door for me. The blast from the AC carried the lingering stink of cigarette smoke back outside where it belonged. The nurse led me to the empty front desk, where I signed in on a sheet of paper.

"One of my brothers?" I asked.

"Both, actually."

Something about that didn't sit right with me. Had something been going on with Mama? I scarcely spoke to my brothers these days. I was so out of the loop. "How has she been?" I asked.

The nurse hesitated, and my heart sank. I knew she had been getting worse. The only way to cure Dementia was a pine box. It was a child's folly to assume their parents wouldn't age when they weren't around. It was a form of denial. You'd think I'd learn the first time, but I was a slow learner.

With Daddy, it all happened so fast. One day he was there, and the next, I was getting a call from Mama and both brothers. I knew before I answered the phone. He was a heavy-set man and diabetic. He refused to change his diet and ended up in the hospital multiple times. I was glad he died in his sleep from a massive heart attack. It was better than watching him get eaten alive by gangrene.

Mama's room was on the top floor. The red carpets in the hallway were freshly cleaned, and there were still lines in the carpet from the morning vacuuming. The potted plants that decorated the corners were probably fake, but they were the realistic kind. Mirrors and paintings hung along the ivory walls adorned with crown moldings. This place was nice. Daddy did right by Mama. When he died, he had all their finances set. Did he know her mind was slipping even then?

Her room was a spacious, airy room that reminded me of some fancy hotel room. Traces of assisted care in the form of a breakfast tray with a silver platter on the dinner table. The curtains were drawn, flooding the room in daylight. Mama was on her beige sofa in front of the flatscreen TV. Her hair was cropped short and was recently set, and her clothes were neat and pressed, but she sagged in them like a bean bag in a case that was a size too big.

"Hey, Mama," I said.

Mama didn't blink; she didn't flinch. Her wrinkled fingers trembled slightly over the buttons of the remote, but there was no other indication that she was even alive. It wasn't the punch to the gut like the mention of my brothers visiting. This was a slow, creeping feeling like someone was squeezing my heart a little at a time. I eased my stiff body onto the sofa beside her.

"Mama?"

She turned to me then. Her eyes were full of distrust. "Who are you?" she asked.

I bit back my tears. It wasn't her fault she couldn't remember me. It was that damned disease and not her. Still, it hurt nonetheless. "It's your daughter," I said, my voice cracking. "It's Jayme."

Her grey brows raised, and she smiled. "I'm sorry, hun. My memory isn't all that good."

Just like that, she was back, but for how long? "How have you been?"

"Oh, they take good care of me here," she said. "The girls are so sweet."

That was good to hear. "What are you watching?" I asked.

"Oh, just the news."

The TV was playing a documentary on cats. Mama hated cats. She never let me have one as a kid, and here she was watching a series dedicated to them. I supposed it was better than actually watching the news; that was just depressing.

"Mama, I need some advice."

She took my hand and said, "That's what I'm here for."

Where to begin? "I got this problem at work, you see. My boss's daughter is trying to get me to help her mama, but I don't know how."

"What are you supposed to do about that?"

"I think her mama is sick," I said. "Something like what you have, only Mrs. Swollas isn't the sort of woman to listen."

"When my mind started going, I knew something wasn't right. I bet this Mrs. Swollas knows too, she's just not ready to give up her independence. Just be patient and ask the daughter to be patient, too."

I gave Mama's hand a squeeze. Whatever was going on with Mrs. Swollas might have been why her daughter was haunting me, and Mama was right. Maybe the reason her daughter was haunting me was because Mrs. Swollas was too stubborn to listen. I doubted she believed in ghosts, but neither did I until one was staring at me in the mirror.

"I think you're right, Mama."

"How is Lars?" she asked.

I swallowed the lump in my throat. I had hoped she had forgotten that, but dementia has a funny way of hitting below the belt. "Lars is good, Mama. He's been married for seven years now. I think they're trying for another baby."

Mama gave me an incredulous look. "What do you mean? He's married with kids? The two of you were engaged."

"We broke things off before we got married," I reminded her.

"Why would you go and do that? He was a good man. You won't do better."

My stomach churned, and for a fleeting moment, I thought I'd have to run to the bathroom. My worst fear laid out so plainly. That's why my parents were so upset when I didn't marry Lars. It had nothing to do with paying for the wedding; it was because they genuinely thought that he was better than I deserved.

"I'm dating someone my own age," I told her. "He's a biology professor at Berry College."

"Is he handsome?" Mama asked.

I nodded, hoping to move past the wound she inflicted. She didn't mean it. Well, she did, but she didn't mean it to hurt me. "His name is Greg, and he's very sweet."

Mama frowned and shook her head. "No, that's not right. You married Lars. I remember the wedding dress and sitting in the church."

Oh Lord, why couldn't she remember at least this part? "I ran at the altar, Mama. It just wasn't meant to be. I'm sorry."

"Now why would you go and do a stupid thing like that?" Mama jerked her hand away. "And now you're working for some witch and her daughter. What the hell is going on in your head, girl?"

She got up and made like she was going to the bathroom only to stop and come back, fury in her eyes. I didn't know what to do. Paralyzed by fear of upsetting her more, I just sat there. Mama was angrier than I had ever seen her before, and I was one hell of a teenager.

I searched the walls for signs of a nurse button. There had to be some easy way to call them. Mama knocked her breakfast platter off the table and was rambling about witches and unholy spirits. What did I say to lead to this? Did she think Mrs. Swollas was a witch or Lars's wife?

Salvation came from the round red button on the remote. There was a nurse button built into the TV remote. I pushed it and then pushed it again just for good measure. Mama was going off the deep end, and I didn't know what to do. She was hollering now but nothing coherent.

"Mama..."

I didn't dare stand. I was afraid she'd attack me. Several nurses came running in, their blue uniforms a blur that swaddled Mama with soothing whispers. "We need a sedative," one nurse said into a walkie-talkie.

By the time the third nurse came rushing in with a syringe, I could scarcely see her through my tears. I couldn't comfort my own mama until the needle pierced her thin skin and she began to relax. They helped her into bed. She was still shouting, but they were weaker and less angry.

"Don't let her take my baby," Mama cried out before succumbing to sleep.

"She needs to rest now," a Black nurse told me.

"I...I've never seen her like that before," I said. "I don't know why she got so upset."

"It's all right," the nurse consoled me as the other two left. "It's not your fault. She's been increasingly agitated lately."

The Black nurse had a northern accent. She must have come from Northeast. Her nametag had the title Residential L.P.N next to her name. "Where are you from?" I asked stupidly. Everyone probably asked her that.

"Pennsylvania," she explained. "I came to Georgia for college, met someone, and decided to stick around."

I was grateful that she did 'cause I sure as hell did not know how to deal with Mama. "When did she start doing that?"

The nurse led me out the door and down the well-kept hallway. "Dementia patients are prone to fits like that," she explained. "Hers started suddenly about a month ago."

I started working for Mrs. Swollas a month ago. But it was just a coincidence. The mind's need to connect dots that wouldn't have connected otherwise. Correlation does not equal causation and all that. I flunked statistics in community college.

"This just hasn't been my day," I told the nurse.

She patted my back. "This is never easy."

Nothing ever is.

"Hey, while I'm here, I have some questions."

I told the nurse about Mrs. Swollas. I described her memory issues and lack of appetite. The nurse's frown grew deeper and more profound with the more details I gave until I was certain there was a problem. "So, you've been working there for over a month, and you've never seen her eat?"

"Yes, ma'am."

The nurse nodded. "She must be eating something. She just doesn't eat in front of you."

"That's what I figured, but there's no garbage. Ever. No sign of food stuffs."

"She might have issues with eating that she doesn't want you to see. Does she have any tremors?"

I shook my head. "No, not that I've seen."

"Sometimes people with Parkinson's don't have a visible tremor but still have difficulty eating. She might even have a feeding tube. Most don't want people to see their feeding tube."

That would explain the long gowns. If she had tremors in her feet or legs, I wouldn't be able to see them under all that. A feeding tube might also explain the strange jokes about how she was always hungry but couldn't eat what I brought home. I suddenly felt like a jerk for bringing all those things to the house.

"What about her memory issues?" I asked.

The nurse folded her arms and said, "It could be any number of things. Does she have a doctor?"

"Not that I know of."

"You should encourage her to see one. I'm afraid that's all I can say."

I expected as much, but the nurse helped explain ailments I hadn't even considered. Maybe that's where Mrs. Swollas was now, seeing a doctor or specialist, and she just didn't want to tell me. There was so much I didn't know about her.

The drive home was quiet, the apartment even quieter. I sat on the couch and allowed myself a pity party. I had no idea Mama was so bad off. Why didn't my brothers tell me? My grief morphed into anger. I had every right to know Mama was on a decline. They could have at least warned me she was like that. Had I known she was going to have a fit like that, I would have been more prepared.

I dialed Tommy's number. He was probably at work, but I didn't care. This was important.

"Hello?"

"When were you going to tell me about Mama?"

"What do you mean?" he asked.

"I stopped by to visit, and she was acting crazy. They said you've been stopping by."

"Jayme, I don't know what the hell is going on with you, but you can't just call me up when I'm on a job site raising hell after being out of the picture for six months. I've been trying to get ahold of you, and you never call back."

This was news to me. I hadn't seen a single call from him or Bradley. "I haven't been getting anything."

"I leave voicemails."

I believed him. Tommy wasn't one to lie no matter how bad the truth was. He was the one that told me Daddy died. "I don't understand."

But I did understand. Greg was deleting my calls and voicemails...but why? He used to take my phone because it had internet before he got his own. He was the only one who had access.

My brother was quiet for a moment as if he understood what was really going on. "Jayme, do you have a place to call me? Somewhere safe?"

"He's not abusive," I insisted. "I just don't know why he'd delete all your calls."

"You can always stay with us if you need to," Tommy said.

"Okay," I said with a deep breath. "I'm sorry. I don't know what's going on anymore."

"I'm here."

"Thanks, Tommy."

I spent the next few hours stewing. With my anger re-directed, I deliberated on what to do. I needed an explanation. He knew I had brothers, he knew their names, so why try to cut me off from them? Was that the real reason he kept taking my phone? Tommy was right to assume the relationship was abusive. Trying to cut me off from my family was something an abuser would do.

Just leave. You don't need to wait for him to feed you more lies or withhold important truths. Pack your things and stay with your brother. Nothing good can come of this.

Were those my thoughts or someone else's? I didn't have time to ponder it as the front door opened, and Greg came rushing in. His briefcase and coat fell from him as he embraced me. "Are you okay? Tell me everything."

13

— • —

A bottle of Pino Grigio later, I had regaled him with my whole day. I left out the conversation with Tommy, still unsure of how to proceed with that. The voice that urged me to leave him was quiet now, and all that was left was me, clinging to the only lifeboat I had.

Greg listened intently. His glass was still mostly full, and he gave it to me at the end. "Jayme, is it possible you might have just freaked out because you were alone and spooked in the house?"

I should have been angry—I wanted to be—but between hindsight and exhaustion, it was plausible. My mind wanted to rationalize this, and maybe he was right. I slipped on the steps, heard things that weren't there. My imagination must have gotten the better of me. "Maybe you're right," I admitted. "I really hate being there alone."

"When does she come back?"

I shrugged, the weight of the day slipping away. "I don't know, but she will be mad if she comes back to find the house unattended."

Greg gazed at the TV, not really watching it. His mind was somewhere else. "Claire is going to get a thousand dollars from each check."

This day was the gift that kept on giving. "That's nearly half your check," I gasped.

"I can keep on fighting it, racking up more attorney bills, or I can just pay it. As it stands, half my check goes to her and a third of it goes to the lawyer. I can't afford to keep fighting this."

If he prolonged the divorce any longer, he'd have nothing. I didn't imagine he would hit rock bottom before finally giving up. I rubbed his back. "Sign the papers; it's only for a few years."

He gave me a weak smile. "She can't do anything else once it's signed."

No, she wouldn't be able to. He was bound to get raises in the future. Once he repaid her the twenty-three thousand dollars, she couldn't get anything else. I shuttered to think about how much that lawyer had cost. Greg might as well have gone in there without a lawyer with the way Claire's team had him bent over.

"I just got in so deep," he said. "I thought the only way out was to keep digging. There was no way she could just get away with it...but she did."

There was a reason for that, but there was no reason to rub it in his face at this point. If I were Claire, going through all he put her through, I'd want my money back, too. "I'm fortunate Daddy didn't try to sue me for the wedding I ran out on."

"Well, I, for one, am glad you did."

That brought me to my next question. "Greg, I talked to my brother today. He said he'd been trying to get ahold of me for months now."

His silence spoke volumes.

"Why?" I asked.

"He kept calling while I was at an interview, so I blocked his number. I forgot all about it until just now."

You don't really believe that, do you?

No, not really, but what other plausible explanation was there? "He was worried you were trying to isolate me from the family."

"The phone works both ways, don't it?" Greg said. He stood and stretched. "I'm beat. You want me to fix you some dinner?"

"No."

It was a truth that slapped me across the face. He wasn't wrong. I could have just as easily called Tommy or Bradley on my own, but I waited. Why did I wait? Deep down, I believed my brothers had given up on me like my parents did. It was my fault. I missed my nieces and nephews' birthdays, never once called to check in on anyone. I couldn't blame Greg for that.

The tension between us that night was silent and awkward. Greg ignored it and went right to sleep. For most of the night, I lay awake, fretting about the future. I wanted Mrs. Swollas to come back. I missed the old bird. What would she make of everything that had happened today?

#

The next morning, I returned to the house to find she was still gone. Not only did I not know where she went, but it occurred to me that I didn't know how she left either. I assumed she got a driver, but how would she? The way old people ordered taxis before cell phones, I guess. Still, she didn't allow anyone near the house... Did she walk down the road until a taxi found her? It was strange.

I eyed the gargoyle as I came in. It was perched in the exact same position as I had left it. Did it have its wings spread in the first place, or was I imagining things? It might have had posable wings, or maybe Mrs. Swollas had a set of wings she stuck on it as a joke. With nothing to do today, I intended to find out.

Her room was unlocked. I stepped inside but made sure to keep my hands at my sides. At any moment, Mrs. Swollas could come home and find me rummaging through her things. The trust I had been trying to establish would have been lost. Maybe if I had a broom with me or a duster, I'd look less suspicious, but I wasn't about to dust the gargoyle.

The Southern heat met me at the balcony doors. The glass revealed the stone monster awaiting on the railing. I took a deep breath and stepped out. Its wings were down, but from this angle, I could see why I thought they had moved. The wings were not entirely folded back or tucked in as they appeared from the ground. They were partially expanded. I'd see their span from directly under the house, but from a distance, I'd only see the arches.

I forced myself forward to touch the thing. It was hard and dense like a rock should be. Red and green Moss was growing on it in patches that almost resembled clothes. It was just stone and nothing more. I scared myself stupid, that's all.

I left her room and returned to the kitchen, where I threw out all the food I bought for Mrs. Swollas. She had touched none of it, and it was nearly expired. I replaced the stuff with my own sandwich and yogurt. I dusted some things that didn't need dusting and wiped down some windows, but there wasn't much to do for an empty home.

My curiosity got the better of me. I wanted to know if I really was being haunted or if I was going crazy. The ghost, if there was one, wanted me to look in that room. There was something important in there. The missing pieces of this jigsaw were behind a locked door, waiting for me.

Greg had me convinced I was scaring myself, but there was no explanation for what I was experiencing. I just didn't know, and I hated not knowing, but I also didn't want to get caught. I could just go home and take the day off. Not like Mrs. Swollas would care. If she did, I could say I started my period; it was due any time now. Lord knows she hated that.

I was zipping up my purse when the whispers trickled down the walls. "I knew it!" I said out loud. "You don't want me to leave, do you?"

The singsong whisper flowed across the walls as if trying to lead me to the stairs. My knees trembled as I forced them to move across the sky bridge and down the stairs leading to the locked rooms I had left yesterday. The whispers grew louder and more prominent, but I couldn't make out what they were saying. It was English but so thickly accented and old, I could not comprehend it. It reminded me of trying to read Shakespeare in high school, only there were no notes at the bottom of the page clueing you in on what was being said.

This time, I went to the door that started all the commotion the other day. Reaching for the frame, I felt for what I understood now to be a key. It was a stick key, so I inserted it into the doorknob itself, and the lock shifted open. I gave one final glance around me to make sure Mrs. Swollas wasn't standing behind me like she sometimes did. The hallway was empty, and the voices had quieted, leaving no sound but my own breathing.

The room would have appeared to be a normal study if it weren't for the giant pentagram drawn on the floor. Each point of the star had three candles of assorted colors. There was an altar as well. Adorned with crystals, pewter bowls, and an ornate dagger. A massive book was centered at the altar.

Stepping over the pentagram drawn with what was probably chalk, I read the open pages of the book. It was a protection spell. This was Wicca. I sighed with relief at that. Mrs. Swollas practiced Wicca, which was known to be a good magic, even in these parts where non-Christians were considered Satan worshipers.

Wicca was mostly associated with recycling and caring for nature. That was something I could respect. They didn't sacrifice animals or praise demons. It was sort of endearing to know she had practiced such a fantastical spirituality.

I wondered if there was something in here about ghosts. How to talk to them, summon them, even. There was no denying something spooky was going on, and I wanted to get to the bottom of it. Was Mrs. Swollas somehow involved? She seemed startled, uncomfortable even when I talked about it. It wasn't until I described her daughter that she left the house for the first time in a month. It was more than just coincidence, but why leave? The ghost was here, or with me rather.

The rest of the study was typical. There was a desk and a computer chair, though there was no computer. The desk had several well-read books hand-bound in leather. I didn't dare sit, but I opened the oldest book and skimmed through the pages. It was handwritten in scrawling cursive, and I was never good at reading fancy stuff.

The words I could make out were in English, but once again, the terms and vocabulary were so different. Even the spelling was weird. I released the frown building between my eyebrows and shifted to the newer book beside it. It had similar penmanship, but it was plainer, and it was in an English I could understand.

I mistook them for recipes at first, but the titles indicated that these were spells of some kind. I compared the newer book to the one I couldn't read and smiled. Mrs. Swollas was translating old witchcraft. That smile was short-lived when I flipped to a page about a potion promising long life. Among the list of things it required, the heart of an innocent was listed at the bottom.

I flipped both books shut and stepped away. That was not any Wicca that I had heard about. She isn't sacrificing babies, I rationalized. She's just transcribing an old book. But why did the handwriting look the same? The ink was the same color and everything. Nausea washed over me, and I was filled with the urge to leave the room.

It was only after I locked the door that it occurred to me that there was no kitchenette in the study. She had been lying about that as well. I checked the other rooms. The pin key unlocked all three. I wasn't surprised to find that not only did none of the rooms contain mold, but none of the floors were soft.

They were extensions of her study. There were books...so many books. The room closest to the stairs was dedicated to modern stuff. Published books I recognized. Fiction as well as nonfiction. The far-left room contained more old books. Not so ancient that they were handwritten, but old enough. There was a worn copy of Don Quixotic and printed editions of Shakespeare, Plato, and even a first edition of Frankenstein. It might have been a forged copy or something, but it looked legit enough to my untrained eyes.

To me, the two rooms were a private collection and not to be confused with the middle room. There were cardboard boxes stacked in the far-left room as well. Addresses from Harvard and Cambridge and several others I wasn't familiar with. She was a collector of sorts.

Perhaps when she said she needed to sort out some affairs, she meant that she had to travel somewhere to add to her collection. That would make sense. A trip to Harvard would take a few days. Maybe she was trying to buy or donate to the college.

I locked all three doors before trudging back up the stairs. Opening the locked rooms only gave me more questions. What kind of a witch didn't believe in ghosts? The word *witch* didn't sit right, and I was suddenly back in my mother's apartment while she was hollering about a witch taking her baby.

"Don't worry, Mama," I said out loud. "I don't think the witch wants to take me all that bad."

14

G reg paused at the door when he saw that I was home before him for the second day in a row. "Hi, honey," he said tentatively.

I leaned forward. "It happened again. I'm not crazy."

He shrugged off his coat and hung it up. "Never said you were crazy, but...you heard the voices again?"

"Close the front door."

He whirled around and shut the door, chuckling to himself. "Now you got me spooked," he said, joining me on the couch. "What happened, exactly?"

I told him about the room and its contents. "And I never did find a kitchenette. She's gotta be eating, but it's not from any kitchen. The nurse at Mama's home suggested she was on a feeding tube, and that might be true, but I don't know."

"So, she has a lot of old books on the occult." I swear Greg's ears perked when I mentioned the books. He had a natural inclination towards books and especially those that were related to his field in any way, but still. He could at least contain his enthusiasm a little; I was being attacked by a poltergeist.

I was being led by ghosts into a room full of witchcraft and books about brewing the hearts of the innocent, and he was stuck on the books? "Yeah, I think she's transcribing an old book to a modern one, but it's Satan worship, Greg."

He nodded. "No, I know, that's awful. I don't know what to make of it."

How could Mrs. Swollas explain all of this? I didn't think she could. Ghosts, witchcraft, her rules. It was all getting to be too much. "Maybe I should quit."

Greg pressed his lips into a thin line. "Between Claire and the attorney bills, I can't afford to help more than I am now. If you got a job that paid less, I don't think we could swing it."

Fucking Claire. I fell against the seat of the couch and sighed. He was right. We needed the money. That was the funny thing about money; the more I had, the more impossible it seemed that we had managed with less. I did not want to go back to that. Fretting over bills, waking up at night in a panic...late fees. Paying more money just because I didn't have it to begin with. No, there was no way I was going to willing go back to that circus. "I'll look for a job that pays as much—"

"Like what?" Greg interrupted. "That woman is paying you forty a year to sweep floors and do the occasional laundry. You just don't have the education to do better."

You can't do better.

My mama said the same thing yesterday, and it stung even harder hearing it come from Greg's mouth. I regretted talking him up to my mama. Maybe she wouldn't remember that I had visited at all. "Just a few weeks ago, you wanted me to quit."

"That was before Claire's cut was taken out of my check. I thought I'd be able to take care of both of us, but I can't."

There was no way out of it, then. I'd have to work with Mrs. Swollas and hope she wasn't eating babies. It was like I was selling my soul to the devil for a decent wage. Greg may have been right, but that didn't mean he was off the hook. Couldn't do better, my ass.

"So, I should just go work with old lady Satan worshiper?"

"Just until you find a job that pays well," he reasoned. "If you quit, you can't get unemployment."

He had a point, damn him. "Maybe I am just overreacting. She might be an exotic book collector."

"Her books are easily worth a fortune," Greg said. "She might have them just to have them. Shit, I still got my college textbooks. I'm not planning on being a psychologist, but I got a book on it."

"Then why did that ghost want me in there so bad?" Did Mrs. Swollas do something to her daughter? I shook my head at the thought. No, she loved that girl. She feels responsible for her death, but she didn't murder her only beloved daughter.

There was more to this story, and like it or not, I would be seeing it through. That night, Greg was stroking my back and inching closer. The last thing I wanted was sex. His hand snaked around my waist and to my breasts before I swatted him away. "After the last two days I've had? What are you thinking?"

"I'm thinking it's been weeks," he grumbled.

I grinned in the dark. It was a smug, spiteful happiness that I enjoyed more than I should have. Poor baby, he hadn't gotten any in weeks. Meanwhile, here I was dealing with all this. Men and their priorities. What if I was just losing my mind? It wouldn't matter to him just so long as what was between my legs was available to him.

There was movement on the bed; he had gotten up. Off to go pout on the couch, probably. A few months ago, I would have stopped him and talked him into getting back into bed. Well, that wasn't the person I was anymore. This person was going to roll over and get some shut-eye.

That night, I dreamt that I was back on that grassy knoll with the overcast sky. There was a massive shadow looming over me. Squinting, I looked up to behold a behemoth of a house. It was a weathered gray with stone around the foundation. I shivered as the ocean breeze blew my light blonde hair all over the place. It wasn't me; I was in the young girl's body again, but this time, I could speak for myself. "Hello?" I called.

"You're here."

I turned and faced a slight, sickly pale girl with black hair down to her waist. She was wearing a black lace gown and little dull leather shoes with roughly made buckles. Behind her was a dense, overgrown forest. Her eyes were dark, and her face was...pointy. She was beautiful but frightening. Like a tiger or a panther. Small, adorable, and yet there was a threat lurking behind her eyes, as if she could turn on me at any moment.

"Where am I?" I asked, my childish voice still held its southern twang.

The girl's eyes went wide, and she stepped back. "You?" she hissed. "How are you here?"

What was she talking about? She asked if I was here, and then she seemed afraid of the fact that I was here. "I'm not gonna hurt you," I said, stepping closer. "I just want to know what this place is. I've been having dreams about it for a while now."

The girl's eyes narrowed, and she approached with jarring speed before stopping an inch in front of my face. "How can this be?"

There was something familiar about her eyes. They were almost totally black. I had never seen anything like it, but at the same time, I felt as though I recognized them. There was something almost predatory about the little girl. I was gulping for air in fear. She wasn't natural. Up close, she was all bony. Beneath the skin, points protruded at her cheekbones and jaw. Her nose was sharp along the bridge. "Are you some kind of elf?" I asked.

She tilted her head before bursting into childish giggles. It would have been charming if it didn't expose her sharp, pointy teeth. With a sharp-knuckled hand, she led me toward the maze. I pulled back. "No, I don't want to go in there," I said.

I couldn't say why, but that place scared me.

"It's all right," she said. "I won't let you get lost."

We walked hand in hand through the maze in silence. In minutes that could have been hours, we came to a clearing where a tree with a swing and fountain emerged. This place felt safe but frightening, just like the girl. I hated not knowing why.

"How many times have you dreamed of this place?" she asked, pushing me onto the swing.

The scent of lavender coiled around me as she moved behind me to push the swing. "A few times this last month, but I can't help but feel like I knew this place even before then."

"I see. Is it possible you dreamt it as a child?"

"I can't remember anything specific," I said. "But I've always felt like I was destined for something. I suppose everyone thinks that."

The world spun in a blur of overcast and green until I came face to face with the girl. "What did you say?"

I wasn't afraid then. The word came out of my mouth so easily, and I was smiling, but it wasn't me. It was someone else then. "Destiny."

The alarm clock was blaring in the distance. It echoed over the shores and through the hedges. The girl heard it, too; she cursed in some old language and spun me so fast, I had to shut my eyes. When I opened them again, I was face to face with Greg.

"Get up," he said before stomping off. "Damn."

I suspected I'd need to make my own breakfast.

15

—•—

When I got to work that morning, I fully expected Mrs. Swollas to be there. She said she was only leaving for a few days, so it made sense, but something in my gut sensed it as well. I had a funky dream the night before, but I couldn't remember much of it. I was at that place again, there was a girl, and then Greg was shaking the hell out of me.

He didn't so much as say goodbye when he left for work. A cold war was brewing between us, and Greg wanted me to wave the white flag first. I still didn't like that he blocked my brother on my phone, and I wasn't that keen on the things he said last night, either. Maybe if I just talked to him. Greg couldn't have known what my mama had said. He didn't know the baggage that came with that phrase. It wasn't fair to hold it against him.

"Morning, ugly," I said to the Gargoyle as I drove into the carport.

I came into the kitchen to find Mrs. Swollas waiting at the dinette table. I had to do a double-take when I saw her. The lines on her face had softened, and her cheeks were plumper. She either put on a few pounds or regrew some collagen. "You get some work done?" I asked, starting the tea.

"In a manner of speaking."

"Got your business all taken care of?" I asked while the kettle heated up.

She rested her hands on the table. "I'm afraid not. It seems I left with more questions than answers."

No small sense of smug satisfaction came from that answer. If I couldn't find answers, at least she couldn't either. I did learn she wasn't hurting for money, and that was a good thing for me. Clearly, she had enough money to get some work done.

I poured some tea and set it down. I wanted to ask her so many things, but how to broach the subject? *Hey, I broke into your library slash witch altar... Do you eat babies?* Once again, she sipped on the scalding hot tea as if it were lukewarm.

I was beginning to entertain the idea that she really was a witch. It was ridiculous. A real, honest-to-God—or Satan—witch. I joined her at the table, deciding my next move. "I had an interesting few days while you were gone."

"Yes, I suspect you did," she said.

"Mrs. Swollas, I don't want to sound crazy, but I've been experiencing things. Things I can't explain. Ever since I started working here."

She eyed me, unreadable and unmoved by my confession. "Having any strange dreams lately?"

I shrugged. "Yeah, at least I think so. I can't really remember them when I wake up."

Mrs. Swollas frowned at this. I got the feeling that I had missed something crucial, but trying to remember a dream after it had been forgotten was like trying to pull the tide back to shore. I still wasn't ready to admit I had broken one of her rules, so I kept that bit to myself.

"Mrs. Swollas, you haven't touched any of the food I brought over. You gotta be hungry."

"Starving," she said with a wry grin. It sent a shiver up my spine. Another one of her private jokes.

"Why won't you eat then?" I asked.

Her eyes fell to her tea. "It's hard to have hope at my age. So many times, I've felt the warmth of optimism only to be shut out in the cold once more. Perhaps it is best to forgo hope at this stage and push on with my original plan."

There was so much sadness in her voice. Mrs. Swollas was trying to slowly kill herself. I couldn't imagine the willpower it would take to manage such a thing. If she wanted to end her life, she could have chosen a quicker way, but I was glad she didn't. Asking about Greg signified that she was done speaking on the subject and that I shouldn't push her further.

"Greg," I said with a sigh. "We've been fighting, if I'm honest. He's stressed out about all this money he owes, and I've been so preoccupied that I haven't been as attentive as I should be."

"If I may ask, do you see yourself with him for the remainder of your life?"

No. No, for the same reason I ran at the altar from Lars. That wasn't my destiny. It was so childish, but that's how I felt. Mrs. Swollas would think that was stupid. "I don't know," I said.

She nodded. "I'll need you to run some errands for me today. I have some mail and packages that need to be picked up from the post office. I need a fan for my bedroom as well."

"Oh?" I asked. "What kind of packages?"

She hesitated before drinking more tea. I think she wanted to tell me to mind my own business, but instead, she told me, "I'm expecting several rare books. I have a knack for old languages, you see. I translate various texts and send them to universities for study."

That explained all the books and the boxes from colleges. I should have figured as much. I could be so stupid sometimes. "Mrs. Swollas, why didn't you tell me?"

"I had to be sure you could be trusted," I blinked, and she smirked.

Those books I encountered in the library were translations. She was probably taking notes in the old language before transcribing it in English. I slouched in the chair, feeling like a total dumbass. "Wow, that's really neat," I said. "I bet you get some strange things."

"Some of it is outright ridiculous and grotesque," she said. "But sometimes, I find lost knowledge that can benefit the people of today."

"What do you make of my...experiences?" I asked.

A woman of her age had likely experienced all sorts of strange things. She pulled her chair out and stood. "I suggest you keep a journal and pen by your bed. Write down your dreams the moment you wake up. I suspect you're going through something, but I honestly don't understand it."

"You mean to tell me that you've read all these strange things and have no idea why a ghost is haunting me?"

"Poltergeist," she said. "A ghost haunts a specific area. A poltergeist haunts a person. They were quite rare and are never benevolent."

I was pretty sure it was her daughter who haunted me. By all accounts, she was a nice woman if Mrs. Swollas could be trusted. She scared the hell out of me, but she didn't do anything to hurt me. "Maybe they only write down the bad ones and never the good."

"Ghosts and Poltergeists are generally useless. They are not here to tell you anything, and they mean nothing except to those who cling to them. That, I am an expert on, I can assure you."

Just like that, she sashayed out of the room. Her burgundy gown ruffled against the kitchen island and was squeezed up the stairway. I remained at the table, stewing over a tea that was too hot to drink and uncertain of what to make of the conversation we just had. It was a lot to unpack.

"Starving herself to death?" I muttered to myself in the car as I backed out of the carport. It was so extreme and self-punishing. She chose a life of solitude because she struggled with modern-day technologies; I could understand that. She came from a place where they didn't have cell phones and washing machines. But it was more than that. She was isolating herself as well, and I didn't think it was out of fear. It was another way to suffer. For whatever reason, she hated herself a great deal.

Waiting in line at the post office, a selection of pocketbook journals caught my eye. She had a good idea about writing down my dreams. I picked one up with a watercolor print of a blue mountain. There were so many packages to pick up that the lady behind the counter wheeled them out with a handcart.

The wheels squeaked with a vengeance as I carted all the books out. It was hot in the post office, and my face was undoubtedly red as every miserable soul standing in line stared at me. I loaded up the backseat, and I swear the tires sank an inch when I finished. Humidity clung to me, and I wiped the sweat off the nape of my neck. I was not looking forward to hauling those into the house.

Greg called me while I was in the post office. He was probably worried, given the last few days. I put the AC on full blast before calling him back right then and there in the parking lot while I still had reception.

"Hey," he said after two rings.

"Hey," I said.

"How are things?"

"She's back," I said. "No ghosts yet."

"They don't show up when she's around?"

"That would be too easy," I said.

He chuckled at that. "So, everything is okay?"

"I guess," I started. "I mean, she basically admitted that she is starving herself to death."

"Holy shit. That can't be right. Jayme, if she's a danger to herself, you have to do something."

"I know," I groaned, resting my free hand on the steering wheel. "But what can I do?

"You can call a doctor. Insist that she see one, something."

And destroy the trust I had built with her? She would see it as a betrayal.

Passersby were eyeing me curiously as they walked by the car. Greg wouldn't buy my fears of mistrust, but there was something he would respond to. "And get fired?"

"At least then you could collect unemployment," he offered. "She'll forgive you when she's in her right mind."

He saw right through me. If only that worked both ways. "I'll see if I can't get her to a doctor," I said.

"Call me if anything weird happens."

"I will," I promised.

For all his faults, Greg was considerate. I stopped by a grocery store and bought some of that gin he liked with some seltzer water. It was the least I could do after the way I had behaved over the last few days. He had been as good as gold ever since he got his job back, and I was the one being the ass.

I stopped by the hardware store to get Mrs. Swollas a fan. I saw a bunch of them on sale last time I came. It was a good thing she asked for it now; come summer, they would be all sold out. Everyone had air conditioning in the south. Even a house as weird as hers, but sometimes it was nice to have something extra at night.

Standing around a forest of fans, it occurred to me that I didn't know what size she wanted. Was she talking about a little fan to dry her face or a free-standing one? I tried calling the house, but she didn't answer.

"Can I help you?" a woman asked.

I whirled around to find a short, stocky woman with a red vest on. "Well, not unless you can read my boss's mind."

"I feel that way too sometimes."

We had a laugh about it. The last few times I was here, I worked with the same old man. Maybe he could recommend a good one. "Hey, where's that older guy? I think he was from Louisiana."

The mood dropped, and her eyes fell to her shoes. "Russ stopped coming into work. He's never missed a shift before. We called his house and the police. No one knows where he went."

My stomach bottomed out. I saw him not even a week ago. He seemed healthy enough. "Oh, I'm so sorry. I liked him. I hope everything is okay."

"They checked his trailer, but it was empty. His car is missing, too."

She made it sound like he was murdered or something. Who would attack a sweet old man like that? "Maybe he met someone, fell in love, and decided to never look back."

The woman's face brightened a little. "I hope so."

I took a free-standing fan to the checkout line. On my way out, I saw posters all over the walls asking for information on the man Russ. Something about it really upset me. Guilt nipped at me, but there was no reason for it. It wasn't like I was the one who killed him. Maybe I just wished I could have gotten to know him more. At least remembered his name.

Greg sent me a text with a little old-school heart out of an arrow and the number three. The track phone didn't have emojis. "I got a little surprise for you when I come home," I texted back.

"I'm trying my best to make you proud. Love you," he responded.

My fingers hovered over the autofill text. *Love you too.* I couldn't do it. I threw the phone in my purse before shoving the fan into the front passenger seat. I hadn't told him I loved him since he started working. What was wrong with me?

Maybe part of me didn't want him to work. If he was a functional, self-sustaining adult, what would hold him to me? Driving down the freeway, I gave myself a good, hard look in the rearview mirror and asked myself a question. Why wasn't I happy he was getting back on track?

You can't do better.

Something my mother and Greg had both told me. A phrase that had been implied my whole life as a Southern woman. Marrying a decent man with money and having children was paramount, and I fucked it up. Greg wasn't intended to be a permanent thing. He was a means to punish myself. Except now he was coming back to a life of success, so I was poking holes in our life raft. Perhaps Mrs. Swollas and I were not all that different after all.

16
— · —

Greg's eyes lit up when I set the bottle on the kitchen counter. He was wearing his blue apron to cook his famous meatloaf. "Good day?" I asked, eyeing the array of bottles of sauce he used to make his 'secret sauce.'

He shrugged and pressed the meat into a log. Greg was irresistible with his sleeves rolled up to the elbows. "I could ask you the same," he said, nodding to the bottle of gin.

Leaning against the counter, I sighed and waved the white flag first. "I've been out of sorts lately. I'm sorry."

"Well," he said. "I can't blame you. Something is going on. I don't mean to be insensitive. I just don't know what to do."

What else could we do? I was convinced I was being haunted and no one else was experiencing it but me. I could swear up and down that it was happening, but there would always be doubt until it was his ankle a ghost was yanking on. Mrs. Swollas's rules were there for a reason, and I had already broken one. I might need to break a few more before this was over.

"I just wish you could have been there," I said.

Satisfied with his masterpiece, Greg put the loaf in the oven and washed his hands. "I don't particularly like the idea of you being alone in that house. Next time Swollas is out of town, let me come with. I know it's breaking her rules, but what if something happens to you?"

I nodded. "If she leaves town again, I'll have you come over."

Would I, though? The place scared me, but inviting people to her house without her consent was flat-out wrong. It wasn't like the haunting was occurring solely in the house, either. Wiping his hands on a towel, Greg turned to face me. His eyes lit with concern as he pulled me in close. "You're a good woman, you know that?"

I started to blush. When I tried to look away, he nudged my face with his until we were kissing. He had me pressed against the cabinetry, and I was fumbling with the buttons on his shirt. I wanted him. Yanking on the apron in frustration, it loosened and fell to the floor while he undid his buckle. Something about watching a man undo his belt was enough to melt me.

A loud hissing followed by a burnt smell severed the mood. Molten brown sauce was bubbling over the pan and dribbling onto the stove-top. It was threatening to set off the smoke alarm with all that sticky sugar on the burner. There was laughter and a mad dash to clean up the mess while we were still half-undressed.

"We'll continue that later," he promised.

The sauce was a little burnt, but it reminded me of the action in the kitchen. Each bite was like a memory of our failed tryst that would no doubt continue later. "You know what," Greg said over a bite of meatloaf. "I think what you need is a night out."

"That would be nice." The last time we went anywhere together was our trip. It wasn't that long ago, but I never went anywhere apart from work and shopping. It would be good to get a few drinks, just him and I.

"You need to be around people other than Mrs. Swollas. Let's go out with my friend Josh and his girlfriend."

It wasn't quite what I had in mind, but dinner with friends wouldn't hurt none. "Sure."

Greg smiled, and I bit my lip in response. He knew what that meant, so he took the plates away, and we picked up where we left off in the kitchen. Afterward, I took the journal and a pen to the bedroom and left it on the nightstand. Mrs. Swollas was convinced that my dreams could tell me what was happening if I could just remember them.

Here goes nothing. I pulled the comforter up and hoped to God I'd sleep well that night.

That night, I did dream, but it probably wasn't what Mrs. Swollas was hoping for. Regardless, I wrote it down and brought it to work with me. She was already in the kitchen when I arrived. Formally dressed in a beige dress this time, but the red broach was fixed at her collar. Her hair was blacker than before, but there were still veins of gray working throughout her bun. Old ladies loved their rinses. I tossed my lunch in the fridge and made the usual tea. "Morning, Mrs. Swollas," I greeted.

"Good morning. How did you sleep last night?" she asked.

"I had a dream, so I wrote it down for you." I placed the tea and the journal before her, wondering what she would make of the entry.

Drinking with one hand, she opened the journal deftly with the other. She knew her way around books. I supposed she had a lot of practice, given her occupation. She didn't need reading glasses, which was curious since almost everybody at her age did. Hell, I needed them, too. She didn't even do the thing where she adjusted the book's distance to see better.

Her tongue slid across her lower lip while she read. It was a short entry, and she finished it in mere seconds before frowning at me. "What is this?"

Yeah, it wasn't what she wanted. "It was what I dreamt last night."

Her scowl wasn't a real one. I'd come to learn that she appeared annoyed out of habit but wasn't actually all that upset by anything. Mrs. Swollas was far more patient than she expressed. Her boundaries were strongly asserted to ward off any shenanigans, but I was beginning to see that she wasn't all that stern once she decided she liked someone.

"In the Piggly Wiggly with no clothes on with a buggy full ground beef..."

I snorted with laughter. "I'm sorry, Mrs. Swollas, I didn't realize how weird it sounded when I wrote it down; I was half asleep."

"Indeed. Can you perhaps translate for me?"

It took me a second to catch on. She had never seen the store. For all she knew, I was naked inside a wiggling pig with ground beef. "The Piggly Wiggly is a grocery market," I explained.

Her heavy-lidded eyes raised. "Oh, I see. You were shopping and realized you were naked."

"Yes, Ma'am."

"What is a 'buggy'?"

"It's what we call a shopping cart. Like a basket with wheels."

She pressed her lips as if she were keeping a sharp remark inside. "So, you dreamt you were shopping naked and had lots of ground beef in the cart. You woke up as you were standing in line, realizing everyone was staring at you and that you were exposed."

"Yep."

"Well, I admit this was not quite what I was hoping for, but I think I am to blame as much as you."

There she went, talking in riddles again. "You don't control my dreams any more than I do."

"Well, no, but perhaps I will see if I can send you a message. I was too weak to do so before, but I think I can do it now."

Why could she do it now but not before? She told me she was on the verge of giving up on life until recently. Her will to live was now tied to me and this ghost. I leaned back and tilted my head. "Is this some kind of witchcraft you're trying to do?"

Mrs. Swollas raised her brows. "You're finally catching on."

Struggling to accept that, I did my best to keep my face from revealing my thoughts on the matter. Religious folks didn't enjoy their beliefs being scrutinized. She truly believed she was a witch and that she could communicate with me in my dreams. "Well, it won't hurt to try," I said at last. "But the only way you're going to get stronger is by eating."

"Yes, I have been doing a little of that. Just enough to do what needs to be done," she assured me. "To truly regain my power, I'll need a substantial meal, but it's too risky."

She had been on this hunger strike for so long that she probably couldn't digest food without going into shock and dying. I hated the thought of it, but at least now I had confirmation that she was eating and that she wasn't trying to kill herself anymore. That would get Greg off my back and help the inklings of betrayal subside.

"More cleaning today?" I asked.

"No," she said. "With all the new additions to my collection, I need you to help catalogue my books and prioritize translations."

Was this the job I was meant to do all along? She hired an assistant, after all. The job description didn't specify how, so I assumed I was a personal assistant. She trusted me enough to allow me near her precious collection. "Does this mean you are going to let me into the library?" I asked with a smirk.

"I suspect you already know the way."

My startled expression amused her. How did she find out? I was only in there for a minute, and I never moved anything. "I didn't touch a thing, I swear."

"I'm well aware. Come along."

An uneasy feeling crept along my skin. She must have had cameras, but how and where? She couldn't manage a telephone, let alone security cameras. Perhaps it was a bluff. I never was good at calling them. On the few occasions Greg played poker with me, he said I made for an easy target. Silently cursing myself, I followed Mrs. Swollas to her library. I made no mention of the non-existent kitchenette. I was walking a fine line, as it were, and I didn't want to lose out on this opportunity to do actual assistant work.

When I brought the boxes in, I set them just inside the doorway. Mrs. Swollas must have brought them downstairs, but those boxes weighed a ton. She must have had more energy than she played at because my back was still sore from hauling them around. "You got all of these downstairs and into the study yourself?" I asked.

"I'm more capable than I look," she said. Plucking the dagger from the altar, she extended it to me handle first. "Open them all. Inside should be letters containing request dates of return. The journal right there has my priority list."

"Yes, ma'am."

Little was said while we worked. I unboxed and took notes of when books were requested back for returns. Several were already late. There were directions for applying for extensions which was simple enough online, but Mrs. Swollas obviously hadn't done it.

After a lot of organizing, I found the letters for the books that needed extensions and put them in my purse. I could do that bit at home. Mrs. Swollas worked diligently at her desk as if no one were there at all. It wasn't until I set a stack of four small, leather-bound books on the desk beside her that she paused. "What are these?"

"These are the books that were due for translations months ago," I said. "I'm going to apply for extensions for them, but you should really get started."

"Pfft," she said, returning to her work. "I've never filed for extensions, and they still continue to send more."

She had a point. Most of these books came from the same handful of universities from Europe. I couldn't read any of it. I had to stare at the symbols on the books and compare them to the ones written on the paper. The one she was translating was the one I found on her desk the day I broke in. The one about eating babies.

"Where is that one from?" I asked.

"It's a compilation of various books I've translated in my career. I have several compilations. Some are dedicated to ancient astrology, extinct creatures, cultures, religion, and this one is ancient potions."

"So, it's like a 'Best of' but for history."

Her eyes flittered to me before returning to the books. She didn't know what I was saying, and it annoyed her. "We do the same with music and short stories," I explained. "Especially if the musician has made a lot of music, they put the most popular on one album, so you don't have to buy all the others."

She nodded, but her pen did not leave the journal. "Yes, that is precisely what I'm doing. Rather than search thousands of books for one thing, I can easily find it, and if I need more information, the citation of the book is on the bottom."

I was impressed. She did all of this on her own and was regarded as a noted scholar. There must have been twelve different languages alone in the books I unboxed, and she could read all of them. I didn't even know if these languages were still in use today.

By the time I was done sorting and prioritizing in her notebook, it was well past lunch. My stomach gurgled loud enough that Mrs. Swollas stopped what she was doing to stare. "Gods, girl, go eat."

"Yes, ma'am."

Exhilarated by my new job that did not include cleaning, I decided to eat my sandwich on the sky bridge. I sat on the short, dense carpet and enjoyed the scenery. The swamps in the distance were in full bloom. Water lilies floated on the low waters, and tiny purple flowers covered the ground. Summer rains would cause the ponds to rise significantly, but for now, they were shallow and murky. The cottonwood had released and was sending a flurry of fuzz that drifted like snow. It was beautiful, but it was also a reminder that I'd need to start packing allergy medication.

I checked my phone and waited for several minutes for anything to load, cursing at the lack of reception before debating just how angry Mrs. Swollas would get if I broke another rule.

So far, I had broken into one of the locked rooms and bled, but the period was just an accident on both our parts. It was bound to start again any time now; I'd need to let Mrs. Swollas know. If I changed my tampon frequently enough, she probably wouldn't notice, but my flows could be unpredictable and heavy. Taking a few days off during that time of the month was a nice perk anyhow. How many women could say they got paid time off every time their period started?

Finishing the sandwich Greg had prepared for me, I stood up and went back to the study. Mrs. Swollas was still working. Not stopping to eat or rest. "Maybe you should take a break, too," I said, standing in the doorway.

She finished writing her sentence before raising her head. "Yes, I suppose you're right. Perhaps I'll take a nap. If you're done before I wake, feel free to leave."

Sounded good to me. I resumed arranging the books in order of priority when Mrs. Swollas paused at the door. "May I ask you for some advice?"

I was so shocked I dropped the book in my hand. "Me?"

"You are the only one in this room. At least I assume you are." Her eyes scanned the room as if she really did think someone else was there.

"I'll try," I said, unsure of what sort of advice I could have for her.

"Suppose you have a chance to reclaim the thing you want most in life. Would you take the chance?"

"Well, sure."

Mrs. Swollas nodded. "But what if, in doing so, it puts others in danger? What if the chance is actually just wishful thinking, and you've made a mess of everything?"

I couldn't possibly know what she was referring to, but it had to do with me. I could feel it in my gut. The protection spell on the altar was likely for me because she had no one else. Then again, maybe it was for herself, and that was why she didn't get pestered by the same entity as I did.

"If you're asking my permission, you have it." My southern drawl was gone then. It was replaced with a crisp, European accent like her own. Speaking in tongues was something that happened in churches. People did it every day. Maybe that's why the notion didn't alarm me as much as it should have, but it wasn't me speaking. There was something comforting in it, like someone else driving or following a museum tour. I wasn't being forced; it was more like I was guided to somewhere I wanted to be, even if I didn't know where that was yet.

Her eyes welled with tears, and I wasn't sure if I had said something wrong or even what I had said in the first place. "I'm not asking you," she said. "This is Jayme's choice."

Her words were a deft blow, confirming something I wasn't ready to accept. I was being possessed by Mrs. Swollas's dead daughter. But it didn't feel that way, not like how they showed it in films. I wasn't vomiting green bile and contorting unnaturally.

"I..." I started to say before swallowing. "I'm not in any danger."

"I don't know if things will remain that way."

"No one does," I countered. "No one knows what the future holds. I could get hit by a bus tomorrow."

Mrs. Swollas chuckled in relief before taking in a deep breath. "Try not to get hit by a bus. It seems your life is no longer solely yours."

About time.

17

The evening air was warm and buzzing with nightlife. The warm glow of streetlights and the thrum of music coming from various bars along the strip. Greg's cologne occasionally cut through the humidity with a sweet smell that reminded me of the ocean. It didn't actually smell like the beach at all, but for some reason, it reminded me of it. Must have been the sandalwood or the blue bottle shaped with waves that made the association for me.

"Hey," Greg said as he pulled me in closer. "You're awfully quiet."

I forced a smile until the tops of my cheeks hurt. Greg laughed so hard, he had to look away. "It's okay to be a little nervous about meeting new people. Josh is a bit of an introvert, too."

That made me feel better. I wasn't the only one in the group that was awkward. "What about his girlfriend?"

Greg shrugged. "I've never met her."

We made our way inside a bar. Downtown was full of them, so I had no idea how Greg could know what was where. Inside, Greg took my hand and led me toward a couple. The man was tall and lanky, with long brown hair in a low ponytail. The woman was heavy set with bright lipstick and a retro dress from the fifties. I pressed my lips together, feeling keenly aware of how bare my face was. I got so used to not wearing make-up that I didn't put any on tonight. My hand was pulled along until we joined the couple at the tall table with the extra-high chairs.

"Hey, y'all," Greg said as we sat down.

I had to climb up into the seat. There was just no way of getting in and out of these things gracefully. I think bars liked them because it was easier to tell who had drunk enough just by watching people risk their lives to get down. Once I was finally situated, I joined the other three, who were all watching me struggle. I was hot and flushed already, and we had just got here.

"Jayme, this is Josh and Brittney," Greg said.

"Nice to meet y'all," I said.

Josh was clutching his phone and nodding despite there being no conversation to nod to. Brittney smiled at him and said, "It's weird making friends in your thirties."

"I know!" I said, my voice a little louder than I intended. "Everything is more awkward than it was in high school."

"I don't know," Josh said. "High school was pretty bad for some of us."

I doubted Greg could relate. He seemed comfortable in just about every scenario. "I'm getting drinks," he announced gracefully sliding off the stool. "Drinks?"

We were nodding, but he was already three steps toward the bar. "So how do you know Greg?" I asked.

"I work at Berry, too," Josh said.

"Oh, okay," I said. "In biology?"

"I'm in IT."

That checked out. Brittney was already a drink or two in. "I work in the Berry cafeteria. That's how I met Josh," she said, smiling at him. They were super cute together. She was really pretty, and she only had eyes for him. He was too nervous to notice, but occasionally, he'd glimpse up at her before returning to his phone.

"That's funny," I said. "I met Greg in the cafeteria, too!"

"Not so different from high school after all," Brittney said.

Everyone's laughter was genuine that time. Greg returned with a waitress in tow. "I didn't know what y'all wanted, so I just got another of whatever Brittney was having, and I got you an IPA."

"Did they have Smash Galaxy?" I asked.

"No, but they had that hazy one you like."

"Good enough for me!"

"You like IPAs?" Josh asked. Brittney's bright pink lips were wrapped around the straw of her fruity drink.

"It's cool, right?" Greg said. "Not many girls like IPAs."

"I don't even know what y'all are talking about," Brittney said.

"It's a type of beer," I explained. "It's kind of bitter and hoppy. People either love it or hate it, like cilantro."

I took a swig of my bitter beer and savored the taste. Greg was right. It was nice to be out with people I didn't know. I got to hear someone else's stories for a change. "This guy," Greg said, pointing at Josh. "He's the one who saved my ass."

"Oh?" I asked.

Josh turned bright red behind his wire-rimmed glasses, and Brittney was containing her laughter.

"You remember that lovely picture you put on my screen?" Greg asked.

I nearly spit out my beer. "Oh no."

"I couldn't figure out how to get it off the screen," Greg explained. "It was mortifying. I found him and was like, 'Please don't judge me.'"

"It was a first," Josh chided. "I've seen the blue waffle, but not a guy who couldn't change his background screen."

Brittney was giggling so hard. "When Josh came home and told me about the blue waffle, I about died!"

"Well," I said laughing. "If it helped you make a new friend, I'm glad I did it."

"To new friends!" Greg said, raising his beer.

We all toasted to that.

Several rounds later, someone turned on the Karaoke. That was usually about the time I'd mosey on out, but none of us wanted to leave yet. I just got a fresh beer, and Greg was talking about sharks in the Galapagos. It wasn't the most fascinating subject, but the way Greg described it had our sides aching from laughter.

"I bet the students just love you," I shouted over the Karaoke. Brittney had dragged Josh up there, and he was mumbling along to her off-key but adorable performance.

His cheeks were already pink from all the beers we had, but he got that much redder with the compliment. "I really enjoy teaching," he said. "I can't believe I was willing to give it up over Claire."

"Now don't you go beating yourself up for the past," I said.

"You do enough of that for the both of us."

I was taken aback by the comment. I had to tell him about Lars and the rift that it tore in my family. He never said anything about it one way or anything until now. "I don't know what to say."

"It's time for you to let go too." His watery, bloodshot eyes were staring deeply into my own. "He wasn't the guy for you, no matter how bad your family wanted him to be. The only mistake you made was trying to please everyone but yourself."

He was right, but I didn't know how. It wasn't like if I thought about it hard enough, I could change it, but my mind always went there anyway. "I just wish I got a chance to reconcile things with Daddy."

Greg took my hand. "I think you're still grieving the death of your father, and the wedding has prevented you from getting closure."

There wasn't much closure to be had. He was dead, and Mama wasn't right in the head. That only left my brothers, but I didn't know if either Tommy or Bradley had spoken to Daddy about what happened. "Maybe I can talk to Tommy and see if he knew Daddy's mind on it."

Greg nodded, but his lips were thin and tight. The last time we talked about my brother, I was mad at him for blocking Tommy on the phone. I wasn't harboring any resentment over it. Greg pointed out that a phone works both ways, and it was just as much my fault as it was his.

The song came to an end, and everyone was clapping for Brittney, who did a little curtsey with her flared skirt. Josh was so eager to get off the stage he nearly knocked over his microphone. "They're a cute couple," I told Greg. "I'm glad you made me come out."

This lightened the mood right in time as our newfound friends joined us. "I'm glad you think so 'cause Josh and I are talking about getting together on a little side project!"

The expression on Josh's face was unreadable in that moment. Brittney tilted her head but said nothing. "What for?"

"Oh, we're just joking," Greg said. There was a quiet exchange between Greg and Josh that left Brittney and I puzzled. Clearly, there was some sort of plan hatching between the two that they didn't want to share with us yet. That was fine by me, but maybe Josh needed to run things by Brittney first. Greg could do whatever he wanted just so long as he kept his day job.

"It's getting kind of late," Josh said. "We should probably get going."

We all agreed that we'd do this again as we made our way to our cars.

"Are you good to drive?" I asked Greg.

"Yeah," he said. "I quit drinking over an hour ago."

"I wish I did!" But I didn't, not really. I hadn't been this elated in a long time. "I'm going to regret this in the morning."

"At least you don't have to work."

And I was grateful for that. I fell into the seat and fumbled with my seatbelt. Greg reached around me to help, and I laughed. "You really can take them down," he joked. "They really liked you, I could tell."

"I liked them," I said. "I can't tell you how glad I am that you made me go."

The gutless wonder rattled to life, and we puttered down the road back to our apartment. I watched the taillights as they passed us by, basking in my intoxication. It wasn't until we turned into the apartment complex that, in my peripheral vision, I saw her in the mirror. While I was looking out the window, she was staring straight at me.

My body jerked, and my heart went into my throat. I sat up real quick, but she was gone. It was just me in the mirror. I must have fallen asleep in the car and dreamt it. My heart was thudding so hard that I thought I was going to be sick.

"Pull over," I said.

The seatbelt was gone, and I was out of the car before it came to a complete stop. I puked in the shrubs next to the sidewalk. In an instant, Greg was by my side. "Hey," he said. "I didn't realize you had that much."

I was drunk, but not *that* drunk. The woman appeared in the mirror again, and it was too much in my current state. It was more than that. She didn't just appear. She had been there all along. Never once had she left my side, and I couldn't help but feel like she had been with me all along. But that wasn't right. None of this started until I started working for Mrs. Swollas. It had something to do with her.

My brain was fuzzy on details. Greg helped me up the stairs and into the bed. "Shh," he soothed. "You're okay."

The soft comforter enveloped me, and a familiar beep followed by the sound of rushing air came from the window. "Greg," I moaned. "She's not just haunting me, she's in me..."

There was no answer. My gaze shifted and played tricks on me in the dark. He wasn't in the room. He must have gone back for the car; we had left it still running on the side of the road. He was so concerned that he had rushed me up the stairs first before going back for it. Just as well. I did not mean to say that. Not in the 'I have no control of my mouth' kind of way, but the normal kind of unintentional blurting. I was so drunk that I no longer made sense to myself, so I closed my eyes and went to sleep.

18

I woke up to a mouth full of fuzzy teeth and an earthquaking headache that refused to relent after several painkillers. The typical hangover for people over thirty. Another punishment for aging. Greg was already up and about when I emerged from the bedroom. I wasn't working, but there was still work to be done.

"Can I use your laptop?"

Greg got up off the couch to retrieve his satchel. He handed it over and sat beside me expectantly. "Job hunting?"

I didn't like the way he was hovering, but it wasn't like there was any great mystery to what I was doing. Just sending a few emails. "No, I need to do some work for Mrs. Swollas."

"Oh yeah? What's our favorite old hag up to these days?"

I gave him a scowl. "Don't call her that."

"Sorry," Greg said, raising his hands in defense.

Pulling the papers out of my purse, I navigated various websites. Stanford, Harvard, Cambridge, Oxford, and ETH Zurich. Greg's eyes widened as I emailed department heads to let them know that Mrs. Swollas still had their books and that she was working on them. I signed as her personal assistant with so much pride I could burst.

"Jesus," he said. "She's got some good connections."

So did I. Now that I was the established correspondence, these people would be contacting me for updates. Consulting me for her notes and anything else they might need. In time, I might even learn a bit from her or type out her translations.

I smiled at Greg, but his eyes were on the letters in his hand. He was reading the various books with a great deal of interest. "Anything you recognize?" I asked.

Tearing his eyes from the page, he said, "Jayme, some of this stuff is said to be impossible to translate. There's no known language for this one," he said, pointing to the paper.

"Oh, yeah?" Mrs. Swollas didn't seem too concerned with any of the titles I wrote down in her priority list.

"She has this," he said, still pointing. "In her library right now?"

It was a title that I had stacked in the second priority stack. "Yeah, that one is from Yale, I believe."

Greg's mouth about dropped on the floor. "Jayme, this is incredible. Speaking as a biologist, this could be the discovery of the century if she deciphers it."

"It's sort of neat the way our jobs are becoming compatible."

Greg was laughing like he just won the lottery. "You have to tell me if she figures it out. I want to know what it says!"

"I will, I promise."

We were just getting into lunch when my phone lit up—which was strange because the only person who ever called me was Greg.

"It's my brother," I said. It was jarring despite knowing he could now call since the number was unblocked. Greg muttered something about getting some dishes done and left me alone to read the text.

Hey Jayme, I need to talk to you if you got time.

I was on the balcony clutching my phone to my ear. My stomach was all in knots and still nauseous from the hangover. I wasn't ready for Mama's death. If he was calling, it was probably that. Please don't let it be about her. I couldn't handle that. Not now when everything was going so well.

"Hello," he answered.

"Hey," I nearly gasped. "What's going on?"

"Aw, Jayme, I didn't mean to frighten you. Everything's okay."

I swayed with relief. "Mama's okay?"

"Well, as well as Mama could be," Tommy said. "That's not why I called. I got an opportunity to buy out a gravel pit in Virginia. I could expand my business, you see."

"Oh, Tommy, that's great."

"Well, it can be, but it would mean I have to move to Virginia until it's totally set up. I planned on taking Bradley with me."

He was worried about leaving me and Mama behind. We lived across town from one another but hadn't seen each other in years. I wondered if he still had that big old beard and if he was losing more hair on his head. Bradley looked like a ginger version of Tommy but lacked my older brother's ambition.

"Tommy," I started. "I'm making damn near forty grand a year salary, and Greg is back to teaching again. We're fine."

"I didn't ask about that boyfriend of yours," he said gruffly. "I was asking about you. You can come with me, you know. I could use an administrator or something like that."

The way he spoke about Greg suggested that they had words after all. Whatever led Greg to block Tommy had to do with a conversation. I didn't imagine Tommy and Greg would ever get along. Tommy was too much like Daddy. He didn't mend broken fences easily.

"I can't leave the lady I work for," I explained. "She's like a second mother to me."

"She ain't as good as our mama."

"That's why I said second mother," I said with a giggle. "But that reminds me. I need to ask you something."

"Shoot."

"Was Daddy still mad at me, you know, after the wedding?"

"He was mad at first," Tommy said. "But after a while, he got real quiet about it. I got on him for the way he yelled at you. He shouldn't have acted like that. Mama blamed herself, and I think Daddy did too."

I didn't understand. "How could they blame themselves?"

"They pushed that wedding hard, Jayme. I told them you weren't ready. Hell, even the pastor knew you didn't want to get married. He tried to talk to them about it after they had to order a new dress 'cause you lost too much weight to take it in. They looked like damn fools, and they knew it. Like getting married would solve everything. I love Katie, don't get me wrong, but damn, it can be hard sometimes."

"I can't tell you how relieved I am," I told him. "I've been carrying that weight for so long."

"That's Daddy for you. He wasn't happy unless we all knew how disappointed he was in us."

Tommy was a millionaire, or at least close to it by now. I couldn't imagine Daddy being disappointed with that, but my brother was right. Daddy was never happy with anything we did.

"I'll keep an eye on Mama. You don't need to worry about her."

"I'm not worried about Mama," Tommy said.

"I'm happy, and I'm real happy for you and Bradley."

It was the truth. Ever since I started working with Mrs. Swollas, I had everything I could have ever wanted or needed. It was like bits and pieces of me were finding places in my heart that were missing. I felt more and more like a whole person for the first time in my life. No longer would I allow others to determine my worth or what I could get out of life.

"All right," Tommy said. "But if you need anything, just call me, and I'll have you flown to Virginia."

I smiled at the thought of my older brother, there to rescue me as he always did when I was a kid. He was stern like Daddy but not nearly as cold. Daddy did forgive me in the end. It felt good to know that. I wished I could have known before he died, but it's not like he would have admitted it to me the way Tommy had. "Love you, Jeff."

"Love you."

I couldn't say why, but I suspected that would be the last time I spoke to my brother. It wasn't sad, rather a peaceful knowledge. He could let go, and so could I. The glass slider shut, and Greg peeked his head around the corner. "Is everything okay?"

I nodded. "Tommy and Bradley are moving to Virginia."

He stared at me for a long moment as if he were waiting for me to explain the rest. But I didn't want to. It was too emotionally draining to rehash. Greg was good at reading the room. "Okay," he said. "Wine?"

Wordlessly, I fell onto the couch, and a red wine was brought to me. "You're a doll," I told him.

The rest of the night was filled with theories and discussions about the book. What it could mean, where it came from. How the greatest minds on the planet couldn't figure it out. It was fun. I couldn't recall a conversation this stimulating between us since... Well, ever. "Do you think she can do it?" Greg asked as we got into bed. "Translate those books, I mean."

"She told me she was a witch," I said, sliding the covers over my bare arms. "Maybe she will use a spell."

Greg let out a groan.

"What?"

"Just...try not to get caught up in all that."

"I'm not," I insisted. "She admitted that she's not eating but says she is starting to again."

"Well, that's good. What kind of person can just stop eating like that?" he asked.

"The witchy kind," I teased.

"Just so long as you don't go on that diet," he said. The slap on my ass made my whole body jiggle. "I like a little meat on your bones."

I was always on the thicker side, but not enough to get me into trouble. I had gone on a lot of diets in my teens and twenties, but no matter what I did, I always came back to this weight. Not too big, not too small, just an average-looking girl, that was me.

The thinnest I ever got was leading up to the wedding. My nerves were so bad I couldn't eat anything without puking it back up. Everyone just assumed I was dieting for the wedding and encouraged it. No one ever questioned the way I ran to the bathroom after eating a few crackers or a biscuit. Looking back, it was obvious I was never going to make it to the end of that altar, but I just didn't know it.

All this time, I was so sorry to Lars and to my family, but never once did I consider that maybe that girl crying in the bathroom every night needed some consoling, too. I was worth forgiveness, and I did deserve better. I simply had to demand it instead of wallowing in my mistakes.

As I drifted off to sleep, it was my mother's voice that called to me. Her last pleas before being sedated were about not giving her baby girl up to a witch. She was talking about Mrs. Swollas. How did she know about the old woman, and what did she mean? My mama knew something about what was happening to me, but it was too late. I was on a different path now, one that I chose, which was more than I could say about most women in the South.

Lukewarm water drifted lazily below my knees. Croaks of bullfrogs and the buzz of mosquitoes were everywhere. Reeds whistled below me. I was in the swamp below Mrs. Swollas's house. I was wearing a white silk slip trimmed with delicate lace, and my tummy was flatter and my breasts smaller. Hair blonder than mine brushed my shoulders.

"Am I you again?" I asked.

Yes.

"What do I call you?"

I'm Destiny.

A pond skater left ripples in the water as it swam by. "So, we're being metaphorical, I take it."

Not at all. My name is Destiny Sallows.

"Oh," I said, shifting my foot in the pond sediment. "Okay. What do you want from me?"

I want to be with you.

"Like, you want to take my body and run?"

The voice tried to answer, but I couldn't pay attention. I was running along short green grass. I was afraid and running from someone. Who was I running from? My heart was pumping in my chest, and I kept falling. The grass scraping against my legs and hands was making me itch, and I was whimpering. I had to do something. There was somewhere I had to go to put an end to it all.

I opened my eyes to find Greg staring down at me. He was rocking me in his arms, tears were falling down his face. The alarm clock was blaring into my consciousness. "Greg?"

"You wouldn't wake up," he whispered. "I shook you and yelled at you, but you just wouldn't wake up."

I bolted upright and began writing down my dream. I had to write it down, or I'd forget. "I'm okay," I said. "Greg, I promise I'm okay."

"You're not!" he was shouting as he got out of the bed. "I thought you were in a coma or something. Jayme, something is wrong."

I had trouble waking up is all. I jotted down as many details as I could before the dream began to fade. "I was having a dream," I told him.

He wouldn't understand. Instead of telling him about Destiny, I came up with another excuse. "I took an Ambien last night. I'm sorry, I should have warned you."

Greg's shoulders eased. He was shirtless, and the perspiration across his chest only highlighted the definition along his brood frame. "Jesus, Jayme."

He bought the lie. Maybe my poker face was getting better. I set the journal aside and crawled out of bed. Wide awake by the shaking he gave me. "I'm thinking about visiting my mama today," I told him as I pulled my jeans on. "You want to come?"

"Sure, why not?"

After my talk with Tommy, I wanted to make things right with Mama. Last time I visited, things didn't go too well, but maybe meeting Greg would put her in a better mood. We picked up some breakfast burritos and made our way to that end of town.

"Brother and mother in one weekend," Greg said. No doubt he wanted to know more about what Tommy and I talked about. I didn't blame him. I wanted to know what he and Jeff argued about that made my brother dislike him so much.

"I'm going for a Coleman record," I joked.

"Yeah, you guys don't really keep in touch, do you?"

I guess not. My grandparents lived in another state, as did most of my cousins. We were always closer to Mama's side of the family because Daddy didn't have many left. He had a brother somewhere who sent a yearly Christmas letter, but that was it.

"Not everyone calls their mother at least once a week."

Greg blushed at this. I didn't mean to tease him; I thought it was sweet. "Well, when my father left, I was all she had, and she was all I had. We were both abandoned by the same guy, you know?"

"I love that you talk to your mama so much." I smiled at him and placed my hand on his. "I wish I could still talk to mine the same way."

His smile faded into a frown in that moment. "It's like you're saying goodbye to them or something."

He was ever the astute one. I was doing exactly that, but I had no intentions of going anywhere. A part of me was letting go, but it was only to make way for what was to come. "I'm saying goodbye to my past, Greg."

"Just so long as that doesn't include me."

I used to believe that love conquered everything, but I think I had the wrong kind of love in mind. It wasn't something I could explain to Greg, but I could never tell him I loved him until I fully loved myself. I could never realize the entirety of my soul or the depths of my potential until I was complete. Greg could not complete me, but that didn't mean we couldn't be together. "Just stay by my side," I whispered. "Stay by my side and always choose me."

19

I tried not to think about the last time I visited my mama. It was like she was a totally different person than the one I was raised by. She had a bad day, but that didn't mean it would be the same this time. "The flowers are pretty this time of year," I said.

"Yeah," Greg said. "Though the pollination rate has been in decline the last few years."

"Why is that?"

Greg shifted in the driver's seat and glanced at me. "Well, only bees can pollinate, and we're losing them."

"Oh, right."

He peered at me again, and I gave up. "All right, you win, I'm just nervous."

"You have every right to be."

I inhaled a deep breath. "I just never know what she's going to be like when I visit. With Tommy and Bradley moving to Virginia, I'll need to visit more often."

Last time, she was hollering about a witch. I knew it had to do with Mrs. Swollas, but how? I could ask, but the answer might just be confusion. How would she even know that Mrs. Swollas was a witch? The whole thing gave me the shivers.

"I'm sure they will call and visit," Greg reminded me.

We rolled into a parking spot, and Greg turned off the car. There was no going back now. He took my hand, and I smiled at him. Words could not describe how happy I was that he was here with me. He was my shield against anything my mama might say or do. I swallowed the dry lump in my throat and made my way into the lobby.

Greg's eyes wandered about the place as I signed in. "It's real nice here."

"Say what I want about my daddy, but he did right by Mama."

"I'd say so."

A gaggle of nurses strolled by us, all in their blue and white uniforms. Black lacquered nametags denoting the type of nurse they were. They were so prim and starched that, for a moment, I wished I had a uniform like that. Greg punched a hole in that desire when I glanced up and saw he was suppressing a giggle.

"What?"

"One of them had poop on their shoe."

There was a lingering odor of feces. I wrinkled my nose and gave him a second look. "Maybe nurse outfits ain't so cute after all."

"No nurse outfit is complete without vomit or shit."

The recollection dawned on me. "I forgot your mama was a nurse."

"And that's why I don't want to roleplay doctor and nurse in bed."

Yeah, that checked out. Lord only knew how many times his mother came home physically and mentally demoralized by working with sick people day in and day out. It was about as sexy as that poop smear on a shoe.

I paused outside the door for a moment. Should I knock? I couldn't remember if I knocked last time. I shook out the tension in my hands, but before I could knock, Greg did it for me. "It's okay," he promised.

"Come in!" a familiar voice from the other side of the door called.

The scent of my mother's room greeted us in the doorway. Clean, polished, and a hint of Mama's Avon perfume. One of the nurses must have ordered it for her. Another reminder that they could take care of her here in a way I never could. Mama's hair wasn't as nice as it was last time. It was crumpled and flattened. Her set had been repuffed, but her hair needed to be reset.

"Hey Mama!"

"Hey!" she greeted me with a hug and stopped short at Greg. "Who is this?"

"Mama, this is Greg."

Her wrinkled mouth made the shape of an O, and she embraced him. Greg's face lit up at the instant acceptance, and he gave me a reassuring nod as if to say, *See? It's going to be a good visit.*

"Come on in and have a seat," she said, gesturing to the sofa.

"How have you been feeling?" I asked, sitting down beside her.

"Oh, just fine," she said. "Y'all want some tea? I gave the recipe to Naomi, and she brought me a pitcher."

I was taken aback that she remembered. "I hope you can give that recipe to me," I said. "Try as I might, I can never get it just right."

"You got it right for the most part. You always did add too much sugar, dear."

The total change in her demeanor from last time was just incredible. She went from angry, erratic, and confused to happy and cognizant. It was like I had my mama back again. She smiled and eyed Greg. "So, how long have you two been an item?"

"A little over a year," Greg said. "Your daughter is just incredible. I can't tell you how much of a blessing she has been for me."

"That's my girl," my mama said with a snap of her arthritic fingers.

"Mama," I gasped. "You look so good."

She frowned and mussed her hair. "Tuesday can't come soon enough. I need my hair permed again."

"Greg took me to Gatlinburg last month."

"Aw, how sweet. We used to go there every summer. She tell you that?"

"Yes, ma'am."

"He took me on the sky bridge!"

Mama laughed and patted my hand. "My girl was always the bravest out of my three kids. She was the rowdiest, too."

I flushed and braced myself for an embarrassing story. Right on cue, Mama started to tell a story about me when I was a little girl. "When she was six, she went through a biting phase. She bit my son Bradley and didn't want to get in trouble, so she climbed up a tree and refused to come down!"

Greg laughed. "How did you get her down?"

"I had to call the fire department!"

Helpless in the throws of old family stories, I leaned back into the couch and sighed. I'd take the same three stories over a dementia-dominated mother any day. Greg was absolutely smitten with the conversation. Leaning forward with his hands folded between his knees. He was hanging on every word. "Was she always so wild?" he asked.

Mama rolled her eyes. "Lord...I can't tell you how many times she snuck out of the house as a teenager. Always getting into trouble."

He knew this much from me. It was a small high school, and I was desperate to fit in. I partied with everyone and got a bit of a reputation for it. "One thing she did that none of her friends ever knew," Mama said with a waggle of her finger. "She never drank! She always put coke in her cup and walked around with it like there was alcohol, but she never got drunk."

Greg looked at me in astonishment. I never told him that—or anyone else for that matter. "Mama, how did you know?"

"Honey, I can smell booze a mile away, and you never smelled like it."

I was taken aback by the revelation. "There was a girl at school," I explained. "She was a senior when I was a freshman. I'll never forget it. She got so drunk she passed out, and some boys took advantage of her. I swore I'd never be that girl."

"The Whitman girl," Mama said. "I remember that. Bless her heart."

If Mama could remember that, then maybe she could remember how Daddy felt about me and Lars. I was hesitant to broach the topic, afraid that the bad memory might send her spiraling. Instead, I took advantage of her good mood. "Hey, remember the time that guy tried to make off with our grill?"

That sent her cackling. Greg was willing to oblige the conversation despite not being part of it. "Oh, my Lord, I nearly forgot."

"Some hillbilly tried to make off with our grill," I explained to Greg. "Only, it was one of those biggins, so the only way he could get it was by chaining it up to the back of his pickup and making off with it!"

"The whole neighborhood watched as it rattled down the road!" Mama finished.

We went back and forth, sharing little stories like that. We talked about Greg and his work, as well as mine. I watched her carefully as I spoke of my job and of Mrs. Swollas, but there was no recognition as far as I could tell. Whatever had her so upset last time wasn't here now.

"What do you think of Tommy and Bradley moving to Virginia," I asked when she brought it up.

"Well," she said with a sigh. "I'm no businesswoman, but I'm worried. The reservation tried to buy that gravel depot, but Tommy offered more. It must have been a lot of money. I just hope it's worth it."

He never told me any of that. The fact that Mama had remained wholly present and herself for the last hour and a half was astonishing. We were having such a good time, it wasn't until the nurse named Naomi came in announcing Mama's water aerobics class that we stood to leave.

"We better let you go," I said, giving her a hug. "I'll come back real soon."

"It was very nice to meet you," Greg said as she embraced him.

"You're a good-looking man, you know that?"

Greg laughed bashfully and left the room, allowing us to say goodbye in private. "I'm real glad you're doing so well, Mama."

"Likewise," she said. "I'm so happy for the both of you."

Hearing those words melted all the anxiety away. "I'm glad you like him so much," I said.

Mama gave me a funny look and said, "I wasn't talking about him. I was talking about that real pretty gal with you."

I shook my head. That didn't make any sense. What was she saying? "Mama?"

She hugged me again and led me toward the door. Naomi was so young, and her smile was crisp, just like her uniform. There was no shit on her shoes. I searched the room for signs of the pretty gal Mama spoke of. "The angel told me all about it, and good for you!"

She gave me a wink as if we were in on some secret together. I turned to Nurse Naomi for an explanation, but she shrugged and went to Mama's bedroom. "Time for your aerobics."

I tried to turn around. I wanted to stop and ask Mama what the hell she was talking about, but she was stronger than I expected, and before I could ask, I was guided out and the door was shut. I stood there, mind spinning. What the hell was that all about?

"Greg, did you hear any of that?"

He wasn't even listening. I found him at the far end of the hallway, looking at himself in the mirror. Mama said he was handsome, and now he was checking his hairline and picking at his teeth. "Should probably see a dentist now that we got dental," he said.

"Yeah."

She said an angel had told her something. I drifted down the hall toward the elevator while Greg chit-chatted about nothing of importance. Mama wasn't the first person to talk about an angel. Renee had said something like that, too. I'd have to talk to Mrs. Swollas tomorrow. Whatever it was, I wasn't the only person seeing it, and I suspected it was no angel.

20

In my haste, I left the university letters on the couch next to the laptop. Mrs. Swollas didn't believe there was any use for them, so I didn't think it would matter anyhow. I kissed Greg goodbye and took the lunch he prepared for me before heading out the door.

When I got to the house, Mrs. Swollas was awaiting her morning tea. She stood when I came in and blurted out, "Anything?"

I groaned as the vision of the journal flashed in my mind. "I left it on the nightstand."

"So, you can remember nothing on your own?" Mrs. Swollas was practically chopping at the bit. I understood why, though. If this were my daughter, I'd want her back, too.

"I remember that she was beautiful," I said, sitting down. "Her name is Destiny."

"Yes!" Mrs. Swollas whimpered. She clamped her hands over her face. "How is this possible?"

"I don't think I'm the only one seeing her." I told her about Renee and now my mama seeing an angel. The old woman stroked her face, deep in thought.

"Montgomery spoke of an angel as well," she said. "But he didn't know you, and Destiny died after I moved in."

Mrs. Swollas was so deep in thought that she'd revealed a truth. She had known Montgomery, and she had lived here for much longer than she let on. It was a strange thing to hide. Even stranger that she arrived young but aged significantly in just a few short years.

"It's more than a coincidence, but ghosts don't haunt dreams," she said with a shake of her head. "What could possibly be going on with you?"

Hell if I knew. I wasn't exactly experienced with ghosts. "I don't really know what to make of all this, Mrs. Swollas. I just know that she needs you to be stronger. I think she doesn't want you to go on the way you have been."

Mrs. Swollas deliberated on that. What was so hard about eating food for this woman? It wasn't like I was telling her to kill someone. Just eat a damn sandwich and get over it. "If you want, I can start bringing you things to eat," I offered. "Just tell me what you want, and I'll get it."

"I appreciate the sentiment, but I can manage on my own. Just see to the house and my affairs."

So, she'd only eat takeout? It was strange, but whatever it took to get her eating on a regular basis. "Fast food isn't good for you, Mrs. Swollas."

"Food seldom outruns me," she retorted from the hallway.

She needed to get out more anyway.

Her study had descended into chaos while I was away. All the books I had stacked in groups based on order of priority were strewn about the room and opened at various points. Not just across the tables but on the floors and chairs as well. She had been searching for something. Cross-referencing her own collection with the new arrivals.

If I could read any of these books, I would know just what that was, but all I had to go on were the scattered notes she had ripped from journals and scrap pieces of paper she had left. I was at a loss as to how I would tidy up in a way that didn't disrupt her research.

"Shit," I drawled. She must have been at this all night.

Starting at one corner of the study, I got down on my knees and inspected the various scraps of paper. There was a method to her madness, at least. She always wrote the citation at the bottom of the note, even if it was a shredded-up bit of paper.

Types of seances, communicating with the dead...

She wasn't doing her job; she was trying to figure out how to speak to her dead daughter. It never occurred to me that she was irked by the fact that her daughter chose to communicate with me instead of her. It must have been frustrating. Why me?

I tucked the parchment into the corresponding book like a bookmark before putting it back on the shelf. Book after book in the first pile was all about how to communicate with spirits and what conditions brought souls back from the dead. Based on the increasingly agitated notes, she hadn't found what she was searching for.

Nothing. Nothing explains how or why. Could this haunting be false? A scheme of sorts or a Daemon in the guise of her?

I couldn't help but take that note personally. I had never lied to Mrs. Swollas, and I wasn't lying about the things I had been experiencing. Still, the alternative was disturbing. She did not believe it possible that her daughter's spirit had returned after all this time and that something else was feeding me lies. I pressed the note into the book and snapped it shut. Putting the books on the shelf in the same group I found them in, I moved on to the next pile in the corner.

A looming dread hung over me. These books had pictures. Horrid illustrations of demons and their attributes. Massive, spiking teeth and feral eyes. Claws in the place of fingers and tails that curled around goat hooves. Her notes were loosely threaded theories of demons that communicated with people through dreams. A wave of nausea came over me, the smell of old parchment, calfskin, and ink overwhelming.

Mrs. Swollas was an expert on the occult, and she was under the impression that I was being tricked by a demon who wanted to possess me. I had the sudden urge to take a shower. Dirty on the inside from an unwelcome violation. The eyes of the illustrated demons stared at me with all their wide eyes and sharp fangs, like that of the gargoyle perched on the balcony. In a rush, I stuffed all the notes in one book before shoving those things onto the shelf.

After several minutes of huddling in the corner, I got up and moved on to the books strewn around the room. I sighed as the rest were translations. Just translations. She had been referring to other books to confirm her translations, which accounted for the mess. Not wanting to derail her work, I was struck by a better idea.

I had seen it many times under the carport. A large, fold-out table wedged between the house and the metal shelving. I pulled it out, dragged it down the stairs, and unfolded it beside her desk. This way, she could move down the table without having to run around the study recollecting what she needed. I was about to arrange the books on the table when I noted the smears of dirt and the spiders crawling in the crack. These books were worth a fortune, and I nearly damaged them.

I went upstairs to get some cleaner and a rag from the kitchen, but Mrs. Swollas was nowhere to be seen. "Mrs. Swollas?" I called.

Nothing. She must have been serious when she said she'd be coming and going. I didn't think she'd be so immediate about it, but I was glad she was doing what she needed to. I had too much work to do to dwell on it anyhow. Mrs. Swollas was rigid in her habits, and even a demonic possession could not stop laundry day.

The image of Mrs. Swollas forcing a demon to do laundry kept me amused as I collected the unused linens to wash them again. I would be cleaning the barely occupied house as well. She didn't like the smell of regular cleaners, so I had to buy the expensive organic stuff from the top shelf. It worked well enough, I supposed. I always bought the off-brand of everything except dishwasher tablets. Dishes just didn't get clean without the good stuff.

I turned the laundry over and went to the sky bridge to clean the glass. Mrs. Swollas complained that I didn't get the roof well enough, so I had to go back and do it again.

"A lot of that stuff is on the outside," I said, pointing at the leaves and clumps of rotting stuff. "We need a professional window washer."

"Can't you do it?" she asked.

"With a pressure washer, maybe, but I'd have to get up on the house itself."

She dismissed my concerns, which were big liabilities in my mind. What if I fell? She'd be the one to pay those medical bills if I survived. Yesterday, I wouldn't have considered this, but I was desperate to be away from the library. If I could just get a hose up there, it would probably be enough. What a pain in the butt. When I first came here, I thought the sky bridge was amazing; now, I just wanted to set it on fire.

There was a rope of hose snaked around a massive iron nail embedded along the side of the house. I unraveled it and pulled it along the side of the house. It reached the sky bridge. There was no nozzle, but I could always do it the redneck way and stick my thumb over the opening.

Staring up at the sky bridge, holding the slack hose, I could tell the hose would reach just fine, but the ladder wasn't tall enough. It would get me to the bottom of the sky bridge, but that wouldn't do me a lick of good. Mrs. Swollas's balcony was close enough to where I could climb to the overhang and simply walk to the sky bridge, but that still left the issue of getting the hose up there.

There was no twine under the carport and none in the kitchen. Just when I was about to give up, I checked the study. I recalled some of the books being bound with a thick, rough twine, and it seemed to me that it was the same on several of the outgoing books. They could have come like that, but I couldn't imagine professors at Harvard feeling the need to do that. It was more likely Mrs. Swollas did it to mark the books she had finished working on.

Rummaging through the drawers, I found the twine on a wooden spool. "Ah ha!"

What would Mrs. Swollas say if she came home to see how I rigged the string around the hose and threw the spool over the balcony. I imagine she'd be amused but secretly admire my ingenuity as well as my throwing arm. No doubt shouting and raging at me for good measure. It took a few tries, but I got the wooden spool slung over the balcony railing.

I wasn't afraid of heights, but my head spun while standing on that roof with nothing but a string in my hand. It was hard to worry about demonic possession on a second-story roof, shuffling downward to what could be an unstable glass ceiling. Re-wrapping my thread around the spool as I went, the roof became dizzyingly steep, so I sat down and scooted the rest of the way. It really wasn't all that far from the balcony to the sky bridge, but trying to pull the hose up with a cord wasn't easy. It kept snagging on things, and the water was on, so it was splashing all over the place.

"Hell yes!" I cried as the nozzle flopped onto the sky bridge. Water ran over the panes of glass, and for a moment, I prayed there were no leaks. Having to explain how I flooded out the sky bridge to Mrs.

Swollas was not something I wanted to do. Then again, maybe she'd decide to hire professionals. I got paid enough, and there wasn't much else to do but dwell on scarier things than a twenty-foot drop.

I was being possessed by a demon. Southern women everywhere would be clutching their pearls and praying for me. I went to church with my family as a kid, but that stopped when I moved out. Most jobs required me to work on Sundays anyway. It wouldn't hurt to talk to a pastor. If Mrs. Swollas couldn't help, maybe they could.

Positioning my thumb over the nozzle, I created a more pressurized stream across the glass rooftop. Crud and debris went flying everywhere, and it was fun for a moment. Like one of those games at the fair where you shot the water into the clown's mouth until the balloon popped.

I had just about finished when something fluttered behind me. As I turned, I slipped and slid off the roof and rolled onto the sky bridge. A slam of pain was accompanied by a cracking sound between my ears. I rolled over, and the sun blasted into my eyes. Icy cold water seeped into my clothes to bite at my skin.

I groaned and tried to sit up, but the world was spinning so fast that I gagged. I laid back down. The nausea and the throbbing in my brain slowed. I fumbled for my phone in my back pocket. It was wet but mostly undamaged. The touchscreen jerked and skipped around as I tried to focus long enough to call for help.

The keypad flipped to my most recent contacts before the phone called Greg on its own accord. I didn't need Greg. I needed an ambulance. I was so tired... I just wanted to let go and sleep.

Stay awake

"No," I moaned. "Get away from me."

You must stay awake and call for help.

"Piss off ghost or demon or...whatever you are. You're trying to steal my body."

If I was a demon who wanted to steal your body, wouldn't I encourage you to fall asleep so I could take over?

The world was spinning faster than the tilt-a-hurl ride at the fair. I was compromised, and this thing was taking advantage of it. I needed to get myself help and fast, or I might not ever wake up. "That's something a demon would say."

Likely story. There was an exasperated sigh from the ghost demon. Greg's voice was shouting through the waterlogged speaker in a garbled noise. I rested the phone on my stomach before succumbing to the darkness.

21
— • —

When I opened my eyes, blaring fluorescent lights hung over me with angry white halos. Strong cleaning solutions and the bitter scent of sterile gauze filled my nostrils. I turned my head to find Greg in the chair beside me, holding my hand. He had been crying, but the rage in his eyes suggested I was in trouble.

"What are you doing here?"

For a moment, I thought he was going to shout at me.

"What am I doing here?"

"Dammit, Jayme."

I was in a hospital bed. The last thing I remember was being on the skybridge. I had fallen and hit my head. "How did you find me?"

"You have a concussion," Greg explained. "You called me and gave me the address so I could come get you."

"I don't even know the address."

"You did at the time."

Then why didn't I know now? The beeping of a nearby monitor was aggravating. Flashbacks to being in the hospital when I was seven came to mind. I broke my arm bouncing on a trampoline. It was so much fun, flying up and letting gravity pull me back down. I tried to do a flip but landed on my left arm and was stuck with an itchy, stinky cast for the rest of summer.

"How did you get me off the roof?"

"You hit your head, so you probably don't remember, but you were lying on the ground when I found you." Greg was shaking his head as he wiped angry tears from his eyes. "I don't know what I'd do if something happened to you. You almost didn't give me the address; I was so fucking scared."

There was no way. I couldn't have climbed it unconscious. Mrs. Swollas was going to be furious when she found out Greg had come to get me. I broke one of her rules. She might fire me. I began to cry. "She's going to fire me."

"Shh," Greg consoled. "She's not going to fire you. It wasn't your fault."

"Yes, it was."

I got on the roof, I slipped and fell, and I called Greg and somehow gave him the address. I must have recalled it from the first time I put it in the GPS or something. I couldn't think of it now to save my life, but I had hit my head.

The rest of the day was a blur of doctors, nurses, scans, and more nurses until I was finally discharged and taken home. Greg insisted on driving, and I was too tired to care. He helped me into the bedroom. "Doctors said you need a lot of rest. No more climbing on rooftops."

"Never again," I promised.

It would be several more days until I was deemed fit to return to work. Once again, I was stuck in the house with nothing to do. Greg had stress-cleaned the house, so I didn't even have that. I tried calling Mrs. Swollas a half dozen times. I left a voicemail, but I doubted she even knew how to check it.

Dread pooled in my stomach, filling me up and making it hard to eat. My lack of appetite didn't go unnoticed by Greg. He sat yet another plate of food in front of me while I camped out on the couch wrapped in a blanket. This time, it was some chicken and greens.

"You didn't need to take time off," I told him. "I'm fine."

"What were you doing up there anyway?" he asked.

"I was cleaning all the junk off the top of the sky bridge."

"That house is really something else," he said. "She lives there all by herself?"

"Did you see the gargoyle?"

Greg frowned and shook his head. "You told me about it, but I never saw it."

He found me below the sky bridge. The Gargoyle could be seen from there. Maybe he just wasn't looking for it, not when I was somewhere in a mud puddle of my own making. "Did you come from the front or the back?"

"What's the difference?" he joked. "I think it was the back side. The car was facing me when I came in."

That made sense. The GPS would have taken him to the back side. He probably walked under the carport and saw just ahead. He had no reason to check the front. "Well, it's probably a good thing you didn't see it; it's hideous. How did you get there, anyway?"

"I got the call in the middle of a lecture," he explained. "I just knew something was wrong, so I answered. I ran and got Josh."

It made me feel a little better to know that our friend was the one to help. Then again, the image of me lying in a mud puddle tinged with piss and having Josh help get me into the car had me blushing. "He saw me like that?"

"What else were we supposed to do?"

I'd have to thank him later. I stared at the lump of greens on the plate. Greens were my favorite, especially the way Greg fixed them. He cooked them with bacon. I just didn't have the stomach for food, not

when I broke one of Mrs. Swollas's rules. Not when I was about to
lose the best job I ever had with a woman I considered my friend.

She was more than a friend or employer. She was fast becoming
a mother figure for me. But I should know better than to look for
a mother in women I barely knew. Grown women shouldn't need a
mama, but I did. She wanted a daughter as badly as I wanted a mother.
I hoped she'd forgive me.

"I need to get back to work," I said.

Greg was hesitant. "Are you sure that's a good idea?"

"I won't feel better until I talk to her. I need to know if we're still
okay."

"Do you want me to drive you?"

I shook my head and laughed. "Lord, no. That would only make
things worse."

It was only a slight concussion. The doctors said I'd be fine after a
few days and that I was lucky I didn't do more damage. I had a great
big goose-egg on the side of my head, but that was it. I emerged from
my blanket cocoon and grabbed my things.

"Jayme," Greg called as I walked out the door. "I love you."

"Okay, you too, bye."

When I got to the house, I could hear Mrs. Swollas shouting at
something downstairs. It was well past teatime, but I figured she'd be
in the kitchen. She was angry. I rushed down the stairs. "Mrs. Swollas?"
I called.

She had a broom and was hitting the washer with the handle. Loose
strands fell from her bun in straight, coal-colored strands. She must
have colored her hair because there wasn't a trace of gray left. "What's
going on?"

Mrs. Swollas gave one final smack to the washer before turning to
face me. Her face was smoother than I had ever seen it. It was like she

went back in time twenty years. I gasped and took a step back. "How did you do that?"

She responded by giving the washer another strike with the broom handle. Mrs. Swollas had no intention of explaining her sudden youth. It was jarring to look at. She must have realized that but refused to discuss it. "What are you doing?" I asked.

"I was trying to get this damned thing open! Someone left my linens in here for several days. When I arrived this morning, I opened the lid to find it had all gone to mold. I restarted it but when found a rogue pillowcase on the stairwell. I thought to add it, but the thing wouldn't open!"

"It locks shut," I explained. "You need to push the pause button and wait for it to unlock."

"Well," she said. "Thank goodness for modern marvels. So, you've returned at last. Did you enjoy your vacation?"

I swallowed that rock in my throat and nodded. "I'm really sorry, I had no choice."

"You left the water running. A man came to the house to notify me of the leak. You have no idea what you've done."

Except that I did. I had to drive over the lake that I had made in the driveway. I was also fairly certain I had cracked a pane of glass in the skybridge. No doubt water was leaking inside. The only carpeted area in the house, and I managed to ruin it.

"You can take the damages out of my paycheck," I offered. "Please, just don't be mad."

"And then," she said with a shrill voice, "you brought that boyfriend of yours here!"

How did she know Greg had come here? She said she had only arrived this morning.

"I had an accident," I said.

She frowned, staring at me with those intensive eyes, only now their brilliant green was darker somehow, almost cloudy. "An accident?"

I explained what had happened. How I fell off the roof and that I didn't remember giving the address or getting off the roof, but somehow, I had. This softened Mrs. Swollas's demeanor. "You can't climb down roofs or give addresses unconscious," she said.

I shrugged. I didn't have an explanation either. "I don't remember any of it."

"Come," Mrs. Swollas said, casting the broom to the side. "I'll make you tea."

We went upstairs, and this time, she brewed the tea. I didn't know if I was forgiven, but she no longer appeared angry. She just appeared young. How did she do that? I wanted to ask, but I didn't dare push her in what was already a delicate situation.

"She was telling me to stay awake," I said. "Do you really think she's a demon?"

"Daemon," Mrs. Swollas said as she waited for her tea. "There is a distinct difference."

I looked at her stupidly, prompting her to explain. "Daemons are not necessarily evil. They are not being masterminded by some fallen angel. They have wills of their own, and they sometimes make pacts with humans to further themselves in the world."

She set the tea down for me. "Is it possible your daughter became a Daemon?"

Mrs. Swollas shook her head. "No, these are beings entirely of their own making. There's nothing human about them."

"So, are you going to fire me?" I asked.

"Fire you?"

"Dismiss me from your service," I clarified. No doubt she had taken the term literally. The image of her lighting me on fire with a torch was amusing, but smiling made my head throb.

Mrs. Swollas shook her head and gave a dismissive wave. "You were injured attempting to do something I wanted done. It was stupid to go up there like that, but I gave you little recourse. No," she sighed. "I will not send you away. Given the circumstances, I am grateful that your boyfriend came to your aid."

That was a relief. There was still the whole invasion of the body-snatching daemon ordeal, but somehow, it felt secondary to being fired. A Daemon wasn't a demon, but being tricked by one instead of the other still didn't sound any better. I preferred the ghost theory, but Mrs. Swollas did not think that was possible. I wanted to believe it was Destiny. That she was somehow reaching across time and space to save her mother and that I was that important piece that could make it happen. That was just the childish complex of believing I was something more than I was. It was hard to deny the whisps of hope with all the paranormal going on though.

Greg would be relieved, too. He had been beating himself up pretty bad over the whole thing. Our finances would be dire if I was sacked. I would be able to collect unemployment, and he was getting paychecks now, so it wouldn't have been as bad as before. Nothing I said soothed Greg's mind. Not after he cost me the last job, too.

"I just keep getting you fired," he groaned last night while I stared at my dinner.

"You didn't climb onto a roof, and you didn't break into one of her locked rooms or bleed all over the place when she specifically said not to."

I had broken all but one of her rules, yet she was letting me stay. She sipped her tea, looking younger by the minute, and wouldn't say why. She was trying to use magic to protect me from Daemons, and I just couldn't hold it in any longer. "Mrs. Swollas, I've broken so many rules and screwed up so many times. Why let me stay on?"

"Like it or not, we are bound together somehow," she said. "Even before all this talk of ghosts and daemons, I always felt that you and I are connected somehow."

I was dumbfounded by the response. She loved me, I realized. She loved me, and she needed me in her life. The rules no longer applied to me.

"What happens after nightfall?"

"Dangerous things come out. You're not the only one who has broken the rules."

My chest knotted. If the last few months hadn't given me any indication of the seriousness of what she said, the gravity in her voice did. I wasn't the only one to break the rules. Did that mean there were other things living here that were not allowed to move in daylight?

"Is that how I got off the roof?"

Mrs. Swollas stretched her arms forward across the table before standing. "He won't harm you, but I wouldn't try to bring the boyfriend for another visit."

A name popped into my mind then. My friendly daemon was at it again. "Is he named Joseph?" I asked.

Mrs. Swollas whirled around, her eyes wide with bewilderment. She stared at me for a long moment before adjusting the brooch at her neck. "That was his name once," she said. "But that was long ago. Goodness, it is disturbing when you do that!"

"I know," I groaned. "Greg hates it, but I sort of like it. Is that weird?"

She observed me for several agonizing minutes. Just when I expected the glass to crack and the floor to give way to hell, she spoke. "Would you be opposed to a séance? I may be able to understand more if I can speak directly with your friend."

Mrs. Swollas was exactly the woman I pictured to be dressed in black, hovering over a magic ball. It made me giggle, and her eyes shifted. For once, I was making a joke that she wasn't in on. "That would be fun."

"A séance is not fun, young lady. Give me a few hours to set up. In the meantime, you can deal with that confounded machine."

"Yes, ma'am."

22

_— • —_

rs. Swollas had me drag two chairs from the kitchen to the sky bridge. My shoes made wet, squishing noises as we walked along the carpet. "I'll get some of those industrial fans—"

"Don't worry about that now," she snapped.

"But come summer, that crack is going to be a huge pain in the ass."

Contrary to most people's belief, Alabama got the most rain out of any state in the US. Seattle was usually the first assumption, but it was wrong. While the north got a sprinkling all the time, Alabama was a monsoon come August. Rain would come down so hard that all five lanes on the freeway ground to a halt. The rain in the summer was enough to fill the swamps for another year.

When the raining season hit, that sky bridge would flood. Being the bridge between the two sections of the house, only the third story would be spared from water damage. If Mrs. Swollas truly had a mold problem now, this would ruin the house forever. It would be too damaged to sell and too wet to burn down.

She waved off my concerns and placed the chairs facing one another less than a foot apart. "Sit down."

I did as she commanded. She sat in the empty seat and took both my hands in hers. "Close your eyes and listen to the sounds around you. I will be speaking in my old tongue—you won't understand. Just ignore me."

I didn't think it would be possible. It was natural for a person to listen to a foreign language at least for a few minutes. Still, I tried my best. There were birds chirping and an intermittent drip from the broken glass. The last few drops of water were falling onto the soaked carpet. There was a giggle from somewhere inside my mind.

Mrs. Swollas was speaking in a low, hushed voice. No matter how hard I tried to focus on the dripping, my attentions were drawn to words I couldn't make out. After several minutes, her voice became background noise as my mind grew fatigued from trying to recognize and translate. *Drip, drip, drip...*

Birds were feeding their squawking hatchlings. Deer were running from the bloodied body of a stag. Ducks jumped into the water. The sound of stone grinding against stone came from above. *Drip, drip, drip...*

Then, all at once, fingers snapped, and my eyes opened. I was face-to-face with Mrs. Swollas. A thin strand of gray had surfaced along her bun that wasn't there before. "Did it work?" I asked.

Her eyes wavered, and she shook her head. "No," she said. "No presence of a daemon or a ghost."

Oh, great. Now Mrs. Swollas thought I was crazy, too. "I'm not crazy—she's in my head!"

"Shh, no need to shout. I believe you," she said. "I just don't know how yet."

"I heard things," I said. "It was like I could see them."

Mrs. Swollas was still holding my hands. "What do you know of seances?"

"You summon ghosts with Ouija boards and talk to your dead aunt?"

She tried to contain her smile, but it was creeping along her cheeks. "A séance is something that provides intense awareness. If a spirit were here, it would amplify their presence. A Daemon can be banished or summoned in one."

"So, the things I was experiencing were real."

"You heard the local wildlife going about their day," she said. "Yes, that happened."

But there were other things, things I didn't couldn't explain. She must have heard them, too, but chose to not disclose them. "Mrs. Swollas," I said. "Won't you tell me what's really going on with you? With this place?"

The old woman sighed. "I tell you as much as you need. To tell you everything would be too much, and the truth is…"

Too much.

She didn't want to scare me off, and she also couldn't explain what was happening to me. I suspected Mrs. Swollas was a woman who always had answers, and her pride did not allow her to admit otherwise. I was someone who never had answers, so I would have to go without. For a little longer, at least.

After the failed séance, I went to the hardware store. I got a few massive tarps, industrial fans, weights, and a taller ladder. I also got some clear epoxy. Mrs. Swollas was not going to allow someone to come and repair the glass, so I would have to do it myself. This time, I'd have a hard hat strapped to my head.

The missing posters of Russ were taken down. My heart sank. He wasn't here, which meant he was found dead. He was such a nice old man.

"Did you ever find Russ?" I asked the cashier. He was a teenager with shaggy black hair and acne.

"They found his car. It had been driven into the river, but there were no signs of him. He might have escaped and got carried away by the current."

It was bitter news. I had secretly held out hope for him, but he was an older man, and sometimes, these things happened. Might have been an accident. I didn't know him all that well, but he didn't seem suicidal.

"Real sorry for your loss."

#

Mrs. Swollas watched me from within the sky bridge as I scaled the new and taller ladder. I applied epoxy to the crack in the ceiling. It would need several hours to dry, so I covered the area with a weighted tarp. Once I was safely off the ladder, I brought the fans inside to dry the carpets. Mrs. Swollas's ears moved back like an annoyed cat when I turned the fans on.

"Is this really necessary?" she shouted over the fans.

"You want more mold?"

Giving up on that argument, she went to look at the repair I did to the crack. Illuminated in a soft blue glow from the tarp, she appeared younger somehow. "It's a bit messy," she complained.

"But it's waterproof," I said. "You want it to be pretty, call a professional."

She didn't like that answer either.

"Got some bad news from the hardware store," I said. "My favorite guy there went missing. They think he died."

Mrs. Swollas was eager to get away from the blaring fans. Distracted and annoyed, I had to practically chase her down to the kitchen. "Did you hear what I said?"

"Yes, that is rather unfortunate."

I don't know why I told her. I didn't expect her to care. "He was the one who said he remembered you. Said you were young when you got off the train."

And she was growing younger by the day. She couldn't keep hiding it from me; there was something at work here. Was it witchcraft or a good surgeon? I knew better than to keep prodding, especially in her already agitated state, but I had to know why he knew her and if it had anything to do with his disappearance.

"Old men often have confused memories," she said. "Pretty young women all start to blend into one in their eyes."

"So, you're saying he didn't see you getting off the train?"

"Of course not."

I watched her fuss with the tea kettle. She was averting my eyes. Mrs. Swollas was lying, but I couldn't prove it. "Did you have anything to do with Russ's death?"

With that, she whirled around, green eyes wide and pointing. "Do I look like I can overtake a man?"

She had a point. Even with her gown, she barely weighed ninety pounds. Maybe more now, she had filled out a little, but with her corset on, it was hard to tell. Her face was a bit fuller, but she still couldn't weigh more than a hundred pounds even after I dunked her in the swamp.

It was getting on in the evening. Greg had sent several messages to ask if I was okay, but only half my responses got sent. "I should probably get going."

"Yes," she said. "How long must we keep the fans on?"

"Until everything is bone dry."

"Bones are never dry, my dear."

Yeah, okay. Maybe someday, I'd get her to understand modern slang.

There was only so much I could catch her up on in one day. I wondered if she would like movies. I'd have to show them to her, even if it was just to see her reaction.

It was only when I got home that I remembered the journal. After my little trip to the hospital, I had forgotten all about it. Opening to the second page, I reread the entry. The daughter's name was Destiny. My fingers traced the name scratched into the paper, and a vision of a cloudy window overlooking climbing red roses came rushing at me.

"These are your memories, aren't they?" I whispered. From what Mrs. Swollas said about daemons, there was no way they had access to memories of another person's life. This was specific and clear as day in my mind, as if I lived it myself. Yet she did not appear before us at the séance, so she was not a ghost. "What are you?"

A new image came to me then. I was fighting a man. I was trying to stop him from something crazed and evil. I was not strong enough to fight him; rather, I pulled him against me. Flames consumed us both. Smoke filled my nose and stung my eyes, and intense pain engulfed me as the fire raged in the room. I held on to the man and refused to let go even when my skin melted away from my body.

I shoved the journal away, and it thumped harmlessly on the carpet, but the visions kept coming. I was being carried through the darkness. Flashes of pale moonlight stung my eyes. I was so cold. I was dropped on the ground like a sack of cornmeal. My head throbbed as it struck something hard. And there I was, abandoned until the warmth left my body entirely. How many times did Destiny die?

A soft knock came from the doorway. Greg was leaning against the frame. "You okay?" he asked.

"I'm fine," I said, ignoring the tremble in my knees and the chattering of my teeth.

"How did work go?"

Setting the memories aside, I gave him a little grin. "Well, Mrs. Swollas had it out with the washing machine."

"Oh, yeah?"

I followed him out of the room. Warmth worked at my numb fingers, and soon, it was as if nothing had ever happened. "Yeah, I walked in on her whacking it with a broom handle."

Greg's head fell back as he roared with laughter. I regaled him over the more humorous aspects of my day over dinner of hotdogs and a side of canned corn. I didn't talk about the failed séance or anything that would draw concern. He enjoyed the conversation, but every so often, his eyes moved in the direction of his laptop.

"How was your day?" I asked.

He nodded as he finished a bite of corn. "Mostly research."

"About what?"

"Oh, stuff for student homework assignments, lectures...actually, I have some papers to grade tonight."

That was understandable. "Finals?" I asked.

"Yup."

After dinner, I did the dishes while he sat on the couch with a beer, going over the essays. I was humming a little tune while I washed. By the time I was drying and putting them away, I was singing the lyrics as well.

"Hey, honey," Greg called.

I grabbed him a fresh beer and gave it to him, only to find his beer was still half full. I stopped singing. "What did you need?"

"What language is that?" he asked.

It startled me because until he mentioned it, I didn't realize that I was. "Oh, I don't know what it is."

Greg's eyes narrowed. "Did you learn it from Mrs. Swollas?"

"Yeah," I said, squirming under his gaze. "She's always singing stuff from her homeland."

He folded his arms. "It's pretty."

I went back to the kitchen and finished up before joining Greg on the couch. I cozied up next to him and leaned my head on his arm. He shifted the screen out of my sight. I tried to pay no mind to it. Perhaps he was just adjusting or wasn't comfortable sharing what his students wrote in their essays; I'd be horrified if I knew my teachers were sharing my horrible essays with friends or family.

The History Channel was playing that stupid show about old machines, so with nothing else to watch, I settled on a sitcom. It was corny and predictable, but I found myself becoming fully engrossed in the characters all living together despite the lack of any real storytelling.

Greg let out a grunt as he stretched his long legs. "I need to get up."

He went to the kitchen to get another beer before looping back to the bathroom. I was too invested in the sitcom's stupid plight to notice until Destiny's voice prompted me.

What is he looking at?

Who cares? I countered and took a swig of my own beer. My face scrunched from the bitterness of it. The smell of it was like a watered-down skunk spray. It was horrid. When I checked the label, it was the same beer we always drank. It must have been a bad batch.

Greg emerged from the bathroom.

"Does this beer taste funny to you?"

"No, it tastes like light beer."

I took another sip and grimaced. "It's so bitter."

"Coming from a girl who drinks IPAs?"

"I guess so."

I preferred bitter beer in the summertime. Nothing helped you beat the heat like a beer full of hops. For whatever reason, I couldn't stomach the light beer I was drinking now. Ever since the séance, I had been feeling a bit off. The visions from the journal didn't phase me half as bad as they should have. I just had questions.

My bed welcomed me when I plopped my head on the pillow. After working on the sky bridge and hauling around those industrial fans, I was exhausted. Greg was still working when I went to bed. I shivered so hard as I crawled under the comforter. It was freezing in the room! Goosebumps sprouted all over my arms and legs, and my teeth were chattering.

I turned off the AC, but that didn't help. No matter what I did, I couldn't get warm. My fingertips were so cold, like I'd stuck them in snow. They ached and resisted as I tried to move them. The second vision returned to me then. Mrs. Swollas said Destiny died in a fire, but for some reason, she was intent on showing me a death Mrs. Swollas didn't mention.

I was lying in the woods against a half-rotted log. My breath made clouds, and my eyelids threatened to close for good. At least it wasn't cold anymore. The freezing gave way to a sense of euphoria. It wasn't bad, going out this way.

Only when I did succumb to sleep, I didn't die. Warmth returned to my body in a swelter that could only be the South without proper AC. I woke briefly when Greg climbed in around one in the morning.

"Damn, Jayme," he muttered, turning the air back on before getting into bed. He was awfully fidgety. Tossing and turning, messing with the sheet. Something was on his mind, but if he didn't want to share it with me, there wasn't much I could do. I fell back into a dreamless sleep.

23
—·—

Wordlessly, I gave Mrs. Swollas the journal. Her hands clawed it as she sat down to read. I got the impression that she didn't care about tea at that moment, but I put the kettle on anyways. When I turned back around, she was staring at me. "I can't believe it," she said. "This actually happened?"

"She has been showing me things," I said. "I think she showed me how she died...twice."

"People only die once that I know of."

That's not what she had shown me. I didn't understand it either, but she died twice. Once in the woods and once in the fire. "Well, she showed two different deaths. One, she was burning alive with someone, and another, she was in the woods dying from hypothermia or something."

Mrs. Swollas's eyes narrowed. "In the woods? Was she alone?"

"When I see these visions, I'm living them. Someone was carrying me."

"Did you see his face?"

I tried to recall. "It didn't matter to me anymore. The heat of his body was the only thing I cared about."

Mrs. Swollas's eyes welled with tears. This had to be difficult for her. I couldn't imagine what it would be like to hear the spirit of Daddy was tagging along with someone I had only known for a few months. She pulled the journal close to her heart and leaned back in the chair.

"I didn't know," she whispered. "I brought a horrid curse on my family." Mrs. Swollas gripped her teacup so hard I thought it was going to break. "I was so focused on her getting married. I thought it would solve all our problems. I was wrong."

I couldn't help but establish a parallel between my situation and Destiny's. My family wanted me to marry a good man, too. They insisted it would be good for me and that it would make me happy. I loved Lars, I really did, but rather than force myself to go through with it the way Destiny did, I ran. Maybe that was why she chose me.

"What was the nature of this curse?"

"It kept us trapped on the island."

"Who cursed you?"

At this, she smiled bitterly. "I did. Not intentionally, of course. I was tricked by a clever man. No one could leave. Not ever."

"Even in death?"

Did I truly believe what she was saying? I drank up the lore this woman told me as if witchcraft was a real thing. Maybe it was easier to believe, given what was happening between Destiny and me. Then again, I blindly accepted that God was real and that Jesus was our lord and savior. Was it such a stretch to believe witches were real when I knew that Jesus once walked on water?

She shook away the thought and drank her tea. Mrs. Sallows probably didn't know. She remained silent. Likely contemplating all the information neither of us could understand. I struggled to word what I wanted to say next. Renee and Montgomery said they saw an angel. There was a connection between the angel and Destiny, but if ghosts couldn't haunt dreams, maybe she was something else. "Was she like you?"

Mrs. Swollas shook her head. "A monster? No. She was nothing like me."

I had a hard time believing she was a monster. The level of self-loathing the old lady had for herself was unpalatable. She couldn't see herself the way I saw her. The way Destiny saw her. Mrs. Swollas was a mother first and foremost. No matter what she did, it was always in the best interest of her children.

"She says she wants to be with me," I said. "What do you think that means?"

Mrs. Swollas shook her head. "I think she means to possess you, to use you as a vessel to reenter this world."

That didn't feel right. Mrs. Swollas would know better than I would on such things, but Destiny was telling me she wanted to be with me, not take over. I couldn't explain it, but I knew she wouldn't hurt me.

"I don't know if that's entirely what she's doing," I said. "She's asking my permission. She wants us to be together."

"That's impossible. There is no known magic that can do such a thing. Two spirits cannot inhabit one body."

An overwhelming urge to say otherwise came over me. Mrs. Swollas's grief was still fresh in her mind, and trying to fight her on something I did not understand myself would only upset her further. Destiny wanted to tell her something, but I could not utter the words.

I would have to accept what Mrs. Swollas was saying until Destiny showed me otherwise. She was staring at me as if she were trying to decipher one of those ancient books.

"What do you think of all this? One day you were living a perfectly normal life, and now you've been flung into a world of witches, curses, Daemons—"

"Gargoyles..." I finished.

Mrs. Swollas was so wrapped up in the ramifications of possession that she didn't catch the humor. This was a serious matter—I understood that. My soul could very well be in danger, but I somehow knew it wasn't.

"Once I figure out what is happening to you, I could make it stop, you know."

She cared about me enough to say goodbye to her daughter forever. Mrs. Swollas could not comprehend it. I was not sure anyone could. What kind of person was this content with being possessed by a ghost? She said it was not possible both of us could coexist together, but Destiny was telling me Mrs. Swollas was wrong.

"I know it sounds weird," I said. "But I don't want to let her go. She is my other half. Don't ask me how. I just know it. She is the reason I could not get married. She is my Destiny."

I took her hands then, prying them from the teacup. Destiny took the helm and spoke, "We need you to get stronger, Helicant Sallows, and you need to reclaim your true name. It's time to stop hiding in the shadows."

The name was an afterthought, but Destiny had told me this in the last dream. Her name was Sallows, so Mrs. Swollas's true name must have been the same. She had spelled her name backward as some sort of alias. Another way to fade into obscurity. But we couldn't let her die. Not when she was the key to uniting us. Not when she was our mother.

Mrs. Sallows stood, grasping the arm of the chair for stability. "You don't know what you're asking for, I doubt Destiny does either."

I searched for what she was referring to, but I found no answer. Mrs. Sallows gave a slow nod as if it confirmed something for her. "I see she does not."

Destiny remained silent. It was up to me to push Mrs. Sallows to do something, but what? If I stalled, she may not survive long enough to help us. A vision of the altar in the study flashed in my mind. It was pristine white marble marred with blood. We needed her to do something in that room at the altar.

"Do it," I said with as much resolve as I could muster. I was living a half-life without her. Incomplete. If something happened to Mrs. Sallows, Destiny might fade away forever. "It's not Destiny asking, it's me."

Mrs. Sallows buttoned her lips and turned away. "I will go," she said. "I'll be back in a few days. See to my affairs while I'm gone. And no climbing the roofs."

That I could promise. The last thing I needed was another concussion. Mrs. Sallows was brisk in her departure. No goodbyes, and I never saw how she left. Maybe she sprouted bat wings or turned into a mist like some kind of geriatric vampire. She was no longer old, though. In my mind, she was still old, but most people would assume she was somewhere in her fifties now. How could anyone explain that other than magic?

I stuck to light housework for the most part of the day. When I bit into my sandwich for lunch, a pungent, gritty taste nearly made me spit it out. It was just mustard, and I always had mustard on my sandwiches, but today, I could not tolerate the stuff. I scraped it off with a butter knife, and the sandwich became much more enjoyable.

I reorganized the chaos Mrs. Swollas—no, that wasn't right—Mrs. Sallows had created in her study before reusing one of the boxes to pack up the translations she had finished. With nothing else to do, I settled down and read a poem that helped explain Epicureanism. It was fascinating, yet somehow familiar. It was not until I finished the book that it occurred to me that it was all in Latin.

"*De rerum natura*," I said without a hitch. Evidently, I could read and speak Latin. It should have been disturbing or unsettling, to say the least, but it felt so natural to me. It wasn't a first language, to be sure, but it was ingrained in Destiny's memory and now in mine.

24

— • —

Having another person in my mind was not always easy. I had started my period, so I had no choice but to stay home for several days. I deep-cleaned the apartment and did some grocery shopping, but with nothing else to do, we watched TV.

Destiny's taste in TV was different than mine. She liked the daytime dramas and sitcoms; I preferred the junk on the History Channel and the news. Given that we had plenty of time, we alternated between the two. When it was time to switch back to the sitcoms, I decided to leave it on the news. Sometimes, it was fun just to feel the stirrings of her within me, making her fuss.

Destiny?

Sometimes, there were no answers or just a vague sensation that she was near, but this time, there was no response. No warm, enveloping hug of her presence. Just silence. I thought her name over and over, and there was nothing. I got all panicky and scratched at my scalp, pleading for her to come back. I was worried she couldn't come back. Maybe she wasn't strong enough after all. If she didn't return before I went back to work, I would have to tell Mrs. Sallows. She'd be devastated.

I pulled up Latin phrases on my phone. Words that were plainly read and even spoken the day before were lost to me. An entire language reduced to a jumble of letters. The mustard on my sandwich once again tasted good, as did the beer I washed it down with. It did nothing to sate the emptiness inside. I was returned to my half-life, reduced to a heap of crying mess on the sofa.

An hour before Greg came home, two words came to mind.

I'm here.

Bursting into sobs all over again, the crying turned to laughter. Whatever our bond was, it was too strong for her to fade away forever. She couldn't leave me any more than I could leave her. She spoke to me in visions, an anchor plunging into the ocean. A small fishing boat bobbing along the waves. I was her anchor. Destiny would never drift away just so long as she had me.

When Greg came home, he cooked dinner and watched TV with us. His eyes would flicker to me occasionally as I switched from channel to channel. "What?" I asked.

"I thought you hated that show."

I shrugged and drank more Pino Grigio. "It's not so bad. I just didn't give it a chance."

He said nothing more about it and let us enjoy the evening in peace. It felt so good to say *us*. She and I were bound together in a way I never could maintain in any relationship. It was an easy, comfortable comradery. We could be different, but we would always be together.

Where are the letters?

Eyeing the coffee table with a frown, I wondered that myself. "Greg, do you know where those letters went?"

"What letters?" he asked.

How could she know that for sure, being stuck with me all day? "You know, the letters from the universities."

Greg shook his head. "No idea. I'm sure they're around here somewhere."

Liar!

Shush. I swallowed the anger building up inside me. Hot rage that threatened to boil over like Greg's secret meatloaf sauce. Mrs. Sallows did not need them anyhow. "Well, I should probably find them," I said, getting up from the couch.

"What were you doing when you last had them?" Greg asked.

I paused to think about it. I was emailing the universities from the laptop. "I was emailing people."

"I didn't use my laptop today. Maybe they are still there?"

Greg rushed to his satchel before I could reach it. He pulled out the laptop, and the papers came flittering out of his satchel. Destiny's rage had quieted, but my own had taken its place. I did not put them there—he did. I knew he was curious about the books. He wanted to brag to his colleagues that he was going to be learning the translations before anyone else. He would need proof for the academics. It was annoying, but nothing to lie over.

"Greg," I said. "Next time, simply tell me you wish to show your coworkers."

He blushed. "I'm sorry. It was stupid. It's just so exciting; you can't understand."

Greg thought I could not understand. I was a community college dropout who had not read a book since. What would I know of ancient discoveries and biological breakthroughs?

Bile rose in the back of my throat, but I swallowed it. I was not about to let him know that inferiority got to me, but Destiny had other plans.

"I wouldn't get too excited over that book," I said with an overexaggerated Southern accent. Was that how I sounded to her? "It's a hoax by European men who fetishized the Orient. A cryptic joke from one scholar to another, nothing more. If you saw the letters between

Mueller and Kircher, you'd know that. Alas, only one of us can read Latin."

Greg and I could only stare blankly as the words came out of my mouth. After several long, painful moments, Greg asked, "You can read Latin?"

"*Ode Ti.*"

His brows nearly crawled off his forehead when I said it, and I silently chastised her for being so mean. For whatever reason, Destiny did not like Greg. I suspected it was jealousy, but there was more to it. She didn't trust him.

Greg was reeling with my newfound aptitude for language. "You can really speak Latin?" he asked. "How?"

I had not prepared a justification. Had I expected him to question me on such things, I would have developed an excuse, but I had none. Latin was a dead language, but it was something Mrs. Sallows insisted on teaching Destiny at an early age. My brain, however, was currently blank.

"Did Mrs. Swollas teach you?"

"Yes," I said straightening. "Mrs. Swollas taught me."

Greg went to his laptop and pulled up some Latin literature. "Can you read this?"

He was showing me an excerpt from Virgil. "It's about the founding of Rome," I explained.

I translated a few passages for him, and he laughed in amazement. "Jayme, this is incredible. You must be a language savant to pick this up so quickly. No wonder Mrs. Swollas wanted to hire you. She probably wants you to be her protégé."

It was nice to see that Greg was not intimidated by my new abilities. On the contrary, a whole new level of infatuation was emanating from him. A level of respect reserved for colleagues and conferences was now mine. What marvels would Destiny show me next?

Destiny quietly sulked the rest of the evening. I felt bad for telling her off, but she should not have said that to Greg. I let her watch sitcoms until bed, and as I relaxed, so did she. Still, that night, when I went to bed, I fell asleep smiling.

25

Since I was still on my period, I would remain home another day. I longed to return to Mrs. Sallows. Remaining in this minuscule apartment watching TV was frustrating. I still had so many questions, and Mrs. Sallows only doled out answers a little at a time. She might not even be home, I reminded myself. She told me she would be going out frequently, working on regaining her strength to help me and Destiny.

With no plans for the day, Greg asked if he could take the car. The prospect of being without my car filled me with trepidation. What if I needed to go somewhere? I would have to walk to take the bus, which was not worth the effort. Especially in the southern summer heat.

"Josh wants to meet up after work," he said. "It would be nice if I could join for once."

"Yes," I said. "Is Brittney going to be there?"

It would be nice to get out of the house again. We had a lot of fun until I started vomiting everywhere. I had a feeling Destiny would no longer be doing her mirror trick now that I was more aware of her existence, though.

"No," he said. "It's just me and Josh. I think he and Brittney are having a hard time."

I slumped back into the sofa. He probably wanted a guy's night out. I really liked her. It was a shame they were having issues. Greg tilted his head before offering, "You can still come if you like."

"Of course not. You boys have fun."

His expression was a queer one. Had I said something strange? "Um, thanks, hun," he said. "I'll be back late."

Most of the day was dedicated to reading books on Greg's shelf. Most of them were about biology, but I found it fascinating nonetheless. There was a big, bold world out there, and I had seen almost none of it. Mrs. Sallows once said I was her link to the new world; perhaps she wished to travel more as well. How I'd get that old lady anywhere was beyond me, but she had been growing younger, as absurd as the notion was.

Her changes in appearance correlated with her departures from the house. Destiny's memories depicted an older woman, except something must have been flawed about them. Her memories as a child showed images of the same withered old face as when she was in her adulthood.

"Did she never age in your lifetime?" I asked.

Destiny showed me glimpses of a child. Her hair was long and black, and her eyes were equally black. Her white skin was as pale as the moon. They were just flashes and then gone. That was all she remembered. The child and the old woman were the same? Destiny did not know.

"She's hiding something from us," I said out loud. "Something awful."

She doesn't think we can accept her true nature.

It was unsettling. I didn't like it any more than Destiny did. It was hard to accept knowing someone your whole life without knowing anything about them. For me, it was just a few months of questions, but Destiny's whole life was full of unanswered questions.

"Are you the angel everyone keeps telling me about?"

She didn't give me an answer, but there was no urge to protest, so I took that to mean the answer was complicated. There was nothing simple about Mrs. Sallows, Destiny, or even myself anymore. At the same time, it was exciting. Everything about this was new and vast, like the view from the sky bridge in Gatlinburg.

The South always moved at a slower pace. It was something I had come to accept once I grew into an adult. The cars always sped, but the grocery lines were always long. Afternoons drifted into evenings within screened porches, and decisions were seldomly made in a day. We watched self-created drama unfold over the course of weeks and spent Sunday mornings in church to mull it over.

Whatever was happening to us was not a Southern thing. It was unfolding by the minute, and not in the panicked rush of being late for work. It was more like a roller coaster. Some moments slowly cranked upward until a sudden, downhill rush of exhilaration took its place. One minute, I was dusting and doing dishes, and the next, I made world-changing discoveries. Would Greg be able to keep up? He'd readily accepted the sudden ability to speak Latin. Maybe one day, we could all be a family...but no matter how I tried to reason it, Destiny wasn't convinced.

26

— · —

G reg had thankfully left his laptop at home. With nothing else to do that day, I checked my emails and sent out a few, letting universities know that at least some of their books were being shipped back to their rightful home. Mrs. Sallows didn't deem it important, but with how Greg carried on, these places were likely concerned about their priceless artifacts.

My hand moved to check the browser history before I could ask her why, but when the links popped up, I understood. Countless links involving the books and their potential values and how to sell them filled the page. My heart stopped. I was so enraged I was shaking.

I called the college admin office and asked to be sent to Greg's classroom only to be informed he had canceled lessons for the afternoon. He knew where Mrs. Sallows lived and that the house might even be empty. No, he wouldn't dare.

Destiny insisted that he would. Deep down, I knew it to be true. Why leave his laptop at home, cancel classes, then create an alibi? That bastard was going to sneak in there and make off with those books. Just one of them would be enough to clear the debt he owed to his ex-wife and the attorneys.

"Mother fucker!" I screamed. He took my car. Destiny was raging inside of me as well, only hers was a quieter, deadlier sort of rage. His presence was a threat to Mrs. Sallows.

"He won't hurt her."

Can you promise that?

We arranged for a driver to take us to the house. Within minutes, a white Prius was at our door. The driver said little past the customary hellos. That was good. I wasn't in the talking mood. Bumping along the freeway, I watched as the cars passed us by.

"Can you go any faster?" I asked. "This is an emergency."

The driver waved and nodded, but he didn't speed up. I fell back into the seat with a sigh. I needed time to think about what to say to Greg if he was really doing what I thought he was. Our relationship could not go on if he were trying to steal from Mrs. Sallows. He must have known that on some level.

Did he really think he would not get caught? That the book would be discovered missing, and all trails would lead back to him? No, he was too smart for that. He must have known all these things and was still desperate enough to try.

Maybe he had no intention of stealing anything. Perhaps he was just curious about the value, and it was Destiny planting seeds of distrust. In my heart, I knew that was not the case. I had always known what Greg was, what he was capable of, but I had it in my mind that I was atoning for what I did to Lars by accepting a relationship with Greg.

You can't do better. It was always a phrase that haunted me, but no more.

The car stopped outside the driveway just as instructed. I tipped the driver generously and made my way to the house. I walked the perimeter first, and there were no signs of him. Sighing a tense breath into the humid air, I went inside.

"Mrs. Sallows?" I called.

There was no answer. It would be dark several hours from now. Another rule would be broken, but if it meant catching Greg before he did something stupid, it would be worth it. It was hard to follow rules without context. If I just knew her reasoning, I would have adhered to them better. Considering the circumstances, I felt that Mrs. Sallows would understand just as she had all the other times.

I paced the house, tidying up as I went. Anything to keep busy and to make the time pass faster. Daylight faded from the house, soft and subtle. As the shadows grew, so did my anxiety. This was the last rule Mrs. Sallows had, and there was a looming threat that came with the night. Someone else was supposedly here in the night. Why he needed the cover of dark was unknown.

Rules were meant to be broken. If I didn't go against every unspoken rule for a good Southern woman, I wouldn't have made it to this point. I would have never found Destiny, my Destiny. Mrs. Sallows would just have to trust us. Warmth enveloped me then. It was soft and kind, like a hug. She was trying to comfort me.

Destiny did not share my concerns, however. Her tenseness was over Greg and what his next move was. What lurked in the shadows of the house was more of a curiosity to her. Whatever I was, it helped me when I was hurt on the sky bridge, and Mrs. Sallows said he wouldn't hurt us, and that was enough for Destiny. We left the lights off. Our eyes had grown accustomed to the shades of night. It would be an advantage should Greg actually come to the house.

It was nearly ten at night when the headlights bobbed along the driveway. The familiar squeak of my car's breaks sounded from the carport. Nausea pitted in my stomach. He really was trying to rob Mrs. Sallows. I stifled the urge to sob. He was willing to throw everything we had away just for some money. He was going to throw away my newfound security when I did nothing but help him through his hard times. I was not enough for him.

I watched from the sky bridge as not one but two figures emerged. The car doors slammed twice, confirming that Greg did not come alone. Destiny was alarmed by this. To confront Greg was one thing, but a second stranger could be unpredictable. Urges to run and hide swelled in my chest, but I refused. I sacrificed so much for him, and he betrayed me.

Destiny understood betrayal as well, but she insisted on leaving. No, I'm not going anywhere. The intruders did not know the house like I did. The study was locked, and I had the key in my pocket. They would need to search the entire house. That would take time. I thought about just calling the police, but I couldn't risk more people around the house.

There was little in the way of self-defense in the house. A shotgun would have been ideal right about now, but I didn't own one, and neither did Mrs. Sallows. Destiny was frantic at the thought of firearms. What if the men had them?

They made their way into the house, stumbling but not daring to turn on the lights. Instead, they used the flashlights from their cellphones. There were hushed voices, but they were too distant for me to understand what they were saying.

My breath quickened as the light cast massive shadows along the hallway. I stepped into the darkest corner I could find and steadied my breathing.

"Where are they?" the voice was familiar. I recognized the ponytail. It was Josh. This was their secret business idea. They had been planning this! I wanted to sink into the darkness. Let him take the books if they meant more to him than me. After everything...

"She has a study around here somewhere," Greg said. "Millions of dollars' worth of books are just sitting there."

"I hope you're right, man."

"Jayme had the papers to prove it."

They walked right by me. I was about to haul off and punch Greg in the head, but Destiny stayed my body. She was right. We didn't know just how far this Josh guy would go. We didn't know how far Greg would go either, for that matter. I could not imagine Greg hurting anyone, but maybe I was wrong. I didn't think he'd drop me for some books. What would someone do for millions of dollars?

I waited until they crossed the sky bridge before stepping out of the corner. They went upstairs first. That was good. It gave me time to figure something out. An image of the carport came to mind. There was a hammer on the shelving.

A grin crossed my face. I think we can do one better. I ran down the stairs and to the car. There, I popped the hood and yanked the terminals off the car battery. Then, I swung the battery as far as I could, sending it splashing into the swamp. They might get to the books, but they couldn't leave.

Tucking the hammer into the pocket in my leggings, I crept along the outside of the house. Bright flashes of light signaled from the windows. They were in the bedroom. So engrossed in the intruder's whereabouts, it took Destiny's pointed stare at the balcony to get my attention. The Gargoyle was gone.

"Holy shit," I gasped.

Where did it go? I searched the ground, thinking Greg and Josh pushed it off the ledge, but it was nowhere to be found. Why would they destroy it? It was ugly, but they didn't want their presence detected. He thought he could steal and sell the books and that I'd be none the wiser. Mrs. Sallows did have a lot of books, so that was a possibility. Maybe he wasn't trying to leave me, but the betrayal still stung.

If the guys didn't move it, there was only one other way it could have left its post. The fluttering of wings and churning of stone...was that thing alive? Destiny giggled in response. I had to clamp a hand over my mouth to stop from giggling myself.

All this time, I had hated that thing, and now, it was my ally. It was the gargoyle that helped me off the bridge when I was unconscious. Mrs. Sallows's little joke about him going wherever she went made sense, and I nearly laughed out loud. That was pretty damn funny, come to think of it. But where was it now? Was it off in the woods, or was it watching our guests in the dark just as we were?

The lights were no longer bouncing around in the bedroom. They must have gone downstairs. It was only a matter of time before they got their greedy hands on the books, but there was nowhere for them to go. I had to put my faith in our ugly little friend to come sooner than later.

I waited for an agonizing half hour before the front door opened, and two men emerged. Hiding behind a tree, I watched as they strolled out with similar satchels. They were so pleased with themselves. It made me sick. How could he be so happy after doing this?

They went around the side of the house, and I waited. It wasn't long until an argument grew loud enough for me to hear. Yes, get louder. Fight and holler—the gargoyle will hear you, and then it will all be over. Except, I didn't want anyone to get killed. I was angry with Greg, but I didn't want anyone to die. Neither did Destiny. I didn't even know if the gargoyle would hurt them, but I wasn't willing to take that chance.

Greg came running to the front of the house. He was looking around everywhere for signs of a person. "Jayme?" he called.

I sucked in a deep breath and stepped into the moonlight. "What are you doing here, Greg?"

Shame lined his face, and he couldn't make eye contact. "I'm doing this for us."

"Us?"

How dare he. This was for him to be rid of Claire and his other debts. He kept his finances hidden for the most part, but I suspected she was not the only one he owed money to. I shook my head. "Bullshit. That's bullshit, and we both know it."

"Jayme, you don't understand. It's not just about the money," he said. "This place is changing you. I'm losing my sweet girl. I feel like I don't even know you half the time. You're talking strange, and you know things now. You don't even like beer anymore!"

"So, robbing my employer will solve that how?" I asked, crossing my arms.

"She'd fire you, but we'd never have to work again. We could go somewhere, like...I don't know, Jamacia or something."

Did he really mean that? Doubt tugged at me, but Destiny said nothing. Maybe he was doing this for us, but he didn't understand. Mrs. Sallows was more than just an employer. If he had all the information, he wouldn't have done this. If he knew just how important it was for me to be with Mrs. Sallows, with Destiny. "You don't understand, and that's my fault. I can explain it to you, but you need to put the books back and come inside now."

"Jayme, she has so many books—she'll never even notice. I took the ones from her collection and not the university books, so she won't get in any trouble."

How would he know which books belonged to whom? He was lying through his teeth to make me feel better. It wasn't too late. Love could conquer all. Greg just needed to understand. I moved closer to him. Shielded my face in the dark to hide my disgust as he took me in his arms. Greg kissed my forehead. "I'm sorry it had to be this way, but Jayme, these books can change our lives in ways you can't even imagine."

"You read them?" I asked.

"There's more than just money," Greg said. In the shadows, his face appeared menacing and hungry. "I did my thesis research on ways to extend life; this shows ways of making that happen."

His voice was feverish with the prospects. Greg was clutching the strap of the satchel like it was his only salvation in this world. That was once the way he felt about me, or was I just deluding myself? I knew the potion he spoke of—it was the very same one that included hearts of the innocent.

Greg was willing to kill for this. He was willing to kill children even. I doubt he'd do it himself. Rather, he'd want to travel to countries where such a thing would go unnoticed. Jamaica, indeed. I knew exactly why he wanted to venture far from the States, and it was not for a vacation. Tears streamed down my face, soaking his shirt.

"We don't need the books," I said. "Let's just leave them and go. You and me."

"We need the money," he said. "We need what's in these books."

I wasn't enough for him. I never was. I was convenience and easily manipulated, the perfect sort of girl who thought that love could solve all our problems. Perhaps love could fix everything, but not with someone like him. The only way love could be such a transformative force was if it was self-love. It was something Greg would need to learn for himself.

There I was in his arms, but it was Destiny's body I imagined I was holding. She and I were one. Loving her was the same as loving myself.

I hoped that one day Greg could experience that for himself, but it wasn't something I could teach him.

As I held him close, I closed my eyes and thought about what would happen if I let him get away. He could run. He might even outrun the gargoyle and sell the books. Mrs. Sallows said it was a load of nonsense, but how many would die to prove that? I couldn't let him go. It was a slow knife through the heart, but I couldn't let him do that.

The sound of footsteps through the gravel approached. Greg released me just enough to turn to his friend. "It's cool, Josh."

The response was a low, rumbling growl. Greg whirled around and staggered right into me. I had to sidestep him. In the driveway, the gargoyle stood staring at us. It was so still that it could have been a lawn decoration. The tongue that hung to the ground was flickering ever so softly. In a heartbeat, it tilted its head, and Greg screamed.

He took off running into the woods, leaving me and the Gargoyle alone. The gargoyle scratched at its mossy belly with a back foot and gave a frustrated yowl. Greg left me with this monster. He left me to die. It would have been a sad accident in his mind but nothing more. I thought back to what Mrs. Sallows said about men who sounded wise but were corrupted with an ounce of power. She was talking about the Greg's of the world.

The gargoyle sniffed at the ground the way a dog would before leaping into the air. Massive, stone wings expanded, and it hovered in the air for half a minute before falling back down again. It couldn't fly any more than a chicken could, but it would be enough to catch up with Greg.

A beam of light flashed through one of the windows. Josh was helping himself to seconds, it would seem. I moved towards the front door, hammer in hand. The house was much darker, and my eyes needed to readjust. I could hear rustling. Like a rat in someone's garbage can, the intruder was in the study attempting to take what he could.

"Drop the bag," I said, holding out my hammer. "Drop the bag and run. Forget this place ever existed."

The man was so startled that he tripped on a stack of books and fell over. He was tall and lanky, with a low brown ponytail and glasses. He scrambled back in fear. "You're not supposed to be here. He said no one would be here."

"Greg was wrong. Get out."

He nodded. Josh wasn't here to fight. Greg must have talked him into it. As he crawled to his feet, he winced and examined his forearm. "I must have cut myself on something."

I recalled the pained expression on Mrs. Sallow's face when she smelled my period blood. She didn't faint at the sight of blood. She was afraid of losing control around it. That was why no one could come to the house. She did not want to drink their blood because she was trying to starve herself to death. Mrs. Swollas was a vampire. If gargoyles were real, vampires must have been real, too.

"You need to run," I said, gasping for air. "Please...before it's too late."

Josh did not need to be told again. He nearly made it to the door when a frail arm with detailed lace cuffs caught him by the neck.

27

— · —

"It is too late, I fear," Mrs. Sallows said, pushing him back in. "It's time you understand what I am and decide whether or not you can accept it. The both of you," she said, tearing her eyes from her prey.

The guilt pained her. I understood now why she loathed herself as much as she did. Why she hated eating. To eat meant to kill. "You're a vampire, we know."

Mrs. Swollas let out a sharp laugh. "If only it were that easy."

The man's face was turning. He was head and shoulders taller than her, but she held him like he was a toy doll. "If I were a vampire, I could drink just enough to leave my victims alive. I have a curse of a different sort. An affliction that has prolonged my life for nearly six hundred years. So evil and disgusting, my whole family was cursed."

The hairs on the back of my neck stood on end. "Please, let him go."

"I can't," she said. "You and Destiny have given me no choice. You're a reincarnation, are you not?"

"Yes." It was Destiny who answered. "My soul departed the island thirty-three years ago, but because of the family curse, my body remained. I could not leave the island."

Mrs. Sallows's eyes narrowed. "Fascinating. And you need me to help the process along, I take it?"

"Yes, Mother."

"I'm afraid I cannot do it in this current state," she said. "If you choose to leave me after I help you, I'll understand."

After everything we'd been through, there was no way we would leave her. She was our mother. She was cranky and full of jokes I didn't understand, but she cared deeply for us. Neither Destiny nor I could imagine what circumstances would lead to us casting her aside.

In one swift motion, Helicant Sallows pulled Josh toward her and latched onto his throat with her sharpened teeth. He screamed until she severed the vocal cords and chewed on them as if they were a piece of chicken. Blood gushed as his legs jerked and flailed. Nausea overwhelmed me, and before I could stop myself, I was on my knees, retching.

Mrs. Sallows didn't stop. The scent of blood filled the room, and she was heaving like a beast. Her skin soaked up the blood like it was water. The body fell to the floor in her embrace as she bit into him over and over. Flesh, bone, muscle, all of it crunched and slurped. I wanted to run, but the stench was overwhelming.

This was why she did not want me bleeding. She could have done this to me. We had to look away for most of it. My body was so heavy with sorrow. Poor Josh. Destiny was sad she couldn't be there for her mother, that she couldn't understand why she was the way she was until now. Mrs. Sallows kept all this from her to protect her. To give her that perfect childhood on a grassy knoll. Helicant was a monster, but that did not mean she wanted us to be.

The shadows mocked us. In every corner of the room was a distorted cast of Mrs. Sallows ripping limbs and gnawing at bones. Sucking the marrow in a frenzied delight. There was no escape other than to look directly at the beast. She was growing younger by the moment.

Her wrinkles smoothed, and her skin grew plump again. Her hair had fallen away from her bun and was a cascade of darkness all around her.

Her eyes met ours as she bit into Josh's liver, wet with blood. The green in her eyes was gone and replaced with black. Josh was nearly gone, too. It had only been a few minutes, but she nearly consumed all of him. Destiny wanted to turn away, she wanted to flee the room, but I refused. Mrs. Sallows needed our support. She was doing this for us.

We wept then. Wept for the man that was killed, for the mother we provoked into such a position. For Greg's betrayal and for the life that was about to change forever.

When it was over. When the blood-soaked carpet and a pile of clothes were all that remained and our tears had dried, it was a young woman who helped us to our feet. It was still our mother, but she was thirty or forty years younger.

"How does it work?" I asked.

"I consume however many years they have left," she said. "The last three were older men, and they didn't have much time left."

The original owner of the house, but who else? She seemed to read the question from my mind and said, "The man at the hardware store."

"Russ," I whispered.

Her eyes softened, and she stroked my cheek. "I'm sorry about your friend, but he revealed too much to you. I couldn't have you looking for answers; I didn't know what you would do."

"Who was the third?"

"The man from the city after you left the hose on."

That was why she was so upset. He came to the house, and she lost control and ate him. She didn't care that I left the water running or that I cracked the roof on the sky bridge at all. "How often do you need to do it?"

"Not often. I am never sated, but I can go years and years without eating. My powers are stronger when I'm younger, though."

"Did you make a potion to become this way?" I asked.

She sighed. "I drank a potion long ago. A gift from a distant traveler. I've been searching for just how it was made, trying to find a way to undo it, but everything I've encountered so far is hogwash. I don't know why I am this way."

I nodded. The potions in the book were not real. Just medieval fabrications. What Greg held in his satchel was not some holy grail, but that did not mean he wouldn't try. Destiny was still wallowing in a corner of my mind somewhere, but she was more saddened by her own downfalls as a daughter than over what had just happened. "We'll be okay," I said, taking her hand.

Mrs. Sallows's chin jutted out, and her bottom lip trembled. She embraced us then. It was a reunion that Destiny had been waiting for my whole life. Our moment was interrupted by screaming from outside.

"Shall I eat him too?" Mrs. Sallows asked.

Served him right, but that would make her young enough to be a child. It was hard to travel with a child. "No," I said. "I'll deal with him."

When I found Greg, he was in a tree, screaming and throwing pinecones at the gargoyle who remained at the base. Now that the intruder was contained and there was no risk of him hurting anyone, the gargoyle was licking and picking out a bit of fabric that had gotten caught between its claws.

Helicant patted the thing on the head. "Good boy."

Greg was in shock. He was shaking all over and screaming hoarsely. The gargoyle must have frightened him beyond sanity. It was not nearly so scary now that it was moving, though. It behaved more like a dog or a monkey, and despite its grotesqueness, it was sort of adorable.

"He won't hurt you, Greg," I shouted into the tree. Just as Greg would not hurt me anymore.

Incoherent babble was all I got in response, and the tree stunk of urine. Helicant and I exchanged an amused glance before she said, "Come away."

She walked back to the house, and the gargoyle hobbled after her.

"There," I soothed. "It's okay now. No one will hurt you. You're safe. Jayme is here."

"Jayme," he whined.

"That's right. I'm here. Come down slowly when you're able."

"What was that thing?" he shouted.

"A very ugly dog," I said.

"He could fly!"

"I think the dark was playing tricks on your eyes," I reasoned. He wasn't the only one who could gaslight a person. He looked so pathetic to me now. It took me nearly two years to see it. He was not worth my time. I deserved better.

Greg trembled so much the entire tree was shaking upon his descent. He missed the last limb and fell to the ground. I helped him up. "Are you okay?"

His satchel was roped around his neck, yet he still clung to it. I held him until the shaking subsided. I was going to miss him in a way, but there was no way I could accept what he chose to become. It would be impossible to convince him the books were false. Some of them might contain grains of truth, and the world was not ready for such things.

"I'm going to give you a choice, Greg," I said. "Leave the books, and we will leave together, forget this ever happened."

He held me close and whispered, "I can't do that."

"I thought you loved me."

I was shoved backward onto the ground. Greg took off running into the woods with the satchel. I lay there on the gravel, stung by rejection, as I stared up at the moonlight. He never truly loved me, not even a little bit. I wasn't surprised, but I just had to give him the choice. He chose wrong. A dark-winged shadow flew across the night. I did nothing as Greg wailed in the distance.

"Such a shame," Helicant said, standing over me. "What a waste."

I knew how much Helicant hated waste. "They will think a wild animal got him. There's been several cases around the area."

"So I've heard."

"Was that you as well? Or was that him?" I asked, clambering to my feet.

"The gargoyle was desperately trying to get me to eat. I think he hoped to lure me with the scent of their blood. I sometimes eat animals to stave off the hunger, but doing so doesn't affect my aging process."

The gargoyle padded through the forest with the satchel hooked on one of his massive teeth. He dropped it at Helicant's feet. She bent down and kissed him on the head.

"Any more surprises you want to tell us about?"

"I'm exhausted of secrets," she declared.

I doubted that. Mrs. Sallows was nothing but shadow and secret.

We went inside before the scent of Greg's blood could rouse her instincts. By morning, his remains would be too far gone to incite her. She took a bath and changed her clothes before joining me at the table for some nighttime tea. None of us spoke as we sipped. The evening's events had brittled our nerves, and all I wanted to do was sleep. Wordlessly, we climbed into Helicant's bed and slept.

28

— · —

Mrs. Sallows sat me down in the entertainment room. The gargoyle hobbled around the room, scratching himself and making little grunts here and there. "So, let me get this straight. Your family was cursed and stuck on an island for four hundred years?"

"It's a little more complicated than that, but essentially, yes."

"And one single day kept repeating itself...like Groundhog Day."

"Perhaps," Mrs. Sallows said slowly. She obviously hadn't seen the movie. "My family was cursed to relive the horrors on the island forever because of me. Destiny was not supposed to be born, but she was."

I rubbed the bridge between my nose. This whole thing was crazy. Not as crazy as the gargoyle with his claw stuck in the shag carpet like a cat, but enough to send my head spinning. Whatever happened in Destiny's life would make sense when we merged. I just needed to know the basics.

"So, you thought Destiny died a few years ago, which is why you didn't think it was possible that she was a reincarnation, but in actuality, she died somewhere around 33 years ago."

"Precisely," Mrs. Sallows said, crossing one leg over the other. "A soul can be reborn, but it cannot simply occupy another person."

"And she would have remained dormant had I not met you."

"I suspect that to be the case."

The gargoyle came over and nuzzled Mrs. Sallows's hand. She patted its head, and it made a purring noise. Destiny had been awfully quiet. The events of the night before exhausted her, and now she remained inactive. She needed time to process and reconcile everything we had learned, and I think part of her feared that I had changed my mind.

"So, it's not normal for people to remember their past lives, but I'm starting to because of," my eyes shifted to the creature licking the carpet. "How did you know where to find me?"

"I didn't," Mrs. Sallows said with a crispness. "I came here because Montgomery was a book collector who swore he could help me find answers for my condition. To my knowledge, I cannot die. I was hoping his books could undo it."

It was a hell of a coincidence. Destiny stirred, and I rethought that. "Where did he get the idea to collect books?"

Mrs. Sallows frowned as she thought. "He was a strange man. He said that an angel told him that the answers to life could be found in books."

I was willing to bet that angel had blonde hair and brown eyes with freckles. Destiny had been communicating to me in dreams; it stands to reason that she found a way to inspire a crazy old man not too far from where she resided.

"Why did you kill him?" I asked.

"It was an accident. He was slicing tomatoes in the kitchen with a non-serrated knife, the dullard. I told him countless times to use a proper knife, but he didn't listen. He cut himself badly and..."

Then she ate him. "Then you had to start all over on the dying thing."

Mrs. Sallows nodded. "He set me back several years, yes. So what happens now?" she asked. "Do you still wish to remember your past life? To join yourself with Destiny forever? I cannot undo it once it is done."

We were one spirit but two minds. It was frightening to think we'd lose aspects of ourselves to this. "Will I—we—be a different person after this?"

"I couldn't say," Mrs. Sallows said. "This is new to me as well."

Right. Much older than she appeared, it wasn't every day she encountered a reincarnation that could remember her past life. This was my great purpose in life. I could feel it. Nothing else had ever felt so right. I wanted to be with Destiny forever. If that meant giving up aspects of myself, then I'd gladly sacrifice them.

#

The ceremony was held in the backyard. We decorated with our favorite colors—white for Destiny, and yellow for me. Paper streamers branched off from the balcony and were tied off along tree branches. Flowers, we had so many flowers.

I even got a little cake from a downtown bakery. When the baker asked me what I wanted it to say, I didn't have an answer. Happy merging? Or maybe joining would be a better word? In any case, explaining that I was a reincarnation who would soon be remembering my first lifetime was a little much.

The cake sat on a table with a white lace embroidered tablecloth. It had white frosting, and the word 'Congratulations' was written in yellow.

"What about the ring?" I asked.

Helicant plucked the brooch from her neck and held it out for us to see. She smoothed the pin with her fingers, and metal materialized into a ring. Magic. I gasped as she gave me the ring with newly withered hands. Using magic aged her. Helicant laughed. "I've seen many things in my lifetime, but I never thought I'd have a family again."

"Me neither."

"Are you ready?" she asked.

I was more than ready. I had waited my whole life to feel whole, and it was finally happening. "I am," I said.

She took my hand and led me to the front of the house. "Close your eyes. I want you to focus the same way you did during the séance."

The sun warmed my eyelids as I closed them. The breeze sent the leaves rustling. One bird in particular was squawking louder than the others, but there were other chirps as well. A doe was crunching on a berry bush. The sickly-sweet smell of Greg's corpse had attracted a variety of animals. Squirrels were pattering along tree branches and fighting over mates.

Helicant was speaking, but this time, I could understand her. She was asking the gods to heal my spirit and make it whole again. The gods she called on were old and long forgotten, relics of an old world just like her. I paid no mind to her call. It was a distant conversation in the midst of so much life crawling the swamps.

Helicant stopped. I opened my eyes and blinked. Had it worked? I gave myself a once over and turned around to see that wrinkles had formed between her brow and along her neck. She had aged, but I felt no different.

"Did it work?" I asked.

She tilted her head to one side and said, "I felt the magic at work. Why do you think it didn't?"

"Well, I thought I'd feel different." It was more than that; I thought I would be a different person. A better person. Like maybe I'd no longer be scared of snakes and get weirded out by the smell of old people. I was still me, as far as I could tell.

"What was your fiancé's name?"

"Well, I had two. Daniel and Lars..."

Oh.

Destiny was afraid of bugs and disliked the smell of old people as well. Particularly one great aunt who enjoyed smoking cigars. I was Destiny, and she was also Jayme. There was no division between us, and now, the memories she once attempted to share flowed through me as easily as my own.

Helicant nodded with approval, and I still brimmed with the same pride in that as I always had. I was always Destiny. I just went by another name and did not remember until now. "Well, what are we to do now?" Helicant asked.

The grin that crept across my face was one of mischief. We could do anything we wanted, go anywhere we pleased, but there was a place in particular I wanted to visit before we left the South.

#

The heat was so intense, even at night. My shorts and tank top were drenched in sweat, but no one cared about sweat stains here. Gold and red firelight illuminated the camp where we lounged on lawn chairs drinking Long Island Iced Teas. It was a new teatime of sorts, but a tea both Mother and I could get behind.

Black people donned colorful sarongs and danced to the multitude of drums that surrounded us. Between the head and the drinks, the scene was hypnotizing. Beaded necklaces swung as they sang in unison.

"This is wonderful," Helicant said of the ceremony. "No wonder the Christians tried to demonize it. They feared the competition!"

Another woman brought us another round. She called Mother a queen and resumed the celebration. "I think they feared women-ruled rituals," I countered.

To that, we toasted.

We had been in New Orleans for several weeks now, learning about Vudu. We didn't intend to remain in the States long, but once the house had closed, we would be free to travel the world. When I thought about how I couldn't do better, it was because it simply did not get better than the life I was living right now.

The dancers went on dancing and singing to their gods without any idea that we were living among them. Mother's eye was fixated on a tall, lean black woman with box braids down her back. There was an exchange of some sort between the two, a nod and a smile. I gave Mother a raised brow, and she laughed.

"The world is ours now, my dear."

Indeed it was. I was whole and embarking on a new life. One that was not defined by the limitations others put on me. A life free from the confines of selfish and untrue love. I once believed that love could save anyone and change any situation. Love is a force of nature, that much is true. It can alter the course of history and sail through oceans and time alike...but that's only true for those of us who are willing to love ourselves first.